## Pulse ha...
## he opened the...

Sylvie lay in a spill of moonlight on the double bed. She smiled, turned onto her back and held out her arms—an innocent temptress in a muslin gown she'd unfastened all the way to her belly.

He knew what would happen if he got into that bed. She had to know it, too. But he needed to be sure she understood the consequences.

* * *

*The Lawman's Vow*
**Harlequin® Historical #1079—March 2012**

# Author Note

We all make vows and promises. Many are swiftly broken or forgotten over time. But some vows are as binding as chains of iron.

This is the story of one such vow.

When his sister is found murdered in an alley, San Francisco lawman Flynn O'Rourke promises to find the man seen pocketing her jewelry and bring him to justice at the end of a rope.

Flynn's journey will test that vow to its limits. Deprived of his memory and transported to a lonely, almost mystical place, he will fall under the spell of an innocent beauty. Will he keep his vow—even though it means betraying the woman he loves?

Untouched by sensual love, Sylvie wakes to desire in the arms of a stranger with no name. Little does she suspect that the man she calls Ishmael harbors a dangerous secret—one that will tear her fragile world apart.

The idea for this book came to me when I was visiting my daughter in Northern California. Standing on a rugged cliff top with the dark pine forest behind me and the sea pounding the rocks below, I imagined a wild storm, a boat shattering against those rocks and a man with a mysterious ring flung onto the sand, more dead than alive. The rest of the story almost told itself.

I love hearing from my readers. You can contact me through my website, www.elizabethlaneauthor.com.

Happy reading.

# THE
# LAWMAN'S
# VOW

# ELIZABETH
# LANE

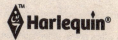

TORONTO NEW YORK LONDON
AMSTERDAM PARIS SYDNEY HAMBURG
STOCKHOLM ATHENS TOKYO MILAN MADRID
PRAGUE WARSAW BUDAPEST AUCKLAND

Recycling programs
for this product may
not exist in your area.

ISBN-13: 978-0-373-29679-8

THE LAWMAN'S VOW

*To my readers—your inspiration keeps me writing.*

# *Prologue*

*Northern California Coast, March 1858*

The storm had slammed in from nowhere, howling with the fury of a banshee run amok. Lightning cracked across the dark night sky. Thunder echoed like mortar fire through the blackness. Lashed by a screaming wind, waves crashed over the fifteen-foot sailboat, threatening to crush its fragile hull.

Wrestling with the tiller, San Francisco police detective Flynn O'Rourke swore into the storm. He cursed the wind and the sea and the hell-damned boat. And he cursed himself for thinking he could sail up the coast to Aaron Cragun's cliff-top hideaway and catch the murdering little weasel unaware. As a sailor he was competent enough; but he was no match for a storm like this one. The sails were gone, clawed away by the wind. Worse, in the swirling darkness, with no stars to guide him, he had lost all sense of direction.

A lightning flash illuminated the sapphire signet ring on the middle finger of his left hand. The ring was the one thing Flynn had inherited from his father—the younger son of Irish nobility, who'd died penniless in the New World, leaving his son and daughter to make their own way. Both had managed well enough. Flynn had recently made the rank of lieutenant in San Francisco's police department. His sister had used her voice and her beauty to become a music-hall star.

Now his sister was dead, strangled in a filthy dark alley after a performance. A shabbily dressed man had been seen crouching over her body, pocketing her jewelry. Witnesses had identified him as Aaron Cragun, a human vulture who collected and sold salvage from shipwrecks up the coast.

Cragun was nowhere to be found. But a police informant had drawn Flynn a map of the coast, showing the remote cliffside aerie where the man lived. When the storm struck, Flynn had been on his way there, bent on dragging the bastard to the gallows or gunning him down on the spot.

Now he found himself fighting for his life.

The hull was filling with water. Abandoning the tiller, Flynn grabbed a bucket and began bailing like a madman. But it was no use. Anytime now, if it didn't capsize first, the sloop would founder and sink.

Flynn was a strong swimmer. If the storm hadn't carried him too far out, he might have a chance of getting to shore. But in the howling blackness, he had no idea which way to go. He could just as easily swim out to sea and drown. Until he could see land, he'd be better off staying with the boat. But as a precaution, he unbuckled his gun belt from around his hips and stowed the .36 Navy Colt in the bow compartment with his store of powder, caps and balls. If he ended up in the water, the added weight could be enough to drag him down.

Sea spray battered his face, the taste of it as salty as the tears he'd devote himself to shedding for Catriona once her killer was brought to justice. His sister had been young and beautiful, eager to laugh, too quick to love and far too young to die. But he couldn't allow himself to mourn her until he'd avenged her murder.

A blinding flash interrupted his thoughts. Stunned by the ear-splitting boom of thunder, Flynn could only be half sure of what he'd glimpsed yards ahead. It had looked like a sheer cliff, towering above rocks that jutted out of the water. Now, high in the darkness, he could make out the faintest flicker of light.

That light was the last thing he saw before the boat shattered against a rock, flinging him over the side. Something struck his head, and the world imploded into darkness.

# Chapter One

"I can't sleep, Sylvie. I'm scared." The boy stood trembling in the lamplight. Dressed in a ragged flannel nightshirt, he was small for his age. His long-lashed eyes, the color of new copper pennies, were filled with anxiety that went straight to Sylvie Cragun's heart.

"Come here, Daniel. I'll rock you awhile." Sylvie put down the novel she was reading and gathered her six-year-old half brother onto her lap. He snuggled against her shoulder, his black hair and tawny skin a rich contrast to her porcelain fairness.

Outside, though the storm battered the quaint cabin they called home, Sylvie had no worries for their safety. Their father had fashioned the outer walls and roof from the inverted hull of a wrecked schooner he'd sawed into sections and windlassed up the cliff. It was sound enough to hold up under any deluge. But the wind was ferocious tonight. It howled like a chorus of harpies, shrieking among the ancient pines that sheltered the clearing. Lightning flashed through the port-hole windows. Rain beat against glass that was thick enough to withstand an ocean tempest. She couldn't blame the boy for being frightened.

Daniel stirred on Sylvie's lap. "Papa's been gone a long time. When's he coming home?"

"He'll be here as soon as he can." Sylvie's arms tightened around her little brother. She was worried, too. Their father had left two weeks ago with a wagon-load of salvage to sell in San Francisco. It wasn't like him to be gone so long. She could only hope he wasn't caught somewhere on the road in this awful storm.

"Will you tell me a story, Sylvie?"

Her breath teased his hair. "What kind of story?"

He mulled over his answer for a moment. "A story about a prince. I like your prince stories."

"All right, let's see…" Sylvie enjoyed telling stories almost as much as Daniel enjoyed hearing them. She usually made them up as she went along, spinning out whatever came to mind. Sometimes her stories surprised even her.

"Once upon a time there was a prince," she began. "A prince who lived at the bottom of the sea."

"How could he breathe?"

"He just could. It was magic."

"Oh." Daniel snuggled closer. Sylvia rocked the chair gently, her voice soft and low.

"This prince was the son of the great sea king. They lived in a palace with gold and jewels and all sorts of treasure. It was a beautiful place. But there was just one thing the prince wanted—and it was the one thing he couldn't have."

"What was that?" Daniel asked.

"He wanted to walk on land. He wanted to see mountains and rivers, birds and animals and everything that was there. But the prince couldn't walk. Instead of legs, he had a tail like a fish. He could only swim, so he had to stay in the water.

"One night, while the prince was swimming, a storm blew in. A huge wave picked him up and swept him right onto the beach. When he opened his eyes, he was lying on the sand. Where his tail had been, he had two fine, strong legs. The prince was delighted. He stood up, took a few practice steps and set out to explore the land."

"But he wouldn't have any clothes on," Daniel muttered drowsily.

"Oh, dear, you're right!" Sylvie exclaimed. "Maybe he could make some out of seaweed. Or just say a magic word, and the clothes would be there. What do you think?"

But there was no answer from Daniel. He had fallen asleep.

Brushing a kiss onto his forehead, she lifted him in her arms and carried him to bed. She'd been a girl of thirteen when her father's second wife, a sweet-faced Mexican woman, had died in childbirth. Sylvie had taken the tiny black-haired baby and kept him alive on goat's milk. Now, after six years, she couldn't imagine a real mother loving her child any more than she loved Daniel.

With a sigh, she settled back into the rocking chair and picked up her book. Her father usually brought her a used book or two each time he returned from San Francisco. By now, the books filled several shelves on the far wall. Tonight she was reading *Moby Dick,* a weighty novel about hunting whales. The book was filled with enthralling description, but Sylvie wasn't sure she liked it. She had glimpsed whales from the top of the cliff. For all their great size, they'd seemed as peaceful as grazing cows, nothing like the monsters in Herman Melville's book. And the story was all about men! The only women in it were the ones who stood on the dock with mournful faces, watching their menfolk sail away.

It wasn't fair. Why couldn't women travel the earth and have adventures, too?

Sometimes when Sylvie gazed into the ribbed ceiling of their ship-turned-house, she wondered where it had journeyed before the sea cast it into the cove below the cliff. Had it beat the battering waves around Cape Horn? Sailed into Canton for a cargo of tea? Brought fortune seekers to the California gold fields?

Through the pages of her books, Sylvie had traveled the world. Paris, New York, Cairo, Zanzibar, Bombay… The names sang like music in her head. She could almost imagine herself strolling the bazaars, fingering silks, sampling exotic foods, wandering through ancient palaces. But she knew it was only a dream. Even if she had the money to travel, how could she ever leave Daniel or take the boy away from his father?

Even a visit to San Francisco would ease her wanderlust, she thought. She remembered the place dimly from her childhood, but she hadn't been there since before Daniel's birth. Judging from the occasional newspaper she saw, the sprawling settlement had grown into a vast wonderland of mansions, docks, businesses, fine restaurants and theaters. She yearned to see it for herself. But her father refused to take her and Daniel along on his trips. "San Francisco's a wicked place," he was fond of saying. "There's danger around every corner and sights not fit for a young girl's eyes. Better you stay safe at home."

Restless, Sylvie laid her book aside, rose and walked to the door. Sliding back the bolt she stepped out onto the porch. Wind lashed her flannel wrapper. Rain streamed off the low eave. From far below, at the foot of the cliff, surf thundered against the rocks.

Heaven help anyone who had to be out on a night like this.

Shivering, she moved back inside, barred the door and prepared to go to bed. Maybe tomorrow their father would be home. They would hear the creak of wheels on the bluff road, the jingle of harness and the wheezing bray of the tired old mule. If the trip had been a good one, their father would be singing in his hoarse, off-key voice. Then Sylvie would grab Daniel's hand and they would run down the trail to see what he'd brought them. Aaron Cragun might not be the most sober of men or the most honest. But no one could deny that he loved his children. And they loved him.

What if something had happened to him?

What would they do if he didn't come home?

\* \* \*

By the time Sylvie awoke the next morning, the storm had passed. Dawn shone through the porthole windows in shades of pewter and rose. A crested jay squawked in the crown of a pine tree.

Pulling on a faded gingham dress and a clean apron, she pattered into the kitchen, added a few sticks to the potbellied stove and put some barley coffee and cornmeal mush on to boil. While breakfast was cooking, she made the bed, splashed her face and pulled her pale hair back into a braid. Then she went outside to milk the three nanny goats.

By the time she'd finished, Daniel was up and dressed in a shirt and overalls Sylvie had remade from some old clothes of her father's. After sending him out to feed the chickens, she sliced some bread and set the table for breakfast.

"Did you wash your hands?" she asked when he appeared at the door a few minutes later.

"Yup, and my face, too." He sat with her at the table and bowed his head until Sylvie had murmured a few words of grace.

"Can we go down to the cove?" he asked. "You can find the best stuff after a storm."

"We'll see. Maybe there'll be time after we've weeded the garden."

"But I want to go now, while the tide's low," he argued. "Why can't I just go by myself?"

Sylvie spooned fresh cream over his mush and poured him some barley coffee. "It's too dangerous," she said. "You could fall, or a big wave could wash you out to sea. And you never know what might be down there. Once I stepped on a sea-urchin spine. My foot was so swollen I couldn't walk for days. I certainly wouldn't want that to happen to you."

"Then come with me. Please, Sylvie. The weeds will only grow this much before we get back." He indicated a tiny space with his thumb and forefinger.

Sylvie had to laugh. "All right. But just for a little while. Now, finish your breakfast."

When breakfast was done and the dishes washed, they set out down the zigzagging cliffside trail. Sylvie carried an empty basket to hold any treasures they might find—delicate shells, chunks of coral, jars and bottles washed up from distant shores. Once, they'd found a brass sextant from a wrecked ship. Another time they'd found a sea chest filled with bolts of soggy cotton fabric, which Sylvie had washed, dried and saved. It troubled her when she thought of it—profiting from shipwrecks in which people had lost their lives. But as her father always said, the things they found would only wash back out to sea and be lost if they left them. How could making use of them be wrong?

His rationale made perfect sense. But there were times when she yearned for a different kind of life—a blessedly ordinary life in a town with friends and neighbors, tree-lined streets, churches, schools and stores. She'd known such a life in the years before her mother died and her father caught gold fever. But now those days seemed as distant as the stars.

Sylvie loved her father and her little brother. And she knew better than to pine for what she couldn't have.

But at times the weight of loneliness threatened to crush her. Most girls her age had friends, relatives and beaux around them. Many of them were even married, with families of their own. Not that she was asking for someone to marry. Not yet, at least. Just to have someone she could talk to—someone real to share her thoughts and dreams—would make all the difference in a world peopled by characters from novels and fairy tales.

As for romantic love, she'd read about it in books, mostly the ones written by her favorite author, Jane Austen. But here, in this isolated spot, the notion seemed as fanciful as the tales she made up for her little brother.

"Hurry, Sylvie!" Daniel called over his shoulder. "I see something down there! It looks like a boat!"

"Stop right there, Daniel Cragun! Wait till I catch up!" Sylvie quickened her pace. The trail was narrow, the sheer cliff more than eighty feet high. Ferns and cascading flowers dotted the rocky face, forming a lush hanging garden. Beyond the black rocks that jutted at the foot of the cliff, a pale crescent of sand, exposed by the low tide, rimmed the cove.

The place was as dangerous as it was beautiful. A fall could mean almost certain death. Daniel was never allowed down the trail without supervision, but the boy always seemed to be testing his limits.

"What did I tell you about running ahead?" Sylvie seized his bony little shoulder. "Do that again, and we'll go right back to the house."

"But look, Sylvie! There's a wrecked boat down there with a big hole in the bottom! Maybe it's pirates!"

Sylvie peered cautiously over the side of the trail. "It's just a sailboat, not a pirate ship, silly. But stay behind me until we know what else is down there."

With Sylvie leading, they wound their way down the trail and over the barnacle-encrusted rocks to the beach. A red crab scuttled beneath a chunk of driftwood. A flock of sandpipers, skimming along the water's edge, took wing at their approach.

The overturned boat lay on the wet sand. Its hull was smashed along the starboard side, leaving a jagged hole. Since the boat hadn't been here yesterday, it must have been cast against the rocks in last night's storm.

Sylvie couldn't imagine anyone surviving such a wreck. But there were thieves and smugglers operating along the coast, and caution was never a bad idea. Dropping her basket to pick up a hefty stick of driftwood, she approached warily.

Not so Daniel. Pushing ahead of her, he raced around the boat, then stopped as if he'd run into a wall. For the space of a heartbeat he stood frozen. When he turned back to face her, his eyes were dollar-size in his small face.

"Sylvie, there's someone under the boat," he whispered. "It's a man! I can see his legs!"

"Get back here, Daniel! Right now!" Sylvie braced herself for what she was about to find. This wouldn't be the first body to wash ashore in the cove. But Aaron Cragun had always taken pains to shield his children from the sight of death. He never let them near a wreck until he'd disposed of any remains, either by burial or by rowing out past the point and dumping them where the current would carry them away. Now, with her father absent, Sylvie would be duty-bound to bury this poor drowned soul. But first she wanted to get Daniel away.

"Go up to the garden, find that small shovel and toss it down," she told her little brother. "Then stay up top and wait for me. Careful on the trail, now. No running."

He took off like a young goat, agile and confident. "I said no running!" Sylvie shouted after him. He slowed his pace, but she continued to watch until he was safely up. Only then did she turn her attention to the wrecked sailboat.

Daniel's feet had left prints in the wet sand. Still clutching the driftwood, she followed their trail around the side of the boat. Just as Daniel had said, a pair of muscular legs jutted heels up from under the hull. The trousers were sodden and caked with sand, but Sylvie had learned to recognize fine wool. The waterlogged brown boots were likewise of excellent quality and little worn. Her father, she knew, would expect her to salvage them. But she couldn't bring herself to rob the dead. She would bury the man clothed, as the sea had left him.

The hull of the wrecked sloop was heavy, but years of hard physical work had left her strong. Grunting with effort, Sylvie managed to lift it by the edge and drag it to one side, exposing the full length of the prone body.

He was tall—much taller than her father. And he appeared younger, too, not much beyond his twenties. His shoulders were broad beneath his tattered white shirt, his haunches taut and muscular. His hair was dark, though not as dark as Daniel's. A few strands fluttered in the sea breeze, catching the sunlight.

He lay with his head turned to one side. Sylvie's gaze was drawn to his profile—sun-burnished skin against the pale sand, black lashes crusted with salt, classic features like the pictures of the gods in her book of Greek legends. He appeared far too young and vital to be dead. But the world was a cruel place. Every piece of wreckage the tide swept into the cove was a testament to that cruelty.

Such a man would be missed, she thought. Somewhere he was bound to have family, friends, maybe a wife or sweetheart. If she could find any information on him, a name, an address, she would write a letter and send it with her father the next time he went to San Francisco.

But the stranger had no coat or vest. Whatever he'd worn against the weather, the sea must've torn it away. That left his trouser pockets as the only place to look.

Leaving the driftwood chunk within reach, she crouched next to him and worked her fingers into his sodden hip pocket. As she'd feared, it was empty. Groping deeper to make sure, she gasped and drew back. One hand reached for her makeshift weapon. A corpse would be cold and rigid. But her fingers had sensed living flesh.

Trembling, she worked her hand under his collar

to touch the hollow alongside his throat. The faintest throb of a pulse ticked against her fingertip. Heaven save her, the man was alive!

"Look out below!" Daniel shouted a warning from the top of the cliff, alerting Sylvie that he was about to fling the shovel down to her.

"No, wait!" she shouted back. "Never mind the shovel. Get some water in the canteen. Close the stopper tight and toss it down."

"Is he alive?"

She hesitated. "Barely."

"Can I come down?"

"No. He might be dangerous. Hurry!"

The silence from above told her Daniel had gone to fill the canteen. Turning back to the stranger, she dropped to her knees and scooped the sand out from under his face to give him more air. He was utterly still, no movement, no sound, but the breath from his nostrils warmed her wet fingers.

What now? With effort, she could probably move him. But what if he had broken bones or internal injuries? Pushing and pulling would only make them worse. Still, there was little she could do without turning him over.

For now, he was lying to one side, his left arm pinned under his body. Maybe she could hollow out the sand on that side and use his sinking weight to help her roll him over. That would be the gentlest way to turn him. What happened after that would depend on how badly he was hurt.

Moving to his left, she began scraping away the

sand along his length, her bare hands hollowing out a space beneath him. She dug furiously, reaching as far under him as his bulk would allow. As he sank into the recess, his body began to rotate onto its side.

So far her idea was working. But the physical contact was more intimate than anything Sylvie had ever experienced with a man. As the backs of her hands rubbed across bone and solid male muscle, she felt herself growing curiously warm. The unaccustomed heat flowed through her, simmering like the ruby-red jam she made when the wild strawberries ripened in midsummer.

Caution shrilled warnings in her head. She was alone here with a child to protect. Her father had taught her to assume the worst of any stranger who showed up. Saving this man could be the most dangerous thing she'd ever done. But Christian decency demanded that she try.

She could hear the breath whispering in and out of his nostrils. She could feel the warmth of his skin and hear the low rumblings of an empty belly. But he hadn't opened his eyes or uttered a sound.

Two years ago her father had brought home a dog-eared medical book. Sylvie had read it so many times that she could quote parts of it from memory. But she wasn't a doctor. And she certainly wasn't a miracle worker. The plain truth was, the man could die right here on the beach.

But she wouldn't let herself think of that now.

Her fingers pawed the sand, widening the hollow

she'd made. His body was already tilted. Now all that
remained was to roll him onto his back.

It was easier than she'd expected. He tumbled over
with an audible grunt, the first sound she'd heard from
his lips. Sylvie's breath seemed to stop as she studied
him.

His eyes were closed, his hair sand-plastered to his
forehead. A purple bruise lay along one cheekbone, a
bloodied gash above his temple. For all the battering,
he had a noble face—almost princely with its chiseled
nose, strong jaw and lightly cleft chin. His features
were marred only by a puckered scar that pulled at a
corner of his mouth. That slight imperfection gave him
a sardonic look, as if he were smiling at some secret
joke.

Was this the face of a good man—a man she could
trust with her safety and Daniel's? Or would saving
him turn out to be the worst mistake of her life?

Transfixed, Sylvie leaned over him. Her finger
skimmed a trail down his bruised cheek. Her touch
sent a quiver through his body. Sensing it, she drew
back, almost afraid to breathe. A sense of possession
stole over her, as if, in saving the man's life, she'd
somehow made him hers.

His closed eyelids twitched. His throat worked. A
moan emerged from between his lips, then a single
labored word.

"Catriona…"

The name stung like the brush of a nettle. It didn't
matter, Sylvie told herself. She'd known all along he
might belong to someone. And wasn't it a good sign,

that the first word out of his mouth was a woman's name? If he had a wife or sweetheart, how bad could he be?

"Here's the water, Sylvie." Daniel's voice made her start. She glanced around to see him standing just behind her, holding the canteen.

"I told you to stay up top," she scolded him.

"I wanted to see." He stared down at the stranger. "Maybe he's a prince."

"A prince? Whatever are you talking about, Daniel Cragun?"

"A prince from the sea, like the one in your story."

Sylvie shook her head. "That's make-believe, silly. He's just a man."

"No! Look!" Daniel pointed to where the stranger's left hand lay against his side. On his middle finger was a heavy gold signet ring, set with a sapphire the size of Sylvie's thumbnail.

Under different circumstances, Sylvie would have been intrigued. Right now she had more important things on her mind.

"Get back and stay back," she told her brother. "I don't want you too close when he wakes up."

Kneeling, she cradled the man's head in her lap, reached for the canteen and twisted out the stopper. She'd need to be careful, lest she cause him to choke.

Raising his head, she tilted the canteen and gave him just enough water to wet his lips. He jerked reflexively, coughing and sputtering.

"Careful," she said. "Just a sip."

He groaned, stirring against her. His eyelids fluttered and opened.

His eyes were a deep, dark blue, as blue as the sapphire on his finger. They stared up at her in blank surprise.

"Where am I?" he muttered. "And who the devil are you?"

# Chapter Two

He was dead, that had to be it. And those silver eyes looking down at him, set in a porcelain face and haloed by a nimbus of spun-gold hair, belonged to an angel. Or maybe to a beautiful demoness.

He felt like bloody hell, which argued for the demoness theory. His head ached. His eyes burned. Every bone and muscle felt as if it had been pounded like cheap beefsteak. The few words he'd spoken felt as if they had been ripped from the raw depths of his throat.

Worst of all, he had no idea what had happened to him.

"Don't try to talk." One cool hand eased his head upward. He felt the metal mouth of a canteen against his chapped lips. "Just a sip for now. Too much might make you sick."

The water was fresh and cold. He craved more than the swallow he took, but she was right about getting sick. His throat and stomach felt as if they'd been scoured with a holystone. Best to take things slow.

Coming more awake now, he could hear the lap of the tide and the sharp mewl of seabirds. His skin, hair and clothes were gritty with sand. Had he been shipwrecked? It seemed likely enough, but he had no memory of being on a boat. The blankness was unsettling. But no doubt everything would come back once his head cleared.

Pouring water into her hand, she splashed the worst of the grit from his face. The palm that grazed his skin was callused. His mysterious rescuer was no lady of leisure. But there was an ethereal quality about her, like a fairy-tale princess dressed in faded calico. Nothing about her made sense.

She eyed him warily as he tested his hands and feet, stretching his arms and legs. He was sore all over, though nothing seemed to be broken. But his ears were ringing, and his head throbbed with pain.

Only as he shifted his shoulders did it dawn on him that he was lying with his head in her lap. His senses seemed strangely acute. He could feel the shape of her thighs through her thin cotton skirts. He could feel the flatness of her little belly and the warmth of her skin. He could hear the soft cadence of her breathing. The close contact was having a most ungentlemanly effect on him. At least he knew his body was functional. But he was well on his way to making a fool of himself.

With a grunt, he heaved to a sitting position. The dizziness that swept over him blurred his sight for a moment. As it cleared he saw that he was in a cove ringed by jagged rocks and pine-crested cliffs. Beyond the entrance, sunlight glittered on the open sea. Nearby, on the sand, lay the wrecked hull of a boat.

The beauty who'd awakened him knelt at his side, one hand resting on a club-shaped chunk of driftwood. Peeking around her shoulder with wide brown eyes was a small, black-haired boy.

Lord, who were these people? Where was he?

The boy stepped into full view. His feet were bare, but his clothes were clean and well mended. He looked the newcomer up and down, his eyes sparkling with childish curiosity.

"Are you a prince, mister?" the boy demanded.

He managed to find his voice. "A prince?" he rasped. "Do I look like a prince to you?"

"Maybe a little." The boy frowned, then brightened. "If you aren't a prince, where did you get that ring on your finger?"

He raised his left hand to look. The fathomless blue sapphire, framed in gold, gleamed in the sunlight. If the stone was real the ring could be worth a small fortune. It was hard to believe these people hadn't stolen it from him.

"Well, what about it?" the boy demanded. "If you're not a prince where did you get that ring?"

"Where are your manners, Daniel?" the young woman scolded. "The gentleman's our guest, not our prisoner." She turned, her expression still guarded. The sea wind fluttered tendrils of sunlit hair around her face. "I'm Sylvie Cragun," she said. "This is my brother, Daniel. And who might you be, sir?"

Her speech was formal, almost schoolbookish. She seemed to be well educated, or at least well-read, he observed. Odd, given her faded dress and work-worn hands. His gaze flickered to the driftwood club. Her manner was friendly enough, but something told him that, at his first suspicious move, she'd crack it against his skull.

Her silvery eyes narrowed. "Your name, sir, if you'd be so kind. And it would be a courtesy to tell us where you've come from."

"My name is…" He hesitated, groping for an answer to the question. But nothing came to mind—not his name, not his family or his occupation, not his home or his reason for being here.

She was watching him, her gaze growing stormier by the second. He shook his head, the slight motion triggering bursts of pain. "I don't remember," he muttered. "God help me, I don't remember anything."

Sylvie stared at the stranger. She'd read about memory loss. The medical book said it was most commonly caused by a blow to the head. The gash above his temple made that explanation plausible. But that didn't mean it was true. Until she knew more, she'd be foolish to believe anything he told her.

"You can't remember your own name?" Daniel asked in wonder.

"Not at the moment." His wry chuckle sounded forced. "Give me a little time, it'll come."

"But if you don't know your name, what can we call you?" Daniel persisted.

He shrugged. "For now, anything. You decide."

Daniel pondered his choices. "Rumpelstiltskin?" he ventured. "I like that story a lot."

"I was hoping for something shorter," the stranger muttered.

"Can't you think of an easier name, Daniel?" Sylvie asked.

The boy's frown deepened. He pondered a moment, then sighed. "I can't think of anything good. Will you help me, Sylvie?"

"Let me think." As Sylvie scrambled to resolve the question, the opening line from the book she'd been reading flashed into her mind.

*Call me Ishmael...*

Ishmael, the wanderer cast up by the sea, with no last name and no home. What could be more fitting?

"We will call you Ishmael," she said.

The scarred corner of his mouth twitched upward. "I take it you've been reading your Bible," he said. "That, or *Moby Dick*."

"Either way, I think it suits you." Sylvie's face warmed as their gazes met. Here was a man who'd read the same book she was reading. A literate man—a gentleman perhaps, who could teach her something about the world. True, he might be pledged or even married to someone else. But surely there could be no harm in a friendly exchange.

As she rose to her feet, the realization struck her.

The man who couldn't remember his own name had remembered a book he'd read.

Memory loss could be selective, she supposed.

But what if he was lying to hide his identity and win her trust? He could be a fugitive running from the law, maybe a ruffian who'd take cruel advantage of a woman and child. There were such men, she knew. Her father had warned her about them. "Keep the shotgun handy when I'm away, girl," he'd told her. "If a stranger comes in the gate, pull the trigger first and ask questions later."

The old single-barrel shotgun lay ready on a rack above the cabin door. Sylvie knew how to load the shot and black powder and set the percussion cap. Her aim was good enough to bring down ducks and pigeons for the cooking pot. But she'd never fired at a human target.

Could she do it if she had to? Could she point the weapon at this compelling stranger, pull the trigger and blast him to kingdom come?

She could, and she would, to protect her little brother, Sylvie vowed. Nothing was more important than Daniel's safety.

But she wouldn't let things get to that point. She would keep the gun close and watch the man's every move. At the first sign of suspect behavior she would send him packing. It sounded like a good plan. But she was already at a disadvantage. The stranger was bigger, stronger and likely craftier than she was. In saving his life, she'd already put herself and Daniel at risk.

Maybe she should have left him under the boat to drown in the tide.

But even as the thought crossed her mind, Sylvie knew she couldn't have done such a thing. She couldn't condemn a stranger who had not yet done them any harm. Every life was precious in its own way. How could she presume to judge who was worthy to live?

She could only do what was humane and what was reasonable—and what was prudent, which in this case meant staying on her guard.

"How did you two get here?" He squinted up at her, the sun glaring in his eyes. "You didn't come out of nowhere."

"Our cabin's up there, at the top of the cliff." She glanced toward the high-water line, where barnacles clustered white against the rocks. "The tide covers this beach when it comes in. You can't stay here, and we can't carry you up the trail. That leaves you with three choices—walk, crawl or drown."

"Well, I don't think much of the last one." He shifted, wincing with pain as he struggled to get his legs beneath him. "Mind giving me a hand?"

She reached for his outstretched fingers. Glinting on his sapphire ring, the sun scattered rainbows over the white sand. The powerful hands that closed around hers were smooth and uncallused. Maybe he was a gentleman after all. Or, more likely, a handsome criminal who lived by his wits.

"Ready?" He pulled against her slight weight. Sylvie braced backward as he staggered to his feet. Standing, he was even taller than she'd realized. Swaying like a tree in the wind, he loomed a full head above her.

"Are you all right?" she asked.

"Just dizzy," he muttered. "Head hurts some."

"Here, have some more water." She handed him

the canteen. "If you want to rest awhile, there's time before the tide comes in."

"No. Might get worse." Lifting the canteen, he drank deeply, then returned it to her. "Let's go now."

Daniel had been standing to one side, watching wide-eyed. Their father was a small, wiry man, and the boy had seen only a few other adults. To him, this stranger must look like a giant.

"Take the canteen and go on ahead, Daniel," Sylvie said. "Be careful, now. Wait for us at the top."

As Daniel scurried toward the trail, she cast around the beach for a scrap of driftwood to serve as a walking stick. Finding a suitable length, she thrust it toward the man she'd named Ishmael. "This will steady you. If you get dizzy, drop to your knees. I'll be right behind you, but if you fall, you're on your own. I can't hold your weight."

"Understood." She could feel his eyes taking her measure, perusing every curve and angle. He'd made no move to touch her, but the intimacy of that gaze sent a thread of heat through her body. She lowered her eyes, staring down at her feet. There was a beat of silence in which nothing moved. Then he took the stick from her, tested it in the sand and turned away to follow Daniel up the cliff.

The trail was slippery from last night's downpour. It was so narrow that in some spots, Ishmael, who was still getting used to his new name, had to turn sideways to fit his shoulders between the cliff and the trail's sheer edge. He couldn't recall having been afraid of heights, but looking over the side was enough to make his stomach lurch.

Well ahead of him now, the boy climbed with the easy confidence of a monkey. A prince, the child had called him. It struck Ishmael as an innocent joke. Right now, the last thing he felt like was a prince. He was damp and filthy, with waterlogged boots, salt-stung skin, a bruised body and a throbbing head that couldn't remember a damn thing worth knowing. So far, all he'd recognized was a name from a book about a white whale and a one-legged captain. He could remember the entire story, but he couldn't remember reading it.

*Call me Ishmael…*

It was the name that had triggered his memory. Maybe, given time, more names would spark more memories until they came together like the pieces of a puzzle, to make his mind whole again.

Meanwhile, it was as if he was wandering blindfolded through a maze with nothing to guide his way.

The sapphire ring could be the key to his identity. But so far it meant nothing to him. He'd been startled, in fact, to see it on his finger. Did it mean he was wealthy? Or that he belonged to an important family? Ishmael grimaced, half-amused at such grandiose ideas. He could just as easily be a thief who'd stolen the damn thing. He'd probably been shipwrecked while running from the law.

From the trail behind him came the light sound of breathing and the swish of calico against bare legs. He checked the urge to turn and look at his pretty rescuer. Dizzy as he was, a backward glance could send him pitching off the trail. The temptation wasn't worth the risk. But that couldn't stop him from thinking about her.

Was she wearing anything under that calico skirt? He imagined those legs walking, thigh brushing satiny thigh…

Damnation! He couldn't let himself get distracted by those thoughts when every step took so much concentration. A fine thing that would be, to survive shipwreck only to tumble down a cliff from fantasies about a woman's skirts. He willed the image away but allowed her eyes to linger in his memory. Framed by thick mahogany lashes, they were the color of a dawn sky in the moment before the sun's rays touched the clouds.

*Sylvie.* The name was as innocent and elusive as she was. He liked the sound of it. He liked *her.* Memory or no memory, it was clear that he had an eye for the ladies. But he'd be a fool to start anything with this one. She was young, not much more than twenty by his reckoning. And she probably had a daddy with a shotgun waiting to blast any man who laid a hand on her. Even if she didn't, he would keep his proper distance. Trifling with such a creature would be like crushing a butterfly.

Ishmael was surprised to discover that he had a conscience. It was puzzling, given that he had no idea who he'd been before he opened his eyes on the beach. Did he have manners? Principles? Was he honest? Had he been taught to respect women?

He could be married, he realized. He could have a

wife and children waiting for him, back wherever he'd come from. All the more reason to keep his distance from the intriguing Miss Sylvie Cragun.

The boy had reached the top of the trail and vanished above the rim. Ishmael willed himself to keep plodding upward. The dizziness seemed to be getting worse. Cold sweat trickled down his face. His breath came in labored gasps, but he pushed himself to keep moving. He hadn't come this far to die falling off a blasted cliff. Besides, there was something else driving him forward, something urgent, he sensed, that had to be done. If only he could remember what it was.

Questions clamored in his head, beating like black wings. So many questions, all demanding answers.

"Tell me where I am." He raised his voice to be heard above the rushing waves below. "Does this place have a name?"

"The only name we call it is home," Sylvie replied. "It's not any kind of town, just a cabin in the forest. Keep moving, and you'll see it in a minute."

"No, I mean *where* is it? Where are we?"

"You really don't know?"

"Would I be asking if I did?" His foot slipped on a clump of moss. He jabbed the stick into the trail, legs shaking as he righted himself.

The next time she spoke she was closer, less than a pace behind him. "You're two days' wagon ride north of San Francisco. Since the boat we found with you is a small one, I'd guess that's where you came from. Does that sound right?"

"No more or less than anything else does."

"You don't remember San Francisco?"

He raked his memory, using the name as a trigger. San Francisco. Fog, rain and mud. The cry of a fish hawker. The smells of tar, salt and rotting garbage. He groped for more, but the impressions were dimmed, like something from his boyhood. He remembered nothing that made him think he'd been there recently. He shook his head. "It'll come. Maybe after I've rested. What…what date is it?"

"It's Tuesday, the twenty-fourth of March. Living here, it's easy to lose track, but I mark off each day on a calendar."

"What year?"

He heard the sharp intake of her breath. "It's 1858. You don't even remember what year it is?"

"I don't remember anything."

"Except the name of a character in a book."

Ishmael had no answer for that. With all that remained of his strength, he dragged himself over the top of the cliff. Breathing like a winded horse, he leaned on his makeshift walking stick and filled his eyes with what he saw.

Close at hand, anchored near the cliff's edge, was a complex system of pulleys and windlasses attached to what looked like a harness for a horse or mule. Best guess, it was rigged to haul heavy loads up from the beach—most likely wreckage that had washed into the cove. In the near distance a low buck fence surrounded a cabin that was unlike anything his eyes had ever seen—at least, so far as he could remember.

The roof and sides were all of a piece, fashioned of

weathered oaken planks that were shaped and sealed to watertight smoothness. Seconds passed before Ishmael realized he was looking at the overturned hull of a schooner, mounted on a low foundation of logs to make a sturdy home. A nearby windmill, for pumping well water, turned in the ocean breeze.

"My father built all this." Sylvie had come up the path to stand beside him. "He cut a wrecked ship into sections and used pulleys like these to haul them into place. We've lived here for almost eight years."

"That's quite a piece of engineering." He willed himself to stand straight and to speak in a coherent way.

"My father is a clever man, and a hard worker. He takes good care of us."

"And your mother?"

"My mother died before we came here. Daniel's mother died when he was born."

"I'd like to meet your father. Is he here?"

Her eyes glanced away. Her fingers tightened around the driftwood club she'd carried up from the beach. "Not right now," she said, "but we're expecting him home at any time. He's probably just coming up the road."

She didn't trust him. Even through the haze of his swimming senses, Ishmael could tell that much. But how could he blame her? She and the boy were alone here, and he was a stranger.

Surely she had nothing to fear from him. Only a monster would harm a woman and child. And he wasn't a monster. At least he didn't feel like one. But how could be sure, when he had no idea what sort of man he was? He could be a thief, a murderer, the worst kind of criminal, and not even be aware of it.

He raised a hand to his temple, fingering the swollen lump and the crust of dried blood that covered it. Pain throbbed like a drumbeat in his head. He'd suffered one sockdolager of a blow. That would explain his memory loss. But would the damage heal? Would his memory return? For all he knew, he could live the rest of his life without remembering who he was or where he'd come from.

Dizziness hazed Ishmael's vision. He tried to walk, but stumbled on the first step. Only the stick saved him from falling headlong.

"Are you all right?" Sylvie's eyes swam before him. She had beautiful eyes, like silvery tide pools, their centers deep and dark. "Can you make it to the house?"

"Try…" The ground seemed to be rolling like a ship's deck under his feet.

"Let me help you." She thrust her strength under his arm, her slight body braced against his. Leaning heavily, he staggered forward. Her muscles strained against his side. Ishmael forced himself to keep going. If his legs gave out, he would be dead weight for her to move.

"Just a little farther," she urged. "Come on, you can make it."

But she was wrong. He knew it by the time he'd dragged himself a half-dozen steps. His legs wobbled; his gaze was a thickening moiré. As they passed through the gate in the fence, the blackness won the battle. His legs folded and he collapsed, carrying her down with him to the wet grass.

Sylvie felt his legs give way, but she wasn't strong enough to hold him. Still clutching his side, she went down under his weight. The grass cushioned their fall, but she found herself spread-eagle beneath him, pinned to the ground. For a moment she lay there, damp, exhausted and breathless. His head rested against her shoulder, stubbled chin cradled against her breasts.

She could feel the rise and fall of his chest as he breathed, hear the rasp of air in and out of his lungs. His eyes were closed, eyelids hooded by inky brows. Black Irish—the term flitted through her memory. She'd heard her father use it, and not in a complimentary way. Was this the sort of man he'd meant?

Whoever he was, he was strangely, compellingly beautiful. But even in his helpless condition Sylvie sensed an aura of danger. A man wouldn't sail this far up the coast on a pleasure outing. What if some dark intent had brought him this far? Whatever the circumstances, she had to get him up.

Working one arm free, she jabbed a finger at his cheek. "Ishmael? Can you hear me?"

He didn't answer. Only then did she realize his body was unusually warm beneath his damp clothes. More than warm. Heaven save her, the man was burning up.

Shoving his face away, she began to struggle. His limp frame felt as heavy as a downed elk, but she managed to roll him to one side. As she scrambled free, he sagged onto his back with a low grunt. When she pushed to her knees and bent over him she saw that his eyes were open, but fever-glazed. She'd nursed her father through a couple of bad spells and she knew the signs.

Heavy-lidded, he gazed up at her. "Whatever we were doing down here, it was nice," he muttered groggily. "Wouldn't mind a bit more…"

"Hush. You're ill. We've got to get you to bed." She scanned the yard. Where was her brother? Why was the little imp always disappearing at the wrong time? "Daniel!" she called.

The boy trotted around the corner of the house, followed by the young spotted goat he'd adopted as a pet. "Where have you been?" she scolded him. "I told you to wait for us."

"Ebenezer was hungry. I was getting his breakfast."

"Ebenezer's big enough to eat grass. Give me the canteen. Then go and fetch the flat cart. We need to get this man in the house."

The canteen was still slung around Daniel's neck by its woven strap. Slipping it over his head, he tossed it toward her, then scurried off to get the two-wheeled cart their father used for hauling salvage from the cliff top to the shed.

She lifted Ishmael's head then tilted the canteen to his lips. He drank as greedily as caution would allow, gulping the water down his throat. Lowering the canteen, Sylvie dampened her hand and brushed the moisture over his face. The coolness startled him. He jerked, blinking up at her.

"Can you get to your knees? My brother's bringing a cart, but we can't lift you onto it."

"I can walk." His voice was slurred. "Just need a little help…"

He began to struggle. Sylvie seized his hands, bracing until he could get his legs beneath his frame. He staggered to his feet, clinging to her for balance. Again she was struck by his height and size. Such a man could be formidable. But right now he was as helpless as a newborn lamb.

Until she knew more about him, it might be smart to keep him that way.

# Chapter Three

Sylvie slumped on the bedside stool in her father's room. Getting the stranger to bed had been all she could do. He'd insisted on walking, but he'd reeled like a drunkard all the way. Only her support had kept him upright. Now he sprawled on the patchwork coverlet where he'd fallen like tall timber under a lumberman's ax. His sand-encrusted boots dangled over the foot of the too-short mattress.

Now what? Sylvie's muscles were jelly. Sweat plastered her dress and her muslin chemise against her skin. Uncertainty gnawed at her mind. Letting this man die was out of the question. She would do everything in her power to save him. But how would she deal with him if he survived?

Like a sick and injured wolf, he was helpless now. But once he recovered there was no guarantee he wouldn't turn on her, with no more gratitude than a wild beast.

If only her father was home. Aaron Cragun understood things that couldn't be learned from books. He would know how to handle this situation. But until he returned, she was on her own. And her first priority was to make him well again. Worrying about protecting herself from him could wait until then.

"Is he going to die?" Daniel stood in the doorway, his small face sad and puzzled.

"Not if I can help it." She willed herself to stand. "Keep an eye on him while I put some willow bark tea on to boil. Then we'll get him out of his wet clothes and under the covers."

She kept a supply of dried willow bark in an empty coffee tin. Daniel's mother had taught her there was nothing better for fevers, and Sylvie had made good use of it over the years. Adding some bark strips to a kettle of water, she set it on the stove to boil and hurried back to the bedroom.

She found Daniel at the foot of the bed, straining to pull off one of Ishmael's waterlogged boots. The boy was leaning backward, about to topple.

"Here, we'll do it together." Sylvie reached around her brother to work one stubborn boot loose, then the other. As she peeled the wet woolen stockings off his feet, Sylvie noticed the hole in one toe.

*A wife would have mended it…* But what was she thinking? Married or single, it was no business of hers. Right now her only concern was saving his life.

"Wash these out in the trough and hang them up where the goats won't get them," she said, handing the stockings to Daniel. "Then you can rinse out the boots under the pump and stick them upside down on the fence posts. Make sure they're in the sun, all right? We don't want them getting moldy."

He scampered off to do her bidding. Such a happy little boy, so full of life and mischief. She would die before she let anything happen to him.

But right now there was Ishmael, half out of his mind and soaked to the skin. She needed to get him out of those wet clothes.

His teeth had begun to chatter. Sylvia darted into the kitchen to check on the willow bark. The water was just beginning to simmer. It would need to come to a full boil, then steep for a few minutes before it was strong enough to do any good. That would just give her time to get her patient undressed and under the covers.

Returning to the bedroom, she resolved to start with his shirt. Cutting it off would be the easiest way. But he would need his clothes when—she wouldn't say *if*—his condition improved. He was too long of limb to wear anything of her father's.

His eyes were closed, his breathing a shallow rumble. Pneumonia from the chilly water, most likely, but she couldn't be sure. She only knew enough to keep him warm, dose him on willow bark and maybe steam him to clear his lungs.

That, and pray.

Her fingers shook as she freed his shirt buttons. The sun had dried the fine linen fabric on the way up the trail, but the woolen undershirt beneath was wet from seawater and sweat. He moaned incoherently, barely aware of her as she worked the garment off him, pulling it over his arms and his dark head. His pale gold skin was nicked with scars, his chest dusted with crisp black hair. But this was no time to pay attention to such things. He was shivering. She needed to get him warm.

Sylvie had left the bedclothes turned up to keep them dry. Now, with his inert body on top of the quilt, there was no easy way to cover him.

Racing into the next room, she pulled the quilted coverlet off her own bed and returned to lay it over him. His eyes were closed. His dry lips moved as if he were trying to speak.

"Don't try to talk," she soothed him. "You'll be warmer soon, and I'll get you some tea for the fever."

The tone of her voice gave Sylvie pause. She was speaking as she might speak to Daniel. But this stranger was no child. He was a powerful male who might take advantage of a woman he saw as meek and tender. She needed to let him know who was in charge here.

And since she needed to strip him of his wet trousers and drawers, there was no time like the present.

The task she faced was a daunting one. She'd cared for Daniel since he was a baby, but she knew little about the bodies of grown men. Her father, mindful of a young girl's sensitivities, had taken care not to expose himself. The very thought of seeing a strange man's nakedness was enough to make Sylvie blush. But she had a plan. Under the cover of the quilt, she could work his garments down and pull them off his legs, leaving him modestly covered.

Crouching at the edge of the mattress, she steeled her resolve, reached under the quilt and began fumbling with his belt buckle.

Through a red fog of fever, Ishmael sensed that somebody was unfastening his trousers. The light touch suggested a woman's hand. Ordinarily he wouldn't have minded. But if the lady was bent on a bit of fun, why was she being so stealthy about it? Why not just wake him up and give him a chance to cooperate?

Only one thing made sense. The little slut was trying to rob him.

His hand flashed out and seized her wrist. With a cry she reeled back, struggling to pull away. But even sick, he possessed an iron grip, and he wasn't about to release his hold.

"Let go of me!" she sputtered. "Don't you know I'm trying to help you?"

He forced his eyes open. His vision swam, but the blurred image of her face bending over him confirmed that she was pretty. "Looks to me like you're helping yourself to my pockets…" The words came out slurred and garbled. What was wrong with his tongue?

"You're sick." She sounded like a schoolmarm scolding a backward child. "I'm just trying to get you out of your wet clothes and into bed."

"Seems t' me you'd have better luck if you got out of your own clothes first."

"Stop it!" she hissed. "If you weren't out of your mind, I'd slap your face."

"A l'il rough stuff might be fun, if that's what you enjoy. I aim to please…" He could feel himself sinking again. It was hard to breathe, even harder to think. His fingers loosened around her wrist. He felt her pull free as the fog closed around him.

"Stay awake!" Her hand seized his jaw and gave it a firm shake. "Once I get your clothes off, you'll need to get under the covers. After that I'll dress your head wound and give you something for the fever."

"Fever…?" He mouthed the word. Strange he should have a fever when his skin had shrunk to shivering goose bumps. And now the woman's hands were fooling with his trousers again, her fingers undoing the buttons and untying the tape that held up his drawers. Not that he was in a mood to argue—the sensation was not the least bit unpleasant. But he was still uncertain whether she was a nurse, a pickpocket or a whore.

"Now!" She yanked the waist of his pants and drawers, peeling them down his body and off his feet in one wrenching motion. By the time she'd left him naked beneath the quilt she was winded from the effort. Ishmael could hear her breathy gasps from the foot of the bed. His head had begun to fog again—a good thing, that. The words his mouth was too muzzy to speak would probably have gotten his face slapped.

He heard the splat of wet clothes dropping to the floor. "I'm going to turn down the bed," she said. "You'll need to get up for a few seconds."

"Try…" He could barely lift his head. He was as weak as a newborn kitten.

"Here." She bent down and slid a hand under his

bare shoulders. "You can move onto the stool by the bed. Hang on to that quilt."

Yes, the damn quilt. It mattered to her that he stay covered, Ishmael realized. Whoever she was, she was a female of tender sensibilities. A lady? She looked too poor for that. More like an innocent, church-bred girl. He'd do well to curb his tongue.

Wisps of corn-silk hair brushed his face as she bent over him. She smelled of sea air and homemade soap, fresh and clean. How could he have misjudged such a creature?

Or was he misjudging her now? His thoughts were wandering like half-witted sheep without a herder.

Her arm was beneath his shoulders now. She was straining to lift him, but his dead weight was too much for her. Gripping the quilt with one hand, he worked his free arm underneath his body and pushed himself up. Caught off guard, she stumbled backward against the wall. Fear flashed in her startled eyes, but only for an instant. As she righted herself, her pretty face took on a look of grim determination.

"It's all right, girl," he mumbled. "Do what you need to. You've nothing to be afraid of."

"And neither do you, as long as you behave yourself," she snapped. "Now, get out of the way while I turn down the bed."

Keeping a grip on the quilt, he hoisted himself onto the stool. Being upright made the dizziness worse. The ringing in his ears was like a howling gale. An impression flashed through his mind—crashing waves, the pitching deck, the blue-white glare of lightning on wave-slicked rocks, then blackness. Was it a memory or only a trick of the fever? Whatever it had been, it was gone.

Sylvie barely had time to throw back the covers before he slumped on the stool. She seized his shoulders, tipping him toward the bed as he fell. He crashed onto his left side, his legs trailing off the bed. The quilt slipped to the floor.

"Ishmael, can you hear me?" She leaned over him. He was breathing, but his eyes were closed. He gave no sign that he'd heard her. Averting her gaze, she boosted his legs onto the mattress and flung the blankets over his body. Then she picked up the quilt and laid it on top of him. Even that, she feared, wouldn't be enough to keep him warm.

He'd begun to shake again. His teeth chattered as Sylvie tucked the blankets around his shoulders. From the kitchen she could hear the faint whistle as steam escaped from the boiling kettle. She raced for the stove to lift it off the heat. A few minutes of steeping and the willow bark tea would be ready. She could only pray it would help. It was the strongest thing she had.

While she waited, she would dress his head wound.

Daniel's Mexican mother had taught her what little she knew about herbs and poultices. One of the most useful remedies was a salve made of pine tar. Sylvie kept a jar of it handy for the scrapes and bumps that befell her active little brother. But she'd never treated anything as serious as the gash on Ishmael's head. She could only hope it wouldn't need stitches.

After tearing strips from an old flannel nightgown, she filled a bowl with warm water and returned to the bedroom. Ishmael lay on his side with his eyes closed. His body shook with chills.

Bending over him, she sponged away the sand-encrusted blood. The wound wasn't as bad as she'd feared, but the bruised swelling around it indicated a fearsome blow, certainly hard enough to cause memory loss.

She applied salve to the wound, then made a cold compress of raw potato slices to bring down the swelling. For the deeper damage, there was no cure but time.

She bound his head with flannel strips and took a moment to check on Daniel. By then the tea was ready. As she carried the first cupful into the bedroom she could only hope he'd be able to swallow, and that the willow bark would do its work.

She would do all she could. But in the end, Ishmael's survival was in the hands of fate.

Breathing was torture. In spite of that, he slept, woke and slept again, drifting between fever and quaking chills. He was dimly aware of a hand supporting his head, a spoon forcing bitter-tasting liquid down his throat. At first he resisted, gagging and sputtering. But he soon discovered that his tormentor would not give up. It was less taxing to swallow than to fight.

Sometimes he dreamed—vague, murky images that floated through his mind, unconnected to any meaning. A woman took form, tall, with cerulean eyes and a glorious mane of dark curls. Draped in burgundy satin, she was laughing, singing, teasing an audience of fantastically dressed skeletons. She glanced toward him with a saucy smile, then turned away and walked offstage to melt into a swirl of darkness. Sensing some evil presence, he called to her—*Catriona!* But there was no answer. She was gone and he knew, somehow, that he would never see her again.

In rare, clear moments, he rose to the surface, like a swimmer coming up for air. At such times, he glimpsed the glow of candlelight and a pair of calm gray eyes gazing down at him. His mind reached toward those eyes in a way that his hands couldn't. They were his link to awareness, beacons to steady him on his way-ward course.

In other moments there were hands smoothing wet-ness on his face, hands spooning the hot, bitter liquid down his throat again and again, forcing him to submit. He had no idea how much time had passed. When he next resurfaced, the flickering candle and the sur-rounding darkness told him it was night. But was it the first night, or one night of many? He had lost all sense of time. The only things that felt real, that anchored him to reality, were those beautiful gray eyes....

Three days later, toward dawn, the fever broke. Sylvie had sagged forward into a doze, her head rest-ing lightly on his chest. So attuned had she become to his labored breathing that the change woke her. She sat up with a jerk. The candle had guttered out, but the fading sky, through the porthole window, cast its pewter light on Ishmael's face. He lay on his back, his eyes closed, his jaw dark with stubble. His cheeks and forehead glistened with sweat.

He was snoring gently, his body relaxed in sleep, and when she reached out to touch him, his forehead felt cool and damp. She'd feared for his life as the fever peaked, but whether by dint of his physical strength, her own feeble nursing skills or the hand of Providence, it appeared he was going to live.

How much would he remember when he opened his eyes? Would he awaken with full recall of who he was and how he'd come here? Or would he still be Ishmael the castaway, the man with no memories?

She had little doubt the memories were there, locked away in the depths of his mind. Last night, while the fever raged, he'd called out *Catriona* again, not once but twice. Whoever this Catriona was, his attachment to her was strong enough to pierce the veil over his memory.

Exhausted, she rose from the stool and stretched her aching limbs. Now that he was sleeping peacefully, all she wanted was to stagger off to her own bed and fall between the sheets. But how could she leave him to wake with no recollection of where he was? In his confusion, he could wreck the house, stagger off the cliff or wander into the forest. Worse, he could harm her or Daniel.

There was no way she dared leave him to wake up alone. But after three long days and nights of nursing she was exhausted. She needed rest.

She took a moment to check on Daniel, who slept in the loft above her own room. At first he'd spent most of the time popping in and out of the sickroom, running small errands and asking endless questions. By now he was worn out. He sprawled on his pallet, eyes closed in slumber. With luck the boy would sleep on for hours.

Returning to the bedroom, Sylvie was struck by a daring idea. Ishmael was sleeping so soundly it would likely take an earthquake to rouse him. And the bed where he lay was the one her father had shared with Daniel's mother. It was big enough for two people to lie side by side.

Her eyes measured the space between Ishmael's body and the wall. There was just room enough for her to fit. She could lie on top of the covers, fully dressed, with the extra quilt pulled over her for warmth. Surely there could be no impropriety in that.

With the last of her strength, she crept into the narrow space and stretched out against the wall. The top quilt was just wide enough to tug over her body.

The wall side was chilly, but Ishmael's body was warm. How would it be, she wondered, to be married to a man and sleep next to him almost every night of her life?

The question was no more than a flicker of thought. Lulled by Ishmael's breathing, she drifted into sleep.

The first sound he heard was the crow of a rooster. Drowsy and disoriented, he blinked himself awake. Sunlight streamed through the open porthole window on the far wall.

A porthole? A rooster? Where in hell's name was he?

He sank back onto the pillow, dredging his memory. Had he been sick? The dull ache in his head told him something was out of sorts. Seconds passed before his exploring hand discovered the wrapping and the soggy poultice beneath it. He wasn't just sick. He'd evidently been hurt. And now he was lying naked in a strange bed.

Only when he tried to sit up did he realize he wasn't alone. A slight body lay on top of the covers, anchoring them to the bed. Not just a body. A warm, breathing body.

Moving cautiously, he rolled onto his side and raised himself on one elbow.

His breath caught.

The girl was lying alongside him, stretched against the wall. Her eyes were closed, her sun-gold hair a mass of tangles on the pillow. In the morning light, her parted lips were a soft, dewy pink. Unlike him, she appeared to be fully clothed.

Scarcely daring to breathe, he allowed his gaze to linger. *Sylvie*—he remembered her name now. And he remembered her bending over him, weary-eyed, to force that god-awful concoction down his throat again and again. Whatever it was, it must have worked. He actually felt as if he was going to live.

What else could he remember? He had a vague impression of climbing a steep cliffside trail, and seeing a house made from an upside-down ship. He must be inside the house now. That would account for the porthole on the wall behind him. And before that, he remembered Sylvie helping him to his feet on the beach, telling him about the tides and christening him with the name Ishmael. But everything prior to that was blank. It was as if a dense fog had closed in, obscuring everything he'd ever known.

Lord help him, why couldn't he remember?

Maybe the girl, Sylvie, knew more than she'd told him. In his impatience, he was tempted to wake her, seize her by the shoulders and shake the truth out of her. But she looked so innocent in her sleep. And it would be farcical to take matters into his own hands while he was as naked as a jaybird under the bedcovers.

What had the creature done with his clothes? If she was trying to keep him prisoner, she'd come up with a clever way. He couldn't get very far stripped and barefoot, could he?

Restless, he straightened his bent legs and stretched them over the foot of the bed. He was rewarded with a hellish cramp in his left calf. Cursing under his breath, he yanked himself upright and seized the knotted muscle.

Sylvie's eyes flew open. She sat up, clutching the quilt to her chest like a shield. "Wh-what are you doing?" she stammered.

"Hurting," he growled.

"What's the matter? Do you need help?"

"Blasted charley horse. Need to get up and stretch."

"I'll cover my eyes."

"I've got a better idea. Go out and get my clothes, wherever you've stashed them."

"I rinsed them, hung them to dry and put them away for you. But you don't look strong enough to be up."

"I'm damn well strong enough to get my clothes on. Now, go get them. *Go!*" With the last word, he swung his legs to the floor, turning the expanse of his bare back toward her.

"Oh!" With a gasp of indignation, she flung the quilt aside, sprang off the foot of the bed and fled the room, slamming the door behind her.

He stood and stretched the agony out of his leg. He'd been hard on the girl. Too hard, given that she'd probably saved his life. But if she thought she was going to keep him locked up and buck naked, she had a few things to learn. He was getting out of here even if he had to wrap up in the sheet like a damn Roman.

Now that he was up, the dizziness had come back. His head felt as if hammer-wielding gremlins were pounding on his skull. But he was on his feet to stay, he vowed. And he wouldn't rest until he knew all there was to know about this place and what had happened to him.

Legs quivering, Sylvie sagged against the closed door. For someone who'd resolved to take charge, she was off to a pitiful start. All the wretched man had to do was snap at her and bare his splendid back, and she was out of the room like a scared rabbit.

But that was about to change. He wouldn't be getting his clothes, or his breakfast, until he'd agreed to her rules.

Moving deliberately, she added kindling to the coals

in the stove and put some coffee on to boil. Two nights ago she'd bundled his clean clothes and dry boots and tucked them under the bed in her own room. They were still there, hidden from sight. And she didn't plan to give them back until she felt it was safe to do so.

After taking a moment to check on the sleeping Daniel, she returned to the closed door. From the room beyond, there was no sound. Sylvie hesitated, one hand on the latch. Was Ishmael waiting to ambush her, maybe lock her in and steal everything he could carry off? Even sick, he appeared strong enough to overpower her.

Walking to the front door, she lifted the loaded shotgun off the rack. Better safe than sorry, she told herself as she thumbed back the hammer, returned to the door and opened it.

Her breath caught in a gasp.

Ishmael lay across the bed, wrapped in the sheet and passed out cold.

# Chapter Four

*Fog and drizzle blended with the dank smell of the harbor. Behind him, lanterns flashed in the night. Crowds of theatergoers surged against the cordon of police officers that kept them from rushing into the narrow alley.*

*Recognizing him, the police had let him through at once. Now he was plunging through the murk toward a form sprawled on the grimy cobblestones. His eyes glimpsed a rumpled satin cloak trimmed in ermine, then the flutter of dark hair. A single silver kidskin slipper lay soaking up the rain…*

*No! Lord have mercy, no!*

"Ishmael! Wake up!"

He was being shaken with a force that triggered sparks of pain. He opened his eyes to the glare of sunlight. Sylvie was bending over him. Her hands gripped his shoulders. Her gray eyes were storms of worry that cut through the remaining fog of sleep.

"What...?" He jerked himself awake.

"Thank goodness!" She drew back, releasing him. "The way you were thrashing and moaning, I was afraid you were having some sort of apoplexy."

Sun dazzled, he raised his head. "Bad dream, that's all. Must've blacked out." His hand moved to his head. The wrapping had come loose, and the soggy poultice was threatening to slide down his face. "If you wouldn't mind..."

She saw the problem. "Of course not. In any case, I'll want to check that head wound. But I'll need you sitting up."

Pushing with his arms, he hoisted himself until the pillow was at his back. Before passing out, he'd used a bedsheet to wrap himself toga style from chest to knee. At least he was decently covered.

He sniffed the morning air. "Glory be, is that coffee I smell?"

"Hold still." Bracing his head, she unwound the bandage and peeled off what remained of the poultice. "It's looking better," she said. "No festering, and the swelling's down. But there's no telling what's happened underneath. Since you just fainted, I'd say you need to stay in bed for a day or two."

"I asked you a question."

"I know you did." She picked up a strip of clean flannel and began winding it tightly around his head. "We'll leave the poultice off for now. And yes, it's coffee you can smell. I'll bring you some after we've had a chance to talk."

He scowled up at her, but she didn't seem to notice.

She was focused on her task, her deft fingers tightening the bandage and tying the ends in a sturdy knot. Her spunk had surprised him. Little as he remembered about himself, it felt natural to be giving orders. Clearly, Sylvie wasn't impressed. She had put him neatly in his place.

"Some breakfast would be good, too," he groused. As if to underscore the words, his stomach gave an audible growl.

"So you're hungry, are you? That's a good sign. When Daniel's up and the chores are done, I'll make us all some cornmeal mush. Nobody eats till the animals are taken care of. That's my father's rule, and it's mine, as well."

She was rolling up the leftover wrapping when he noticed the old single-barrel shotgun leaning against the door frame. His hand flashed out to catch her wrist. "What were you planning to do with that gun, Sylvie? Shoot me?"

Her eyes held a glint of steel. "Yes, if it came to that. I have property and a young child to protect. A woman alone can't be too careful. Now, let go of me this instant."

He released her wrist. She snatched her hand away and spun toward the door.

"You said we needed to talk," he called out, stopping her in her tracks. "How about now?"

She turned back, her eyes wary.

"That is, unless you're planning to shoot me in the next couple of minutes," he added, his mouth tightening in a twitch of a smile. "Don't be afraid, Sylvie. I'm so weak I can barely stand. And even if I could hurt you, I wouldn't."

"How do I know that? And how do *you* know that? You don't even remember who you are." She hesitated, her gaze narrowing. "Do you?"

He shook his head. "Not yet."

"Then please understand if I don't trust you."

"Not sure I even trust myself. But I can't believe I'd harm you or your little brother. If I'm wrong, you're welcome to use that shotgun. Now, what is it you want to talk about?"

Her small hands bunched the hem of her apron. She cleared her throat. "Just this. Until my father comes home, I'm the one in charge here."

"I'm aware of that." He also sensed that part of the picture was missing. Did she even have a father, or had she invented him as a means of protection? Clearly, the girl hadn't built this cabin by herself. But there had to be more to the story than what she'd told him.

Sylvie Cragun... Why did the name sound familiar? Blast it, why couldn't he remember?

"There are rules," she was saying, "and as long as you're here, you're to follow them. First of all, you're not to lay a finger on Daniel, or on me, or on anything that doesn't belong to you."

As if he would. "What else?"

"Once you're strong enough to be up and around, you'll be expected to earn your keep. Daniel may believe you're a prince, but I don't care if you're the emperor of Japan. You work or you don't eat."

"Fair enough. Is that all?"

"Just one more thing. You're free to go anytime you wish. But I want to watch you leave. No sneaking off in the night with the jewelry and silverware."

Her feeble attempt at humor wasn't lost on him. He gave her a wry smile. "In other words, I'm to conduct myself as a decent, responsible human being. You saved my life, Sylvie. I'm not ungrateful."

Color flashed in her face. "Fine. I'll get that coffee now." She spun away and dashed for the kitchen, pausing to snatch up the shotgun she'd propped next to the door.

The room seemed strangely empty without her.

The coffee splashed onto the stovetop, hissing as droplets danced on the hot iron surface. Sylvie steadied the aim of the spout into the chipped porcelain mug. Did Ishmael like cream in his coffee? She should have asked, instead of making that silly joke about the jewelry and silver. He probably thought she was an empty-headed little bumpkin.

At least he'd accepted her rules, almost as if he'd found them unnecessary—as if the courtesies she demanded were actions he'd have performed anyway as a matter of course. Maybe she should've just kept her mouth shut and assumed he'd behave himself. After all, what did she know about proper manners? She'd lived in this isolated spot since her girlhood. Most of what she knew about dealing with strange men she'd learned from books. Clearly it wasn't enough.

Finding a saucer on the shelf, she nested the mug in its center. The saucer was chipped, too, and the pieces didn't match. For all she knew, her patient was accustomed to gold-rimmed china, but this was the best she had. Heaven save her, it had been less wearing to deal with the man when he was out of his head.

She returned to the bedroom to find him propped against the pillows with the quilt over his legs. At the sight of her, or perhaps the coffee, one black eyebrow quirked upward.

"If you'd like cream I can get you some," she said. "I'm afraid we're out of sugar."

"Black is fine." He took the cup and saucer. "And if you wouldn't mind getting my clothes—"

"You just fainted. You need to stay in bed."

"Let me be the judge of that, Sylvie." His eyes narrowed, giving him a wolfish look. "You can bring me my clothes, or I'll get up and find them myself." He paused, his look making it clear that he'd tear the place apart if need be—and that he'd have no scruples about displaying himself in the altogether until the clothes were found.

Sylvie met the challenge in his gaze. For an instant she was tempted to call his bluff. Then she imagined the chaos of a naked madman staggering through the cabin. "I'll get your clothes," she said. "Then I'll leave you to finish your coffee while I go out and milk the goats." She turned toward the door.

"Sylvie?"

Her pulse skipped. She glanced back at him.

"I don't enjoy drinking alone. The goats can wait while you pour yourself some coffee and join me."

An excuse sprang to her lips. She nipped it back.

The goat shed might give her a respite from those prob-ing sapphire eyes and that sardonic manner of his. But she needed to learn more about her unexpected guest. Flee the cabin, and she'd be passing up her best chance.

"I suppose I can spare a little time," she said. "But only a few minutes. The goats are used to being milked early, and they'll be getting anxious."

The scar twitched at the corner of his mouth. "Don't worry, I won't keep you long. I don't want to take the blame for curdled milk."

"It doesn't—" Sylvie began, then realized he was teasing her. Crimson-faced, she dashed into her room, found the clothes and returned long enough to drop them at the foot of his bed. In the quiet of the kitchen, she poured herself a mug of strong coffee and added a bit of the cream she'd set aside for the butter churn. Stirring it, she waited for her pulse to calm.

What a dolt she was, too bashful and addlepated to hold up her end of the simplest social exchange. Why couldn't she be like Elizabeth Bennett in *Pride and Prejudice,* tossing off witty repartee and clever little barbs that left the cynical Mr. Darcy begging for more?

As she'd read that book, she'd tried to imagine what it would be like, meeting a man, holding him spell-bound with her charm. What a joke. She seemed to have only two modes of expression when dealing with Ishmael—either she was railing at him like a shrew, or she was barely able to meet his eyes. Either way, she was sadly lacking in anything intelligent or charming to say to him.

But it was silly, letting him unsettle her like this.

Ishmael was no Darcy and certainly no fairy-tale prince. He was just a man, perhaps not even a good man. The sooner she got him on his feet and on his way, the sooner she could get back to her safe, predictable life.

Setting her mug on the counter, she took a moment to replace the shotgun on its rack above the door, out of Daniel's reach. Ishmael had probably laughed behind his teeth when he noticed she'd brought the weapon into the bedroom. But even if it meant looking like a fool, it was her job to protect Daniel and their home.

Taking her mug, she returned to her patient. He was sipping his coffee, already looking brighter than she'd left him. Gesturing toward the stool, he motioned for her to have a seat.

"No memory yet?" she asked him.

He shook his head. "Maybe if you tell me about this place, and how you found me, it might spark something."

"I'll tell you what I can." Sylvie glanced down into her mug. She had yet to bring up Catriona. She wasn't sure why she'd waited, but she probably shouldn't wait much longer.

He studied her as she sipped her coffee. She looked ill at ease, like a tethered kestrel straining for flight. "Where would you like me to start?" she asked.

"You told me this place is north of San Francisco. What brought you here? Maybe I can figure out why I might've come this way."

"It's a simple story. We lived in Indiana till my

mother died. Then my father caught gold fever and the two of us joined a wagon train for California."

"I take it he didn't find much gold."

"Not a grain. But while he was looking, he stumbled across this cove. He soon discovered he could make a better living from salvage than from prospecting. We've been here ever since."

"And your brother?"

"My father remarried. Daniel's mother died here, birthing him."

"So you raised the boy yourself?"

She nodded. The girl hadn't had it easy, he thought. Losing her mother, getting dragged across the country by a gold-hungry father, living under conditions no young girl should face and taking on responsibility for a motherless baby when she was little more than a child herself. Sylvie Cragun looked as fragile as a violet. But she possessed a core of tempered steel.

She lowered her eyes, as if trying to mask her thoughts. Ishmael was suddenly struck by another aspect of her situation—its isolation. It had to be lonely here, especially for such a pretty young woman. Lonely, and perhaps dangerous.

"This place seems pretty secluded. Do you any have neighbors? Any friends who come to visit?"

Her eyes narrowed. He caught a flicker of distrust.

"We're not talking about me. I'm only telling you about this place to help you remember."

"All right, I just thought you might be able to tell me if there was anyone else out here I might have been coming to visit. Since you and your brother clearly don't know me, it hardly seems likely that I came this way to see you." He sipped the hot black coffee, taking time to think out the next question. "Would I know your father?"

"You might, if you've come from San Francisco. He drives his wagon there every few months with a load of things to sell. That's where he's gone to now." A worried look passed across her face. "He should be home any day now. Maybe he'll recognize you. His name's Aaron Cragun."

"Aaron Cragun." He repeated the name aloud, wondering at the dark flash of memory, like distant lightning through a storm. He'd heard the name before. If only he could remember where. "What does your father look like?" he asked.

"About five foot six, red hair, red beard. Drives a homemade wagon with a lop-eared mule. You'd remember him if you'd met him."

Remember? He mouthed a silent curse. "So far I can't remember a blessed soul I've met. Tell me how you found me."

"You don't even recall that?"

"Not all of it. Tell me."

"It was pure chance. Daniel and I went down to the cove to see what the storm had washed up, and there you were, your legs sticking out from under a wrecked sailboat. You had no identification on you, only your clothes and that ring." Her gaze brushed the sapphire framed in gold. "Do you remember Daniel asking you whether you were a prince?"

"Barely," he muttered. "Don't tell me you're thinking the same thing."

"Of course not. But that ring had to come from somewhere."

He shrugged. "I'm guessing it was made for someone with a bigger hand than mine. If it had been made, or bought, for me it would fit my ring finger, not the middle one. That's the only clue I have."

"And you don't remember how long you've had it?"

He shook his head. "For all I know, I could've had it all my life. Or found it in the street last week."

Thoughts chased each other across her expressive face, like light through a stained-glass window. She was as transparent as a child, he thought, and yet not a child at all. "I have an idea," she said. "Take the ring off."

He met her gaze, hesitating for half a heartbeat before he did as she asked. His first thought was to check for engraving inside the ring. But as he worked it up over his knuckle, he realized what she was looking for.

Where the gold had circled the base of his finger, the flesh was slightly recessed, the skin as pale and smooth as ivory. Wherever the ring had come from, he'd worn it a very long time.

"That ring belongs to you," she said, "and I think it must be very important. If you asked me, I'd guess it's something from your family."

"And what else would you guess, Miss Sylvie Cragun?" He checked the ring's inner surface for engraving. Finding none, he pushed it back into place on his finger.

"I would guess that your family is wealthy, or would have been at the time they acquired the ring. And I would guess that you've never been in dire need of money. Otherwise you'd have sold it. Am I right so far?"

He had no idea. But she looked so fetching next to his bed, with sunlight making a halo of her hair, that he found himself wanting any excuse to keep her with him.

But even from where he sat, he could sense the strain in her—the hands that gripped the mug a bit too tightly, the taut posture of her body, the eyes that darted toward the door as if seeking escape.

"What is it, Sylvie? What's bothering you?" The question came out sounding harsher than he'd meant it to.

She glanced down at her hands, then looked straight into his eyes. "There's one thing I haven't told you. On the beach, when we were trying to wake you, and then again last night, you spoke a name—a woman's name. I'm thinking she might be your wife."

"What name?" Wife or not, that name could be the key to everything he'd forgotten.

"It sounded like Catriona. I couldn't be sure. You were muttering…" Her voice trailed off. Her eyes watched him intently, as if measuring each breath, waiting for some sign of recognition.

He repeated the name in his mind. The memory was like a firefly, sparking for an instant before it vanished into the dark. Nothing. He remembered nothing. Suppressing the urge to snarl in frustration he shrugged and shook his head.

"You don't remember," she said.

"Not yet. I know it sounds familiar, but I can't recall anything more than that. Maybe I just need time."

She rose. From somewhere outside he could hear the bleating of goats, impatient to be fed and milked. Through the ceiling above him came the sound of scurrying feet. "Daniel's awake," she said, moving toward the door. "If he comes down here, tell him to get dressed and come outside to help me."

"I'll do that." He set his empty mug on the stool and reached for his clothes. "Sylvie."

She paused and turned back, the doorway framing her like a portrait. *A Vermeer,* he thought.

Now, where the devil had *that* come from? How could he remember a long-dead Dutch artist and not the face of his wife, or even whether he had one?

"What is it?" she asked. "Are you all right?"

"I just wanted to thank you," he said. "If you and your brother hadn't gone down to the beach—and if you hadn't followed that rescue by nursing me to health—I wouldn't be alive this morning."

The color deepened in her face. Then she lifted her chin and gave him a curt nod. "Don't try to get dressed yet. Stay in bed till you're stronger. I'll bring your breakfast when the chores are done."

She was gone in a swirl of gingham skirt.

For a moment he settled back against the pillows and closed his eyes. *Catriona.* His lips formed each syllable as he struggled to focus his memory. The name was so familiar, as if there had never been a time when he hadn't known it. But there was no face, no recollection of how Catriona, whoever she was, had fit into his life.

Maybe he really was married.

A name and a ring. Two puzzles. *Damn!*

Impatient with himself, he reached for the pile of clothes Sylvie had left on the bed. He might be too weak to walk very far, but by Jehosephat, he wasn't going to stagger around wrapped in a sheet. A man had his dignity.

He was pulling his undershirt over his head when he became aware of two large brown eyes watching him. The boy stood in the doorway, his hair mussed from sleep, his rumpled nightshirt hanging to his ankles.

"Are you better?" the boy asked.

"Looks that way, doesn't it?"

"I thought you might be dead. I've never seen anybody dead. Have you?"

"Don't know. Can't remember. You're a grim little pippin, aren't you? Daniel, is it?"

The boy nodded. "And you're Ishmael. Sylvie says I'm supposed to call men Mr. so and so. But I don't know your last name."

"That makes two of us. Ishmael will do fine for now." Ishmael reached for his clean, dry shirt. "Your sister wanted me to tell you something if you showed up. You're to get dressed, go outside and help her. All right?"

Daniel looked crestfallen, then brightened. "I'll be

helping if I stay right here and keep an eye on you, won't I?"

The boy had the makings of a good lawyer. "I don't think that's what she had in mind," Ishmael said. "Now, get going. I'll see you at breakfast."

"I still think you might be a prince," Daniel said. "I can call you Your Highness if you want."

"God, no. Who put that balderdash in your head, anyway?"

"Sylvie. She tells me bedtime stories about princes all the time. They're good stories. Ask her to tell you some tonight, before you go to sleep."

"Your sister needs you," Ishmael growled. "Go. Now!"

The boy vanished. Seconds later Ishmael heard the scampering sound in the loft overhead. Did he have children of his own somewhere? he wondered. Surely he would remember his own offspring. At least, if he was used to children, he might've been more patient with Sylvie's curious little brother. *If the child really was her brother.* In a place like this, anything was possible.

Reality had taken on a new meaning here. It was as if he'd awakened in the middle of Shakespeare's *The Tempest,* on a wild island with a beautiful, innocent girl and a sprite of a boy. Only Prospero and Caliban were missing.

Hellfire, he was doing it again—remembering something he'd read or seen. Why couldn't he remember anything about his real life?

*Catriona...*

The name had to mean something, but again, the connection eluded him. He swore as he reached for his drawers. Everything he needed to know was inside his head. But where? Why couldn't he find it?

Sylvie herded the first nanny goat into the milking stall. Crouching on the low stool, she found the teats and aimed a stream of milk into the bucket. Lulled by the rhythm of the task, she laid her cheek against the animal's sun-warmed side. The rank smell of goat and the aroma of fresh milk crept through her senses, warm, familiar and comforting. She needed that comfort this morning, needed the sense of familiarity it gave her.

Back in the cabin was a man who'd turned her secure little world upside down. Nothing she'd read or imagined had prepared her to deal with the stranger she'd named Ishmael. He was every hero she'd ever read or dreamed about, as handsome and compelling as any fairy-tale prince. But he was also as mysterious as the bottom of the sea, with an aura of danger that made her skin prickle whenever she came too near. Like a wounded wolf, he lay at rest, waiting for his strength, and his memory, to return. When he came back to his true self, who would he be?

Every protective instinct warned her away. But the need to understand the man lured her ever closer. She could no more resist than the tide could resist the pull of the moon.

She had saved him from the sea. If this were one of the romantic tales she'd made up for Daniel, he would fall in love with her and carry her off to his kingdom on a white horse.

But this wasn't a story. This was real life.

In real life, you couldn't count on anything being the way you wanted it to be. Storms came. Crops and businesses failed. People robbed, killed and betrayed each other. The ones you cared about were gone when you needed them most.

In real life, if you were lucky, you had a few moments of pure joy. But that joy was balanced a hundredfold by grief, disappointment and backbreaking toil. Sylvie didn't need books to tell her that—or to caution her against pinning her hopes on a stranger's smile.

Before starting her morning chores, she'd walked to the edge of the cliff and gazed down into the cove. Last night's tide had receded, leaving the wrecked boat buried deeper in sand. It would be prudent to go down and take a look at it, she thought, before the craft broke up and washed away. Maybe she'd find some clue to Ishmael's true identity, or at least something that would prick his memory.

She would have gone right then. But there were goats bleating to be milked, chickens waiting to be fed and eggs needing to be gathered. After breakfast she'd planned to mix bread and set the dough to rise, do a batch of washing and mend the fence around the vegetable garden before the goats got through. And of course, Ishmael would still need care and watching. But if she didn't make time to go down to the boat, the tide would come in again, and she could lose her chance.

Finishing with the first nanny goat, she herded the next one into the milking stall. While her hands moved with practiced efficiency, her mind raced ahead. Learning all she could about the man was the most urgent thing she had to do. The bread and the washing could wait while she took time to go back down the cliff and check out every inch of the wrecked boat. Maybe there was nothing there to discover. But she needed to look.

Daniel popped into the milking shed, his hair still cow-licked from sleep. Sylvie sent him off to the hen coop to feed the chickens and gather their eggs, then resumed her work. The boy would want to go down to the cove with her. Ishmael, weak as he was, might insist on going, too. But she wanted to go by herself. Alone, she could search without distraction and make her own decision about whatever she found.

It shouldn't take long. Maybe while her brother and Ishmael were eating breakfast, she could make some excuse and steal away. By the time they missed her, she'd be back.

Lost in thought, Sylvie was unaware of anything happening outside until a long shadow fell across the floor of the milking shed.

Startled, she glanced up, thinking it might be Ishmael. But the figure silhouetted in the low doorway wasn't Ishmael. It was a burly man she'd never seen before.

Only when he stepped inside, turning toward her,

could she see his face. He was unshaven and dirty, with a jagged white scar cross his left cheek. His little pig eyes glittered in the dim light.

"Well, well, what we got here?" He grinned, showing a mouthful of rotten teeth.

Sylvie rose to her feet, her heart pounding. "What do you want?" she demanded. "If it's money, we haven't got any."

His grin broadened to a sneer. "Truth be told, me and my partner was lookin' for Aaron Cragun. Little bird told us he lived up this way. Reckon you'd be his daughter, less'n he's got himself a purty young wife."

Sylvie's stomach contracted, but she willed herself not to show fear. "My father isn't here."

"Then I reckon we'll just wait for him, an' have ourselves a little fun in the meantime." He glanced out the door. "Hey, Rigby, lookee what I found!"

A second man appeared in the doorway, scarecrow thin, with a pockmarked face and a greasy red bandanna around his throat. At the sight of Sylvie, his pale eyes lit. "Tarnation. Didn't know what old Aaron was keepin' hid up here, or I'd sure have showed up sooner."

Gulping back her terror, Sylvie glanced around for a weapon. There'd be no way out except to fight for her life.

As the two men edged toward her, one last thought flashed through her mind.

*Daniel!*

# Chapter Five

*She couldn't let them get Daniel!*

Sylvie seized a garden rake that was propped against the inside wall of the shed. It wasn't much of a weapon, but it had sharp iron prongs. So help her, she would kill these men before she let them lay a hand on her little brother.

*What if he was outside? What if he heard her and came running?*

She mustn't cry out, she realized with a sickening lurch of her stomach. If they got her down, she would have to grit her teeth and endure whatever they did to her.

But she wouldn't go down without the fight of her life.

Grinning, the two men edged closer. The thin man laughed, eyes glittering in the shadows. Sylvie clutched the rake handle, a prayer in her heart.

At that moment, the skittish nanny goat reared and

bolted out of the stall. The bucket went flying, splattering milk in all directions as the animal fled.

The distraction lasted only a second or two, but Sylvie used it to swing the rake with all her strength. The impact wrenched her arms as the prongs struck.

The shorter man staggered back, swearing. The blow hadn't been hard enough to disable him, but blood was streaming down the side of his head. "Damn hellcat bitch!" he rasped. "When we're done with you, you're gonna die. An' you won't die easy."

Sylvie readjusted her grip on the rake handle, but the two men were wise to her now. They separated, moving in at different angles. If she attacked one of them, the other could dart in and grab her from behind. She wouldn't have a chance.

Making a split-second decision, she went for the uninjured man. But he was too quick for her. As she swung the rake, he ducked, grabbed the handle and twisted it away from her. With a triumphant leer, he tossed the tool aside. "I like a feisty woman, but enough's enough. Don't worry, you'll get to like this, darlin'. You might even beg for more. Most women do."

Sylvie backed into the corner. She tried to kick out at him, but he sidestepped and seized her wrists, jerking her off her feet.

Now the other man was on her, too. Sylvie went down like a cat at a dogfight. Rough hands tore at her skirts and clutched her legs. The thin man was fumbling with his belt. The bleeding man gripped her ankles. She willed herself not to scream.

"That's enough, boys." The deep male voice rang
with authority. Ishmael stood braced in the doorway,
the shotgun at his shoulder. "Let her go and reach for
the rafters, or I'll blow you all over these walls."

The two thugs peeled off their prey to stare at the
newcomer. "Holy Mother, is that who I think it is?"
one of them whispered.

Ishmael gave no sign he'd heard. "On your feet, you
gutter slime." His voice crackled like ice. "Sylvie, get
out of here. Go on in the house with your brother."

Sylvie scrambled to her feet, pulling down her skirts
as she squeezed past him through the narrow doorway.
She was wild to get away, but she had no intention of
going to the house. Instead, she ducked around the
corner of the milk shed, where she could hear and see
through a crack between the boards.

Only now that she was safe did she give in to fear.
Her heart thundered. Her breath came in tearful gasps.
The thought of what would be happening if Ishmael
hadn't shown up sent spasms of nausea shuddering
through her body.

But this was no time to be sick. She needed to keep
still and listen. The two thugs hadn't shown up by accident. They'd asked about her father. And they seemed
to know Ishmael.

"Toss your weapons over here," Ishmael barked.
"All of them." Two knives and a pocket pistol clattered
to the ground. "Now, talk. What are you doing here?
Who sent you?"

The two men exchanged frantic glances. After a beat
of silence, it was the thin man who spoke. "Nobody

sent us. Aaron Cragun cheated us out of fifty dollars gold. We come to find the little weasel and beat it out of him."

"And when you didn't find him, you bastards decided to rape his innocent daughter." Ishmael's voice was a snarl, so coldly menacing that it chilled Sylvie's blood. Who was this man?

"We didn't mean no harm," the bleeding thug whined. "We just figgered, since Cragun owed us, we was entitled to a little fun. Then that hellcat got me with a rake. Damn lucky she didn't put an eye out."

"Maybe I ought to finish the job." Ishmael raised the shotgun. The men cringed. "At this range, I could blast you both with one shot. Probably blind you, at least, if you didn't die." His finger tightened on the trigger. Sylvie could hear one of the men blubbering. Her heart was threatening to smash through her ribs.

Ishmael exhaled, breaking the tension. "But if I shot you, then I'd have a filthy, stinking mess to clean up, wouldn't I?" He stepped clear of the door, keeping the shotgun level. "Leave your weapons and get going. Whoever sent you, you can tell them that Cragun isn't here, and that his children have a protector who'll blast anybody who comes within range of this place." He motioned with the barrel. "Run, before I change my mind! The next time I see your ugly faces, you'll be buzzard bait!"

Sylvie shrank against the shed as the two thugs burst out the door. They bolted for the trees, where they'd probably left their horses.

They'd said they were looking for her father, that he'd cheated them. Could it be true?

*Oh, Papa, what were you thinking? How could you have put us all in such danger? And where are you now?*

Ishmael slumped in the doorway, as the sound of hoof beats faded down the road. The shotgun in his hands felt as heavy as a cannon. Releasing the hammer, he let the gun slide to the ground. It was a good thing the lowlifes ran for it when they did—he couldn't have held it steady for another thirty seconds.

It was the boy, slipping into the house, who'd alerted him to the arrival of the two men. Luckily, he'd been dressed by then, and he'd found the shotgun loaded. But it had taken all his strength to remain standing and keep the gun leveled on the two thugs until they fled.

The sight of Sylvie, pinned on her back with her skirts bunched around her thighs had triggered an explosion of pure rage. In the heat of his fury, he'd been on the verge of pulling the trigger. Then something had held him back. Maybe he'd just been concerned about hurting Sylvie. But there was more to it than that. Even when Sylvie had fled, he still hadn't been willing to kill the men. Whoever he was, he sensed, he wasn't a killer. But he *was* a protector, it seemed. Coming to Sylvie's defense had felt so natural, so right. He hadn't even hesitated to take up the shotgun and face down two armed men.

What would have happened if he hadn't been here? The thought of what the bastards would have done to her was enough to make him wish he'd gone ahead and blasted them to kingdom come.

At that moment, rumpled and shaken, Sylvie appeared around the corner of the shed. With a little cry, she stumbled into his arms.

Whimpering, she burrowed against his chest. He held her with agonizing restraint. She fit against him as if she belonged there, but a voice in his head whispered that he had no business doing this. What if he was married or running from the law? What if she was getting wrong ideas about him—that he might stay with her, even marry her? He needed to stop this.

But her need for comforting was so great that he couldn't bear to let her go. She was so innocent, so precious, and she'd come so close to experiencing the worst that could happen to a young woman.

Her low whimpers had stopped, but she remained in his arms. Was she waiting for him to kiss her? For a moment he was sorely tempted. But that would be the worst thing he could do. It would complicate everything.

Summoning his self-control, he eased her away from him. Her silver eyes brimmed with unshed tears. A dirt smudge marred her cheek.

"I told you to go in the house," he growled.

She drew herself up, her spunk returning. "I couldn't very well go and leave you, could I?"

"You could have, and you should have. I managed fine on my own."

"Maybe so. But you should see yourself. You're as pale as a ghost. What if you'd fainted again?"

He swore under his breath. "If you'd gone in the house like I told you, it wouldn't have mattered. You could've barred the door and kept you and Daniel safe."

"And left you out here at their mercy?" She shook her head, then bent and picked up the shotgun. "Come on. We need to get back to Daniel, and you need to rest."

"I'm fine." In truth, he felt like hell. His head was swimming and his legs were as unstable as manila rope. When she moved close, offering him support, he laid an arm across her shoulders. A slight shudder passed through her body, but she didn't move away.

"Have you ever seen those men before?" he asked her.

The breeze lifted tendrils of sunlit hair as she shook her head. "My father hardly ever brings people here, not even his friends. He's very protective of us and this place."

"But they claimed to know him. And they knew enough to come here."

"My father's been selling salvage in San Francisco for years. Plenty of people would know him. And it wouldn't be all that difficult to find the road he takes." She pulled away and turned to face him. "Those men, they knew you, too."

Her words rocked him. He stared down at her.

"When you first stepped into sight, one of them said, 'Is that who I think it is?' Didn't you hear, Ishmael?"

"No, I didn't." Lord, had they really recognized him? Those two butchers?

"I had the impression they were afraid," Sylvie said. "And it wasn't just because you had the shotgun. They were scared of *you*. Did you recognize them?"

"I don't recall ever seeing them before in my life." Ishmael shook his head. What had he done, driving them away without questioning them further? Those two filthy bastards might have given him the key to his identity. Now they were gone, and it was too late to go after them.

Not that it would have been a good idea, Ishmael reminded himself. The two men were a danger to Sylvie and Daniel, and even with the shotgun he was in no condition to hold them off for long.

But they had left him with one more piece of the puzzle. Sylvie had said the pair knew him, that they might have even been afraid of him.

What did it mean? Was he part of their dark world? Could he be one of them?

If so, Sylvie could be in more danger than she knew.

"Listen to me, Sylvie." They'd begun to walk again, but he stopped her short of the front porch. "I'm hoping those men are gone for good, but we can't know for sure. Keep your eyes open, and keep Daniel close to you. Don't either of you go far from the house alone. You mustn't trust anybody, not even me."

She stared up at him. For all her years in this place she'd felt safe. Now that had changed, and she didn't understand any of it. Ishmael had saved her and threatened her attackers with death if they came back. She was counting on him to protect her and Daniel.

"What are you saying?" she demanded.

His eyes narrowed, giving him the wolfish look she'd come to recognize. "I'm saying that I don't remember who I am. For all I know I could be a danger to you."

"I don't believe that. Not after what you just did."

"You said those two thugs recognized me. They're not the sort of people you'd meet at a church social. How do you know I'm not like them, maybe worse? How do you know I didn't come here for the same reason they did?"

"Because you're a decent man. I can tell."

"Can you?" His hands gripped her shoulders. His voice deepened to a growl. "Damn it, Sylvie, you're so innocent. You have no idea what the real world is like, or what people are capable of doing to each other."

She recoiled from the sting of his words. "That's not so. I may not have traveled, but I've read—"

"You can't learn everything from books!" he snapped. "I'm not your knight on a white charger! I could be anybody. I could hurt you or your brother! You've got to stop being so damned trusting!"

"I'm not stupid, Ishmael," she flung back at him. "Don't you think I've had my doubts and worries about you?" She twisted out of his clasp. "I told you, you're free to leave anytime you want. That offer still stands."

"And if those men come back, or others like them?"

"Then I'll shoot them myself." Spinning away, she stalked toward the porch. "Breakfast may be a little late. I'll call you when it's ready."

Willing herself not to look back at him, Sylvie

mounted the porch. Daniel stood in the doorway, looking small and scared. Leaning the shotgun against the door frame, she gathered him into her arms and held him fiercely tight. "It's all right," she whispered. "Those men are gone. We're safe now."

He pushed away a little. "Ishmael saved us. Why did you get mad at him just now?"

Sylvie sighed as she set her brother down and returned the gun to its rack above the door. How could she explain her emotions to a small boy when she didn't fully understand them herself? Was she at risk of falling in love with a man who couldn't even remember his own name?

But what a foolish question. Ishmael was right. She was too naive, too trusting. Now, with so much danger afoot, she needed to be cautious. She couldn't afford to trust anyone she didn't know.

And she didn't know Ishmael. Not really.

Daniel's eyes were as appealing as a puppy's. "I like Ishmael. He's brave and he's nice. Why are you mad at him?"

Sylvie measured water, salt and cornmeal and put the mush pan on the stove to boil. "I'm not really mad at him, Daniel," she said. "It's just...well, men can be difficult sometimes. They always want to be the boss."

"Can I be the boss when I get to be a man?"

Sylvie hid a smile. "That will be up to your wife," she said. "Now go and finish gathering those eggs. Mind that old brown hen. Don't let her peck you."

The boy scampered outside. Sylvie watched him go, then scanned the yard for Ishmael. He was coming out of the milk shed with the two knives and the pocket pistol the two thugs had left—something she should have thought of herself. It wouldn't do for a curious little boy to find those weapons.

For a moment her eyes lingered on him. He was still unsteady on his feet, but he moved determinedly, using the rake as a walking stick. Was he really a danger to her? Sylvie still found that hard to believe. But she'd seen his very appearance strike terror into two armed criminals. Clearly there was a side to the man she'd barely glimpsed.

Returning to the stove, she stirred the lumps out of the simmering mush. She owed it to herself and to Daniel to learn all she could about the stranger. And she would start with the wrecked boat that had brought him here.

As soon as breakfast was served she would make the trek down the cliff and examine every nook and cranny of that hull. If there was a clue to be found, she would find it.

Ishmael and Daniel sat on opposite sides of the table, feasting on sliced bread with chokecherry jam, fried eggs, barley coffee and cornmeal mush. Daniel was entertaining their guest with the story of how his father had once shot a black bear fifty paces from the house. Sylvie judged it a good time to slip away.

Murmuring a vague excuse, she stepped outside and made for the cliffside trail. The morning was sunlit, the ocean breeze brisk enough to batter her skirts as she made her way down to the cove. Gulls dipped and squawked above the waves. Overhead, a frigate bird circled on outstretched wings.

The wrecked sailboat lay at the water's edge, its brown painted hull already peeling in the sun. The scouring sand and smashing waves had begun to do their work. Before long the weakened timbers would fall apart and wash back out to sea.

Leaving her shoes and stockings on the rocks, Sylvie dropped to the wet sand. Water rose in her footprints as she splashed toward the overturned hull. Her heart sank as she studied the boat. The tide had been lower when they'd found Ishmael. At the time, she'd managed to shift the boat a few inches to clear his body. But she wasn't strong enough to careen the hull. As for digging away the sand and crawling underneath, the job would be wet and dirty and would take more time than she'd allowed herself.

But there was another way. Where the hull had smashed against the rocks, there was a hole the size of a dinner plate. Widen it, and she should be able to get through to the inside. Heedless of the splinters, her hands tore at the weakened boards. Within minutes she'd opened the hole far enough to fit her body through.

But she'd used up precious time. Much longer, and Ishmael would be wondering where she'd gone. Her eyes flickered upward to the top of the trail. Satisfied that no one was there, she clambered onto the hull and dropped through the jagged hole.

The air under the boat was damp and cool, the water deep enough to cover her feet. A crab scuttled out of the way, startling her as she dropped to a crouch. The light that fell through the hole was as bright as she needed; but the space was wet and cramped. By the time she got out, she'd be soaked.

There wasn't much under the boat. A quick look around confirmed that most of the loose objects had washed overboard in the storm. But there was a latched compartment in the bow. Maybe there'd be something inside.

Clearing the sand away from the small double doors, Sylvie worked at the stubborn latch. Her fingers were numb, the wood swollen. The sound of her breathing filled the confined space. She'd always hated being closed in. Worse, the tide was rising fast. She fought panic as the water deepened around her. There was plenty of time, she assured herself. And if the water came in too high, she knew the way out.

After frustrating seconds, the latch parted. Sylvie tugged at the swollen doors until they opened. What she saw made her gasp.

A heavy pistol, sheathed in its holster, gleamed in the shadows. Tangled in the belt lay a tin powder flask, sealed with wax, and a closed leather pouch that doubtless contained a supply of caps and balls.

The water was getting higher. Clasping her arms around the lot of what she'd found, Sylvie shoved herself up through the hole she'd widened earlier. A jagged board caught her dress, ripping the bodice, but never mind. She was out in the sunlit air, the tide swirling around her and the cries of seabirds like music in her ears.

Climbing off the wreck, she splashed her way to the rocks where she'd left her shoes. Soaked and sandy as she was, there'd be no hiding where she'd been. The easiest explanation would be a version of the truth— that she'd gone outside and, impulsively, decided to check the boat before the tide washed it away. But should she show Ishmael what she'd found?

As Shakespeare might have said, aye, there was the rub.

If any doubt remained that Ishmael was a dangerous man, it had vanished the moment she laid eyes on the pistol. He wouldn't have brought such a weapon along unless he planned to use it. And a gun of that sort was designed for just one purpose. Ishmael, whoever he was, had likely been planning to shoot someone.

Sylvie pulled on her stockings and shoes and knotted the laces. She couldn't just show up with Ishmael's gun—not until she knew more about him. The swollen compartment doors had protected the pistol from too much water damage. It could be dried, cleaned and used again, as could the caps and balls. Even the powder could be salvaged if the flask hadn't leaked. But a man with a serious head wound wasn't ready to have such a weapon at his disposal.

Partway up the trail, above the reach of high tide, was a deep niche in the side of the cliff. She could shove the pistol inside, along with the other things she'd found. The weapon would be safe there until she decided what to do with it.

Wrapping everything in her apron, she climbed the trail to the hiding place she'd chosen. The niche was so high she had to stretch on tiptoe to push the articles inside. Getting them out would be even more difficult. But at least Daniel wouldn't be able to reach it. Like most small boys, her brother was curious about weapons. It took her constant care to keep them out of his hands.

After jamming the niche with moss, she strode on up the cliffside trail. In the cove below, waves were already pounding the hull of the boat.

Maybe she should have left well enough alone. The discovery of the pistol had raised more questions than it answered. She still didn't know why Ishmael had been headed in their direction when the storm struck. And she still didn't know the identity of the mysterious Catriona.

As she rounded the last bend in the trail, she saw Ishmael waiting for her, the shotgun resting against his leg. The sunlight behind him cast his face into shadow. But she didn't need to see his expression to know he was upset.

"What were you doing, sneaking off like that?" Up close, his eyes were storm clouds, crackling electric bolts of fury. "When you didn't come back to the house, we thought those hooligans had shown up again and dragged you off. I was looking all over for you, and your brother was scared half to death."

"I'm sorry," Sylvie murmured, meaning it. She never would have wanted to frighten Daniel. "I should've said something."

"You're damn right you should've. I told you not to go off alone. And as soon as I wasn't looking, that was the first thing you did! What were you doing down there, anyway?"

She lifted her chin. "The tide was coming in. I thought it might be the last chance to look under the boat."

"Look for what?" He glared down at her.

"For something you might've left behind. Something you might have recognized."

"And did you find anything?"

Sylvie shook her head, hating the lie. "It was a waste of time. Now, if you'll give me that gun, I'll be getting back to my brother."

Snatching up the weapon, she pushed past him on the path. His hand caught her shoulder, whipping her back to face him. "Don't make this any harder than it is, Sylvie." His voice was a low rasp. "Right now, you and Daniel are the only people I can recognize or remember. That makes the two of you damn important to me. Until I can track down my missing life, I need to know you're safe. A stunt like the one you pulled this morning—"

"I said I was sorry. And I promise not to do it again. What more do you want from me?"

He loomed over her, his dark blue eyes smoldering with heat. Sylvie felt that heat seep into her, shimmering like water over her skin. A warm weight stirred and tightened in the depths of her body. Her pulse raced, fueled by a heady mix of fear and awe. He looked almost savage, like a caged animal who, if let loose, might devour her. How would that kind of devouring feel? Would it be so wrong to find out?

That morning she'd come sickeningly close to being raped. She'd tried to put the awful experience out of her mind, but the memory of those filthy hands on her body had lingered like a bad smell. Part of her never wanted to be touched again. But what she really needed was to forget. Letting Ishmael kiss her would blot out the memory as nothing else could.

Alarms shrilled in her head, but she stood rooted to the spot. His eyes seemed to darken. His fingers tightened on her shoulder. Sylvie lifted her chin, her lips parting. From somewhere below the cliff she could hear the wild mewl of seabirds.

He cleared his throat. His hand dropped to his side, releasing her shoulder as he stepped back.

"Go on back to the house, Sylvie." His voice was thick and husky. "Go back to your brother."

His message was clear. She was a silly girl who'd come perilously close to making a fool of herself. She would not let it happen again.

Wheeling away from him, she strode up the path toward the house. Only her shattered dignity kept her from breaking into a run.

Ishmael muttered curses as he watched her go. He'd been drawn to Sylvie the first moment he laid eyes on her. From the beginning, he'd warned himself to keep his distance. But despite his best intentions, things were getting complicated.

Too complicated.

Just now, it had been all he could do to keep from crushing her in his arms and kissing her till she begged for mercy. The hell of it was, she'd behaved as if that was exactly what she wanted. Standing there with those rosebud lips parted and waiting… Lord help him, how could any man resist that kind of temptation?

Sylvie was so blasted innocent. She had no inkling of the effect she had on him. If she knew what he'd fantasized about doing to her, she'd probably run him over the cliff with the shotgun.

If he had any brains he'd leave right now—trust to luck that he could find food and shelter, and that his memory would come back. But how could he go away and leave a woman and child unprotected? If those two buzzards came back here, Sylvie and Daniel wouldn't stand a chance.

He had no choice except to stay, at least until her father came home. *If* he came home.

*Aaron Cragun.* He turned the name over in his mind, puzzled once more by the familiar ring of it. The two thugs had known Cragun. And they'd appeared to know *him,* as well. Was there a connection? Had he known Sylvie's father in San Francisco?

Damn, if only he could remember.

Seating himself on a boulder at the top of the trail, he stared down into the cove. Waves swirled around the hull of the wrecked boat. Before long, as the tide rose, they'd be crashing against the rocks—effectively hiding what could be the answer to a mystery.

But one mystery had already been removed from that boat today.

He'd spotted Sylvie from the cliff top, just as she was climbing out of the hole in the boat. She'd been holding something in her hands, but at that distance he couldn't see what it was. As she neared the rocks he'd lost sight of her, catching only glimpses as she mounted the winding trail.

When he'd met her at the top, she'd been empty-handed. Not only that, but her apron, which she'd had on earlier, was missing.

Plagued by questions, he stared out at the choppy sea. What had Sylvie discovered inside the boat? Why had she hidden it, and why had she lied to him about it?

Ishmael needed answers. He would get them any way he could.

# Chapter Six

"We were worried about you, Sylvie." Daniel stood in the doorway as Sylvie mounted the front porch. "I wanted to help look for you, but Ishmael said I had to stay in the house."

"Ishmael was right." Sylvie bent to hug him. "This isn't a good day to be outside alone."

"You went outside alone."

"I know, and I shouldn't have done it. I promise I won't do it again." She touched a fingertip to his nose. "And you promise me the same, all right? Now, go and get the books for your lessons."

As he scampered off to the bookshelf, Sylvie replaced the shotgun on the rack above the door. After changing into dry clothes, she tied on a clean apron and began clearing away the breakfast dishes. When she'd finished wiping the table, Daniel sat down with his slate and books. He was a bright little boy. Hopefully, one day he'd have the chance to attend school.

Meanwhile, Sylvie wanted him to be well prepared. She made sure he spent at least an hour a day on his lessons, even in the summer.

"Let's see if you can do ten subtraction problems, while I wash the dishes," she said. "When I'm finished, we'll go over the answers together."

"Bet I can get them all right!" Daniel opened his arithmetic book, then glanced up. "Ishmael said I could help him mend the garden fence today."

Sylvie poured hot water from the kettle into the dishpan. "Ishmael's been sick. He'll need more rest before he's ready to work."

"He says he can do it if I help him. I can hand him the tools and hold the posts steady while he hammers them. Please, Sylvie. He can't do it without me."

"Finish your lessons. Then we'll see." It wouldn't do for the boy to get too attached to a stranger with no memory. But Sylvie could tell it was already happening. Daniel had scarcely been able to take his eyes off his new friend at breakfast.

*His new friend...* Sylvie sighed as she soaped a plate and dunked it in the rinse water. Her brother was a lonely, impressionable little boy. Ishmael could break his heart.

*And hers, if she wasn't careful.*

"Ishmael is nice," Daniel announced. "Why don't we ask him to stay?"

Sylvie shot the boy a despairing glance. The explanation couldn't wait. "Think about this, Daniel. What if you went somewhere for a visit and got hit on the head, and when you woke up you couldn't remember anything—not Papa or me, or your home, or even your own name? How would that feel?"

"Scary." Daniel's eyes widened.

"And what if, later on, you remembered again—remembered everything about who you were and where you came from? What would you do?"

"Come home, I guess."

"Well, that's what's happened to Ishmael. He belongs somewhere else. He has a home, maybe even a wife and children. What do you think he'll do when he gets his memory back?"

The boy looked crestfallen as the answer sank home. Then he brightened. "What if Ishmael never gets his memory back? Then can he stay?"

Sylvie soaped another plate. "I can't imagine he'd want to. He'd probably choose to go back to San Francisco and try to find someone who knows him."

"But maybe he'll decide to stay. Maybe he'll fall in love with you and want to marry you. Wouldn't you like that?"

"Daniel…" Sylvie sighed. This discussion was headed in the wrong direction. "Things like that only happen in fairy tales," she said. "Besides, even if he did, how could I marry a man who doesn't even know his own name?"

Daniel looked thoughtful, then giggled. "That would be funny. You'd have to be Mrs. Nobody. Sylvie Nobody."

"That's enough." Her face was burning. "Get back to those subtraction problems, young man. If you finish on time, and get all the answers correct, you can help

Ishmael with the fence. But only if he's well enough to work."

She glanced over her shoulder. Daniel's dark head was bowed over his arithmetic book.

Ishmael returned to the house twenty minutes later. As he stepped onto the porch he could see Sylvie and Daniel at the kitchen table. Her wheaten hair contrasted richly with his dark curls as they bent over an open book.

Stepping back a little, he watched them. With no schools nearby, it stood to reason that Sylvie would be teaching the boy his numbers and letters. But something more was going on here. He could sense Daniel's excitement as they checked the arithmetic problems. He could almost feel her tenderness and patience as they worked together. This wasn't just rote recitation. She was instilling the love of learning in her bright little brother, molding him into a scholar.

His gaze wandered to the shelves crammed with books and to the hand-drawn maps on the wall above them. Sylvie Cragun was no ignorant, backwoods girl. Despite her isolated life, she'd managed to give herself a good education. She was well-spoken and well-read, and with a little refining her manners would be suitable in any society.

All of which led him to wonder about her father. The two thugs he'd run off that morning had been looking for Aaron Cragun. They'd referred to him as a little weasel and claimed he'd cheated them out of fifty dollars. How could such a man have raised two children like Sylvie and Daniel?

Was there something here he wasn't seeing?

The more he thought about it, the more sense it made that Aaron Cragun was the missing piece of his puzzle—the central piece that connected all the others. But how did the pieces fit together? And where did his own piece fit? Ishmael wondered. Had he been headed here when the storm struck? Had he been looking for Aaron Cragun, too?

Sylvie glanced up just then and saw him. "Shouldn't you be resting?" she asked.

He shook his head. "Being up seems to agree with me. I'm feeling better by the hour. And since you've made it clear that I'm expected to work, I thought I'd start on that broken-down garden fence."

A shadow of caution flashed across her face. "Daniel asked if he could help you. He'll be free as soon as we finish checking his subtraction problems—*if* he gets all the answers right."

Daniel looked up from his slate and grinned. "Almost done," he said. "And all right so far."

Ishmael chuckled. "They'd better be. Your sister is one tough teacher. Almost as tough as Miss Hawthorne, back in my grammar school days. She used to whack us with—"

He broke off as he realized Sylvie was staring at him. "You remembered," she said. "You remembered your teacher."

And so he had. The image of Miss Abigail Hawthorne—pince-nez spectacles, a ratty bun atop her

head and a mouth perpetually pursed in disapproval—
was crystal clear in his mind.

And utterly useless.

His fist clenched in frustration. So far he'd remembered lines from a book, the plot of a Shakespearean
play, the name of a long-dead Dutch artist and the
teacher who'd left bruises on his knuckles. He was
glad he was finally remembering something from his
personal life, but still…

Why in hell's name couldn't he remember anything
helpful?

Daniel finished his last subtraction problem with a
perfect score. Whooping, he raced outside to fetch the
tools from the shed. Sylvie sighed as she watched him
go. Ordinarily the boy wouldn't have been so eager to
work, but he'd seized on the chance to spend time with
Ishmael.

Glancing out the window, she could see Ishmael
waiting by the garden. He'd pushed a thick log up to
the fence so he could do most of the work sitting down,
a sign that he might not feel as strong as he'd claimed.

For a few moments she allowed her gaze to linger.
He was keeping an eye on Daniel, making sure the
boy was safe. Did he have children of his own? Sylvie
wondered. He was so good with her little brother, it
did seem possible. But how tragic it would be to have
a family and not remember them.

Somewhere there could be a woman searching for
him, maybe young children crying for their father.
Sylvie could imagine how they must feel, how their

hearts must ache for him. How could the memories of a man's life be wiped out by such a simple thing as a blow on the head?

Was Ishmael's memory coming back? She'd been startled when he mentioned his teacher. The recollection hadn't led to anything important, but it could be a sign that he was getting better. Everything Ishmael needed to know was buried in his mind. All he needed to do was find the connections.

*Did she want him to find them? Did she want him to remember?*

The sea wind blew his hair back from his face, revealing the dark, bruised gash on his temple. He'd taken the wrapping off after breakfast, which was probably just as well. The poultice had done its work. His flesh was healing. Was his mind healing, as well?

She reminded herself of the pistol she'd found in the boat. Ishmael was a man of secrets, perhaps dangerous secrets. But watching his gentleness with her little brother, it was becoming difficult to see him as a threat. Children had innate instincts about people, or so she believed. Daniel trusted the stranger. And in her woman's heart, Sylvie realized, she yearned to trust him, too.

As her eyes traced his profile, she remembered her own warning to Daniel. Somewhere Ishmael had a home. When he remembered, or even if he didn't, he was bound to leave them.

What should she do, when every minute he stayed made that leaving harder to accept? There was only one right answer to that question. She would do everything she could to help him remember. The sooner he was able to go, the less pain it would cause. She had found Ishmael and saved his life. But that didn't mean he was hers. He belonged to another place and to other people. She needed to give him back before it was too late.

Daniel had returned with the tools. Laughing and chatting, he and Ishmael planned their repair job. Sylvie watched the pair a moment longer. Then she forced herself away from the window and set herself to mixing bread.

Ishmael and Daniel had gathered a stack of branches blown down by the storm. Using a saw and a knife, Ishmael began cutting them into stakes with sharp ends that could be hammered into the ground. The job wasn't as easy as it had first appeared. Goats were as clever as they were nimble. They'd butted several openings in the present fence and eaten off most of the carrot tops. It would take a higher, sturdier fence to keep them out of the vegetable garden.

While they worked, Ishmael kept a lookout for the two thugs he'd run off earlier. He'd taken their weapons and given them a good scare, but that didn't mean they wouldn't be back—especially if they expected Aaron Cragun to show up.

"What do you think, Daniel?" Ishmael surveyed the first stick he'd hammered into the ground. "Does it look straight to you?"

"This is what my pa does." Daniel picked up a string with a heavy nail tied to one end—an improvised plum bob. Holding the string to the top of the stick, he let the nail hang, creating a vertical line with the string. "A little bit more this way." The boy motioned left. "Pa says it's important to start straight. If you don't, the whole thing will be crooked."

Ishmael tapped the stick until the line of it matched the string. "Your father must be a very smart man," he said.

"My pa's the smartest man in the world. He built our house and all the stuff you see around here." The boy glanced toward the road, a wistful look on his face. "He's been gone a long time. I can tell Sylvie's worried about him. But he'll be home soon. He always comes home, and he brings us presents."

"What kind of presents?" Ishmael positioned another stake, lining it up with the first one.

"Books, mostly. But sometimes other things, too. Last time he brought Sylvie some cloth to make a dress. And he brought me some shoes. They're too big but he says my feet will grow."

"I'm sure they will. Here, hold this." He reached for the hammer while Daniel held the stake in place.

"Do you like my sister?"

The hammer slipped, barely missing Ishmael's thumb. "Of course I like her," he said. "She's a nice person."

"Sylvie likes you, too." Daniel was all wide-eyed innocence. "I think she likes you a lot. But she's afraid you might have a wife already. Do you?"

"Not that I know of." Ishmael aimed a blow at the

stake and struck home. "But since I don't remember, I can't say for sure."

"If you knew you didn't have a wife, would you fall in love with Sylvie?"

Ishmael shot the boy a good-natured scowl. "Now, what kind of question is that? Since I can't answer the last one you asked me, how would I know?"

Confused by the twist in logic, Daniel frowned. "Are you sure you're not a prince?" he asked.

"I'm not sure of anything, but there aren't many princes in this world. It would be pretty surprising if I was one of them, wouldn't it?"

Daniel shrugged. "I wish my pa was here," he said. "He'd know whether you were a prince or not. Pa knows everything."

Ishmael wished the boy's pa was there, too. If he knew everything, then Aaron Cragun just might know Ishmael's real name.

Supper was savory rabbit stew with dumplings and fresh buttered biscuits. After a long afternoon's work, Ishmael's appetite had come roaring back. But Daniel was worn out. By the end of the meal he was nodding off over his gooseberry pie.

"Come on, sleepyhead." Sylvie eased her brother out of his chair. "You worked hard today. Time to get ready for bed."

"Will you tell me a story, Sylvie?" the boy murmured.

"Maybe, if you're not too tired. Let's get you washed up and into your nightshirt. Then we'll see."

She led him off to the bedroom. Ishmael busied himself with clearing the table. That was the least he could do after such a generous meal.

A few minutes later they were back, with Daniel freshly scrubbed and wearing a clean gray flannel nightshirt. Sylvie settled herself in the rocking chair with her little brother on her lap. It seemed the boy was going to get a story after all. And so was Ishmael. Quietly, so as not to interrupt, he began soaping the dishes.

"What kind of story would you like to hear, Daniel?" she asked softly.

"I want to hear what happened to the prince from the sea," the boy said. "We didn't finish it before."

"Then help me remember," Sylvie said. "Tell me how it started."

Daniel snuggled closer, his dark head resting against her shoulder. "The prince wanted to walk on land, but he couldn't because he had a tail like a fish. Then a big wave washed him onto the shore, and when he woke up, he had legs."

"Oh, I remember now," Sylvie said. "Let's put some clothes on him, shall we? We can just pretend it was magic."

The boy nodded with a little sigh of contentment.

"Let's see…" Sylvie's voice had taken on a mystical quality. As he listened, Ishmael felt himself being pulled into the spell of her story.

"At first, the prince had a hard time walking on his new legs. His knees wobbled with every step. But by the time he'd climbed up the dune to the forest on the other side, he was doing better. He strode along the path, marveling at everything he saw—the trees and flowers, the birds, the animals…" She glanced down at her brother. His eyes were still open, but his head began to droop as she continued, "And the sounds—the wind, the rustle of leaves, the songs of birds. The prince had only known the sound of the sea. He had never heard anything so lovely."

Ishmael watched her from the kitchen. The lamp-light fell like a halo on her spun-gold hair. Her arms were tender as she cradled the child she'd raised. Her face was as serene as a Madonna's.

Sylvie Cragun was beautiful, he thought. So beautiful she made his throat ache. Her voice crept around him like fragrant smoke, low and sensual, stroking him like a caress. Under different circumstances, he would gladly have swept her out of the chair, carried her into the bedroom and spent the night showing her the kind of pleasure she'd never known. But thoughts like that were leading him down the wrong path. The sooner he put them out of his mind the better.

"The prince wasn't used to walking far," Sylvie continued. "Soon he began to get tired and thirsty. Ahead of him, at the bend in the road, he saw a pretty little house with a thatched roof and a garden. 'That looks like a good place to stop and rest,' the prince said to himself.

"Walking up to the house, he knocked on the door. It was opened by the most beautiful girl he'd ever seen. She had long, black hair and eyes as green as the trees in the forest. The instant she and the prince looked at each other they fell in love.

"Now, the girl was dressed in rags. The prince could tell she was very poor. That didn't matter to him, because he had a palace and a fortune in gold and jewels under the sea. But there was one problem. Can you guess what it was?" She glanced down at her brother. "Daniel?"

The smile that crept across her face was as soft as moonrise. The boy was fast asleep.

Sylvie carried Daniel into her room and tucked him in her own bed. Until a few months ago, it would have been easy to carry him up the ladder to his loft. But he was growing fast, getting taller and heavier. Maybe later she could wake him, or ask Ishmael to help her. Otherwise she'd be facing a restless night on the child-size loft bed, or trying to share her own bed and sleep around the margins of his sprawling arms and legs.

Returning to the kitchen, she saw that Ishmael had finished washing the dishes. He was standing near the stove, warming himself against the night air that had grown chilly.

"That wasn't necessary," she said, stacking the clean plates. "I didn't ask you to do my work."

His smile weakened her ankles. "I needed an excuse to stay and hear your story. How does it end, by the way?"

Sylvie felt her face warm. "I won't know until I tell it. And that won't be until Daniel wants to hear more."

"Then I can only hope I'll be here to listen. Otherwise I'll spend the rest of my life wondering what happened to the prince."

His words struck her with an unexpected sting. She'd told herself over and over that he was bound to leave. But this was the first time she'd heard it implied from his lips.

"Is your memory coming back?" she asked, remembering her resolve to help him.

"No more than before. Trying to remember anything useful is like looking for a grain of coal in the dark. But I've been thinking..." He turned away from the stove. The lamp cast sparks of flame in his night-blue eyes. "Those two men I ran off said they knew your father. And you said they knew me, too. That has to mean something."

Sylvie spun toward him, her defenses prickling. "Those men were liars. They said my father cheated them. Aaron Cragun would never cheat anybody."

"I'm not saying he did. But they knew his name. That had to come from somewhere."

"Did you recognize the name?" In the silence that followed, Sylvie realized she was holding her breath.

At last he shook his head. "Not really, though it did have a familiar ring. That's what started me wondering. Do you happen to have a picture of your father? Maybe that would spark something."

Sylvie hesitated. Whatever might connect Ishmael to her father, she needed to know it. So what was holding her back?

"I have an old daguerreotype," she said. "But my father's changed a lot since it was taken."

"May I see it?" Ishmael's voice was gentle but insistent. Sylvie sensed that he was accustomed to getting what he asked for.

"It's in the chest at the foot of my bed. I should be able to find it without waking Daniel."

She walked into the dark bedroom and knelt on the rug to open the chest. Since it held mostly clothes and linens, and since she'd always kept the picture on the bottom, her fingers had no trouble finding the rigid corners of the frame. Lifting it out, she rose and carried it back into the light.

The photograph was smaller than the span of Ishmael's hand, but the image, protected by glass, was clear. It was a family portrait, showing a young couple, seated, with a little girl about five years old standing between them.

Ishmael recognized the child first. Clad in a lacy dress, she was as delicate as a white violet, with large, intelligent eyes and a nimbus of pale blond ringlets. Her rosebud mouth was drawn into a childish pout, as if she was being forced to pose when she wanted to run and play.

"I didn't want to hold still," Sylvie said. "My mother threatened to send me to bed without supper if I so much as moved a muscle."

"You look like her now." Ishmael studied the beautiful, fair-haired woman in the portrait. Sylvie had the same fine-drawn features, the same high cheekbones, long-lashed eyes and small, firm chin.

"Her name was Alice," Sylvie said. "Before she

married my father, she was a teacher. She taught me correct grammar and good manners and insisted I use them. And she taught me to love stories. When she died, it almost destroyed my father. If I hadn't been there to take care of him, I think he might have died, too."

*And you've been taking care of people ever since,* Ishmael thought. While most young girls enjoyed the carefree years of growing up, Sylvie had taken on a woman's responsibilities while she was still a child. Any dreams she might've had, any chance for a life of her own, had been sacrificed for the sake of her father and brother.

So far, Ishmael had avoided a close inspection of Aaron Cragun—perhaps because Cragun's wife and daughter had drawn his eye first. Now he took a long look at the man, or at least the man Cragun had been.

What he saw surprised him. Aaron Cragun was small and wiry, with a jutting nose, sharp, bright eyes and a shock of hair that looked as if it might have been red. That such a homely little man could have married a beauty like Alice and fathered a child like Sylvie seemed ludicrous, if not impossible.

"So, does my father look familiar?" Sylvie asked.

Ishmael stared at the image. Nothing stirred in his memory. "What does your father look like now?" he asked.

"He's older, of course. The portrait was taken just fifteen years ago, but he's had a hard life, and it shows. His hair has some gray in it, and he's grown a beard.

He dresses like a prospector and he loves to talk. I'm guessing he wouldn't be an easy man to forget."

Ishmael shook his head. "Well, if I ever met your father, I can't remember him now."

"I'm sorry. I know you were hoping the picture might help you." She lifted a woolen shawl from the back of the chair, walked to the front door and opened it. "I'm worried about him, Ishmael. He's been gone far too long."

Laying the portrait on the table, Ishmael followed her out onto the porch. The moon was rising above the pines, spilling its light across the yard. Below the cliff, the tide boomed and whispered.

"What will you do if he doesn't come back?"

A shudder passed through her slim body. "I don't know. It's too soon to think of that."

He checked the urge to wrap his arms around her and pull her against him. "You need to start thinking about it, Sylvie. After meeting those two men, I get the feeling he's run into some trouble. If something's happened, you won't be safe here."

She stared across the yard, her back rigid. "I'm not proud of the way my father makes his living," she said. "But he's a good man, and he loves us. If there's any way he can get back here, he will. Daniel and I need to be here when he arrives."

"And if he doesn't?"

"Don't say that. Not tonight." She walked to the edge of the porch. Beyond the garden, the goats stirred sleepily in their pen. "What about you?" she asked.

"What will you do if your memory doesn't come back?"

"My answer's the same as yours. It's too soon to think about it."

What *would* he do? Ishmael wondered. But there was only one right answer to that question. This place was a refuge, a little piece of heaven, complete with an angel who would steal his heart if he let her. But he couldn't stay. He owed it to himself and to anyone he'd left behind to find the missing pieces of the puzzle.

Yet, how could he go? How could he leave a woman and child at the mercy of at least two predators who might still be lurking in the woods?

"Have you thought any more about Catriona?" She spoke carefully, as if every word had been planned ahead. "Her name could be the key to everything."

Ishmael shook his head. He'd racked his brains trying to remember, but the name was still just a name.

"And the ring? You can't remember any more about that?"

"Nothing." He glanced around the yard, listening to the night. Except for the usual sounds—the whisper of wind in the pines, the stirring animals and the muted hiss of waves below the cliff—all was peaceful. But something inside him was on alert, like a hound straining at the leash. Ishmael's instincts warned him to pay attention.

"I'll be spending the night out here on the porch," he said. "Those two thugs could come sneaking back in the dark. You'll need to lend me the shotgun. What did you do with that little pocket pistol I gave you, and the knives they left behind?"

He sensed her hesitation. Even after today, she didn't trust him. But how could he blame her?

"If you're worried about me—" he began.

"Of course not. You saved my life this morning. You can have anything you want. But you've been ill and you need your rest. I'll get you a blanket and pillow." She turned toward the door. He stopped her with a hand on her arm. Even that brief contact sent a jolt through his body. He swore silently. It was getting harder and harder to keep his hands off the woman.

"The rocking chair will do me fine," he said. "I don't want to sleep too soundly. Don't trouble yourself, I'll carry it outside. The shotgun, too."

"I'll fetch the pistol and the knives. And I'll be praying you don't need them."

She flitted into the house. Ishmael could hear her rummaging in the cupboard for the things she'd put away. Retrieving the chair and the shotgun, he carried them out onto the porch. It was going to be a long, uncomfortable night, but after that morning's encounter he'd be a fool not to keep watch.

Sylvie returned a moment later with the pocket pistol and the two knives the men had left behind. Ishmael chose the larger knife. "You keep the smaller one and the pistol," he told her. "If anything should go wrong—"

"Stop talking like that!" Her silver eyes were huge in the moonlight. "You're scaring me, Ishmael. Anyway, those men were looking for my father. Now they know he isn't here."

"But that won't stop them from coming back. If they can't get their money, they might decide to settle for revenge." Ishmael left the details unspoken. Even without weapons, the two butchers could do plenty of damage. He imagined Aaron Cragun coming home to find his house burned, his daughter raped and his son—

He couldn't even finish the thought.

"If you hear anything, promise you'll wake me," Sylvie said. "You might need help, and I'm a good shot."

"Have you ever shot a man, Sylvie?"

Fear flickered in her eyes, to be replaced by a fierce determination. "No, but I've shot deer for meat. And I'd kill to protect my little brother."

"I'm guessing it won't come to that." He smiled, making an effort to put her at ease. "More than likely I'll spend a long, boring night out here and wake up grumpier than an old bear."

"I can wait up with you," she volunteered. "I'll even take my turn watching while you sleep."

For the space of a breath he weighed her offer. A chilly night on a moonlit porch with a beautiful woman…that could be downright tempting. But no, it could be dangerous. Sylvie could be hurt, or she could distract him when he needed to keep a lookout.

And given the way he'd been reacting to her lately, Ishmael wasn't certain how far he could trust himself.

"Well," she demanded, "do you want me to stay or not?"

He loomed over her, a thunderous scowl on his face. "I can name half a dozen reasons why that's not a good idea. I need you inside where it's safe. Whatever happens, whatever you see or hear, don't come rushing out to rescue me. You'll just be in the way."

Her pretty face froze. "In the way? But I could—"

"You heard me. Go in the house like a good girl. Bar the door and keep the gun with you. Hear?"

She made a little huffing sound, turned on her heel and stalked toward the door. Ishmael squelched the urge to call her back. Whatever happened tonight, he needed to know that she and Daniel were safe.

Moving the chair back into the shadows, he settled the shotgun across his knees. With luck, the night would be quiet, the danger gone. But his instincts told him that the two strangers hadn't gone far.

If they came back, he would do his best to capture at least one of them alive. If Sylvie had overheard them correctly, the two thugs had something he wanted, something that could make all the difference.

They could tell him who he was.

# *Chapter Seven*

Sylvie closed the door and slammed the bolt shut. How dare Ishmael speak to her as if she were a backward child? She could handle a gun, kill a rattlesnake, drive a wagon, chop wood, mend a leaking shed and do all a woman's chores. She had dragged him out from under the boat, dressed his wound, nursed him through a fever and probably saved his worthless life. Yet the wretched man had ordered her inside as if she didn't have a brain in her fluttery female head.

Taking a deep breath, she counted slowly to ten. In his own maddening way, Ishmael was right, she conceded. This was a dangerous time, and her first responsibility was keeping Daniel safe. To protect her little brother she needed to be with him, in the house.

So why hadn't Ishmael put it that way, instead of behaving like a superior male jackass? Why did men always feel they had to put women in their place?

Walking to the front window, she pressed close to

the pane. She couldn't see Ishmael from where she stood. He'd probably moved back into the shadows. Or maybe he was prowling the yard, looking and listening.

Over the course of the busy day, Sylvie had managed to block out the scene in the milk shed. But now, alone in the dark, the memory came crashing in on her—the sour smell of the strangers' clothes, their laughter, their rough, dirty hands holding her down, groping her, touching her...

As her thoughts careened ahead to what would have come next, Sylvie began to shake. She'd grown up around animals and read enough to know the facts of life. She knew what happened between men and women, and that sometimes the act could be a horrific violation. Before today that had been unimaginable. But no longer. Now in her mind she saw the hands unbuckle the belt, felt the brutal force spreading her legs...

Clutching her ribs, she doubled over and began to sob.

Ishmael walked the brushy ring between the yard and the trees, keeping the house in sight. His senses were on high alert, the shotgun balanced in his hands. Every few steps he paused to listen to the night sounds around him—the whine of insects, the distant hoot of an owl, the rise and fall of surf below the cliff. Nothing seemed out of place. Maybe he'd imagined the sense of lurking danger.

The house was dark, its porthole windows quiet. There was no sign of Sylvie. He'd been rough on her tonight, but how else was he supposed to keep her safe? If their visitors returned, it was her they'd go after. He needed her inside the house so he could do his job.

*His job.*

It felt strangely natural, patrolling the night to protect innocent people. Was that a clue to the kind of work he'd done? Once more Ishmael cursed his missing memory. He felt helplessly adrift, and he hated it. He wanted to be in charge of his life again. He wanted to know who he was.

And he wanted Sylvie to know.

A faint rustle in the bushes put him on instant alert. He froze, nerves straining in the darkness. After a moment something stirred. He exhaled as a wood rat scurried across his path. He was getting jumpy. Maybe it was time to go back to the house and keep watch.

On the porch, he moved the chair deeper into the shadows. From the height of the moon, he guessed the time to be about eleven o'clock. He had hours to wait before dawn. Glancing through the window into the dark house, he saw no movement. He could only hope Sylvie was getting some sleep. She'd been through a rough time, and it was bound to catch up with her.

The moon crept higher. By midnight Ishmael had begun to doze. His head sagged, then jerked upward. Rising, he prowled the yard again, listening for any sign that he wasn't alone. Nothing.

As he settled back on the porch, his thoughts returned to Sylvie. He remembered her face in the moonlight, eyes like silver pools, lips moist and tempting. So vulnerable. Damn, but it would've felt good to hold her, to taste her...

He imagined her lying in bed, her moon-colored hair fanned on the pillow, one arm flung outward in childlike innocence. He could picture the rise and fall of her breasts beneath the worn flannel nightgown...

*No, scratch the damn nightgown. This was his fantasy, and he'd have it his way.*

*Naked as Venus, she lay in the moonlight, her breasts gleaming pale, her hips barely covered by the sheet. She made a little catlike sound as he bent to kiss her mouth. Her body strained upward. Her lips parted, giving him the tiniest flick of tongue.*

*The contact blazed. Heat surged through his veins. He wanted her. His body was straining to take her here and now. But he knew this was no time to rush. Making love to Sylvie would be like eating ice cream, letting each delicious spoonful melt slowly in his mouth.*

*He deepened the kiss. She moaned, catching his head in her hands, weaving frenzied fingers into his hair. The taste of her was dark, wild honey. Muttering insanely, he kissed her eyes, her chin, her throat, then returned once more to plunder that tantalizing mouth.*

*His hand found the satiny mound of her breast. The fit was perfect, molding like warm butter to his palm. She arched upward, her head falling back as his thumb teased her nipple to a swollen nub. The press of her fingers in his hair urged him downward until his mouth took it in. She gasped, then moaned, pushing against him, her hips making instinctive little thrusts.*

*Sliding his hand around her back he cupped her*

*firm little rump, cradling her against him as he suckled her breast. Heaven... He could have died happy right then. But he wanted more. So did she.*

*Her thighs quivered at his touch. She was trembling—he could feel the fear of her first time. "It's all right, love." His mouth moved against her belly as he eased downward. "I won't hurt you, Sylvie. I'd die before I'd hurt you..."*

*He stroked her, holding back with a tenderness that almost made his teeth ache. Beneath the veil of crisp hair, she was a closed bud, her tight folds slick with moisture. Thrusting against his hand, she whimpered as he opened her petals to his touch. She was ready, so ready, and he ached with wanting her...*

Ishmael jerked awake as the dream dissolved. Any other time, he'd have paid good money to go back to sleep and pick up where he'd left off. But tonight dozing was dangerous. Lives could depend on his staying watchful.

What had alerted him? Keeping still in the chair, he held his breath and listened. Was that the snap of a twig he heard? The whisper of a voice? Something had pricked his senses enough to wake him.

Seconds ticked past before he realized it was the goats.

Penned for the night, they were agitated, milling restlessly about in the confined space, as if they'd sensed a predator close by.

Ishmael rose quietly, the shotgun in his hands. It could be an animal that had spooked them, maybe a cougar or a coyote. Or the unseen invader could be human. Flattening himself against the shadowed wall, he eased around the corner of the house. In the moonlight, he could see the goat pen, with its sheltering plank roof along one side. The goats were moving, their brown-and-white spots flowing eerily in the shadows. The small one—Daniel's favorite—had begun to bleat. It sounded frightened.

Keeping to the dark side of the house, Ishmael peered around for what might have spooked them. If the intruder was an animal, a gunshot and some loud yelling would likely be enough to scare it off. The same tactic might work for their morning visitors. But he didn't want to chase them away. He needed to find out what they wanted, and what they knew.

Dropping to his haunches, he crept toward the goat pen. Through the milling bodies, on the far side of the fence, he detected a crouching silhouette. A head raised in the moonlight. Ishmael recognized the taller, thinner man from their morning encounter.

But there'd been two men. Where was his partner? Circling the house, maybe looking for a way in? Did they know he was here? *Damn, I don't like this,* Ishmael groused. If he'd been wide-awake, he would have seen them sooner. Now he needed a way to draw the missing man out, or he could be in for a nasty surprise.

Picking up a thumb-size pebble from the ground, Ishmael tossed it into the front yard. It landed in the grass with a thud. The man on the far side of the goat pen started, lifting his head. But he remained where he was. There was no sign of the second man—which could mean the fat bastard already knew where Ishmael was. He could be just out of sight, waiting for the right moment to rush him. For all he knew, there could be more than two of them, and they could be armed. Hellfire, there could be a dozen of them out there.

No use throwing a second pebble. The first one hadn't worked. For now, all Ishmael could do was sit still and wait for something to happen.

In the stillness he thought of Sylvie and her innocent young brother, asleep in the house. He was here to protect them. If need be, he would give his life to keep them safe. In the short time he'd been here, they'd become the closest thing he had to family.

Minutes crawled past. The night was chilly, but Ishmael could feel the sweat beading on his body. Where was the second man? Why hadn't he made his move?

He would lay odds that neither of them had a gun. If they did, they'd have tried to use it by now, so they could get to Sylvie and sack the house. The pair hadn't impressed him as very patient or very smart. But what if he was wrong?

He could blast the man behind the goat pen and take a chance that the partner, wherever he was, would run. It might not buy him what he wanted to know, but at least Sylvie and Daniel would be safe.

On the other hand, if he fired without knowing about the second man, all hell could break loose, putting them all in peril.

Shifting, he got his legs under him. He would wait a little longer. Any move would entail risks. If the unsavory pair managed to kill him, then Sylvie and the boy would be at their mercy.

Except for the surge of the sea and the restless movement of the goats, the night was still. In the silence, Ishmael heard a sound that galvanized him—the crunch of a boot on gravel. It had come from the walkway on the far side of the house.

Ishmael's muscles screamed as he shifted position and raised the single-barrel shotgun. He had enemies on both sides and just one chance to fire. He would blast whichever one came at him first and take his chances with the second man. He was too weak for a prolonged fistfight or chase, but he would give it all he had. Lives depended on his actions.

Another footstep. Ishmael was rising when he heard the pop of a small-caliber weapon, followed by a gurgled obscenity that died into silence.

*Sylvie!*

The man on the far side of the goat pen jumped to his feet and bolted for the trees. Letting him go, Ishmael sprinted around the house.

A man's thickset body lay on the gravel below the open porthole. Blood, flowing from the punctured vein in his neck, pooled tar-black in the moonlight. His open eyes were already glazing.

Ishmael's first thought was for Sylvie and Daniel. Since they were nowhere in sight, it appeared they were safe inside the house. His second thought...

Panic surged as he dropped to a crouch and seized the dying thug by the collar. "You know me!" he rasped. "Who am I?"

There was no response.

"Answer me, damn you!" He shook the man in desperation. *"Who am I?"*

But he was already too late.

Rising, he hurried back to the front porch. Sylvie stood in the open doorway, clad in her nightgown. Her hand was locked around the grip of the pocket pistol. Framed in shadow, her pale face was frozen in horror.

Without a word, Ishmael put the shotgun aside, eased the pistol from her fingers and gathered her into his arms.

Trembling, she sagged against him and pressed her face into his shirt. Her body shook with dry sobs.

"It's all right, Sylvie." His lips grazed her hair, her forehead, her eyelids. "You're safe. Those butchers won't hurt you now."

She stared up at him, her hands gripping his shirtfront. "Tell me what happened."

He hesitated, wondering if she was up to hearing the truth. "One man ran off," he said. "The other one's dead."

"I killed him, didn't I?" Her eyes were huge in the darkness. "Oh, no!" She was shaking harder than ever. "I didn't mean to, Ishmael. I saw him through the open window. He had a knife. I thought maybe I could wound him with that little gun, or at least scare him off. I was so afraid he might kill you." She'd begun to sob again. This time there were tears. "I'm sorry. I know you needed to talk to him."

"Hush. It's over."

"I know he was bad. But I never knew how it felt to take a life—a soul. It's awful..."

"Sylvie. Hush." His arms tightened around her. He could feel her heart pounding against his chest. She was so precious, so vulnerable. What if he'd lost her tonight?

He bent his head and covered her mouth with his. For an instant she went rigid with shock. Then, with a little whimper, she melted against him.

Sylvie had read about kissing and imagined it in her girlish daydreams. This time it was real—and as overwhelming as a storm at sea. Her heart slammed. Her pulse raced. Ishmael's smooth, cool lips were masterfully gentle, tasting of her own salty tears. Her first impulse was to jerk away, but as the kiss continued, something changed. Suddenly she couldn't get enough of him.

Her hands caught the back of his head, pulling him closer. Her muscles strained upward until her toes were barely touching the porch. Through her thin nightgown, she could feel the full length of his big, masculine body. Heaven save her, she wanted to feel him all around her. She wanted to lose herself in him, to huddle against him and let his strength block out all the terror and ugliness that had invaded her world.

What was wrong with her? She'd just taken a life and her emotions were a swirling maelstrom. But all she could think of was this man, his arms holding her, his hands caressing the curve of her back. She was wearing nothing beneath the threadbare nightgown. The feel of those strong hands, so close to her skin, sent hot shivers pulsing through every part of her.

Something stirred and tightened, clenching like a fist in the deep core of her body. The sensations were so powerful that she almost wept.

Ishmael's breath rasped in and out. Through his trousers, his arousal jutted hard against her belly. The pressure was exquisite, as if—

"Sylvie! Where are you?" Daniel's cry from the bedroom broke them apart.

"It's all right, I'm coming!" Guilt-torn, she stumbled back from Ishmael. When she looked up at him it was as if a mask had slipped over his face. "Keep the boy inside," he said. "I'll get rid of our visitor and clean up."

Sylvie rushed into the house and closed the door behind her. Daniel was sitting up in her bed, his eyes huge and bewildered.

"I heard a noise," he whimpered. "It woke me up."

"It's all right." She cradled him close. "We're safe. You can go back to sleep."

"Did those men come back?"

"Yes. But Ishmael scared them away. That's what you heard."

"Will they come back again?"

"I don't think so. But if they do, Ishmael's outside. He'll keep us safe. You can go back to sleep now."

"I'm scared." He clung to her. "Will you stay here with me, Sylvie?"

"I'll be here. I promise."

"Will you sing to me?"

"Only if you lie down and close your eyes."

With a little sigh he snuggled into the pillow. Sylvie

tucked the covers around him and began to sing. The childish lullaby was one her own mother had sung to her. Daniel had always loved it.

As the boy's eyelids drooped and closed, Sylvie's thoughts returned to that heart-stopping kiss on the porch with Ishmael. If she could have stopped time right there and stayed in his arms forever, with his mouth on hers, she'd have been tempted to do it. Never in her young life had she known a more thrilling moment.

But she knew she couldn't let it happen again. Falling in love with Ishmael would be the easiest thing she'd ever done. But loving a man who might not be free was both wrong and foolish. She was a better person than the reckless girl who'd shared a stolen kiss on the front porch. In the trying days ahead, she would remind herself of that.

Daniel had slipped back into dreamland. Restless now, Sylvie thought about getting dressed and going outside to see if Ishmael needed her help. But she'd promised not to leave her little brother. It would devastate him to wake up and find her gone. As for being alone with Ishmael... Sylvie's breath caught as the memory swept over her—the texture of his hair, the smell of his skin, the taste of her tears on his lips... Forcing the moment from her mind was like pulling a blade out of her flesh.

Never again, she vowed. She couldn't be alone with him, couldn't go near him or encourage him to touch her. If she was tempted—and she would be—she would think about Catriona. She would say the name in her mind, say it out loud, shout it if she had to. The thought of another woman loving Ishmael, waiting for him somewhere, would be enough to keep her strong.

Fitting herself into the space around Daniel's body, Sylvie closed her eyes. But she knew she wouldn't sleep. Not tonight.

Ishmael picked up the dead man's feet and dragged the body into the trees. Leaving it for the moment, he went back to the path and used a bucket to rinse as much blood as he could from the gravel. It was grim work, but at least it kept him from thinking about Sylvie and the way she'd felt in his arms.

Damn, but he'd wanted her. With nothing except a worn out nightgown between him and that lush, willing body... He forced the thought from his mind. It was a good thing the boy had awakened before things got out of hand.

There was a shovel in the milking shed, along with the rake Sylvie had used against her attackers. Retrieving both tools, Ishmael smoothed the gravel path and washed it down again. He'd check it once more in the morning. He didn't want Daniel to see the blood.

Some distance back in the trees, he scouted a patch of soft ground and set to digging. It was hard work, especially given his weakened condition. But he wanted every trace of the death gone. He wanted Sylvie to wake up to a new day with nothing to remind her of what had happened in the night.

Nothing except him. There wasn't much he could do about that.

He thrust the shovel against a root, grateful that Aaron Cragun had left the blade sharp. If Cragun had caught him with his daughter last night, the man would probably have run him off with the shotgun—or dragged them both to the nearest preacher.

Lord, he never should have touched her. Sylvie wasn't the sort of young woman to be trifled with. She deserved real love, the security of marriage, the joys of a family—all the things he couldn't give her. For now he had nothing, not even his name.

*Who was he? Who was Catriona?*

Sweat poured down his body as he drove the shovel blade into the rocky earth. Until he knew the answer to those questions, he'd be little more than a disembodied ghost with no name, no identity and, except for Sylvie and Daniel, no human connections.

Pausing for breath, he stared down at the sapphire ring. The stone was smudged with dirt, but its depths still caught the moonlight, gleaming like a secret pool. Its very presence on his finger seemed to mock him. Ishmael fought the senseless urge to rip it off and fling it into the night. What was the use? The harder he tried, the less he was able to remember.

What would Sylvie expect of him now that he'd kissed her? Love? Courtship? A proposal? Ishmael shook his head. The only good thing he could do for her was leave. And he would, as soon as he knew she and Daniel would be safe.

But her innocent passion in his arms was something he'd never forget.

As he scooped another shovelful of earth, Ishmael

remembered watching Sylvie come up from the cove that morning. He'd seen her take something out of the wrecked boat. But when he'd met her at the top of the trail her hands had been empty. Whatever she'd found, she'd gotten rid of it somewhere on the trail.

He'd meant to wander down and look for it. But the eventful day hadn't given him a chance. Now he began to wonder all over again. Anything she'd found on the boat would likely have been his. So why hadn't she given it to him?

Had she discovered something she didn't want him to know about?

He glanced at the sky. The night was clear, the moon full enough to light the trail down the cliff. The grave would take him another hour, less if he didn't stop to rest. When it was done, he'd trek down to the cove and try to find what Sylvie had chosen to hide from him.

The next step would be to find out why.

Sweaty and exhausted, Ishmael packed the earth over the grave, raked it smooth and camouflaged it with brush and dry branches. It was a better burial than the bastard deserved, but it wouldn't do to have animals digging up the remains for Sylvie and Daniel to find.

Returning the way he'd come, he checked the cabin. The windows were dark, the goats dozing in their pen. A glance at the sky told him there was plenty of time to go down to the cove. Replacing the tools in the shed, he found a walking stick and set out for the trail.

By moonlight the cliff was as treacherous as it was

beautiful. Shadows fell across the trail, creating illusions of line and shape. Lower down, sea mist shrouded
the rocks. Ishmael was forced to take his time, testing
the path with his stick. Once, after slipping, he nearly
gave up. But no, he resolved, he'd come this far. He
would finish what he'd started.

Searching for a hidden object had been impossible
on the way down, but going back would be easier. He'd
be climbing up and wouldn't have to watch his feet.
With luck he'd be able to find what Sylvie had chosen
to keep from him.

Below the rocks, a silvery crescent of beach gleamed
in the ghostly light. By now the tide was going out,
the waves hissing their retreat down the sand. There
was nothing left of the boat but a few planks on a half-
buried frame. Soon that would be gone, too. Whatever
Sylvie had salvaged from the wreck, it had probably
been the last chance to find it.

Leaving his boots and stockings on the rocks, Ishmael climbed the rest of the way down to the beach.
The wet sand was silky under his aching feet. The
cool waves foamed around his ankles. Digging the
grave had been a dirty, miserable job. The thought of
washing his sweat-encrusted clothes and body in the
sea was too tempting to resist.

Racing down the beach, he plunged into the surf.
The cold water sent a shock of pleasure through his
body. Instinctively he began to stroke and kick.

For a man who couldn't remember being able to
swim, he was surprisingly at home in the sea. With
easy confidence, he knifed through the waves. Pow-

erful strokes carried him out into the cove. Treading water, he paused to catch his breath. Above the beach he could see the rocks, with the cliff towering against the moon.

Something stirred in his memory—that cliff, rising out of the storm in a flash of blue lightning. He remembered the howling wind, the smashing waves, the jagged black rocks jutting out of the waves, and then…nothing.

With easy strokes, he swam back toward the beach. Water streamed off his hair and clothes as he strode out of the waves. The breeze raised goose bumps on his wet skin, but Ishmael barely felt the cold. He was tired but alert, revitalized by the swim. He headed for the rocks, then paused and turned toward the wrecked boat.

The battering tide had done its damage. Sand had washed around the hull, covering most of the stern. The exposed bow had been stripped of most of its covering. Only the foremost end of the prow remained intact.

Seating himself on the wreck, Ishmael closed his eyes and willed himself to concentrate. He could hear the storm in his head, hear the snap of the mast as it broke off and flew into the darkness. He could see the cliff, see the dim flicker of light at the top. He could feel the shattering impact as the boat struck the rocks.

Was it only his imagination, or was he really beginning to remember?

## *Chapter Eight*

Weary once more, Ishmael mounted the top of the cliff. The windlass and pulleys loomed above him, creaking in the wind. Waves whispered in the cove.

He'd inspected every visible inch of trail on the way up. But if Sylvie had hidden anything along the way, he'd failed to find it. Maybe she'd moved it later. Or maybe he'd imagined the whole incident. When it came to what was or wasn't real, Ishmael no longer trusted his own mind.

Did he really remember the storm that had brought him here?

Or were the pieces pulled together from other memories and stories he'd heard?

Was he getting better or was he getting worse?

The wind had dried his clothes on the way up the trail, but he would need to rinse the salt out of them and hang them on the clothesline to dry. It was irksome, having nothing else to wear. But that was a minor problem compared to the loss of his memory.

The house was dark and quiet. Walking to the pump, Ishmael stripped out of his clothes and sluiced his head and body with fresh water. While the breeze dried his skin, he found a tin washtub leaning against the side of the house.

A length of toweling hung over the line. Twisting it around his hips, he felt less exposed. Returning to the pump, he tossed his clothes into the tub and began running water. A glance at the moon's angle confirmed that he had a couple of hours before dawn. Maybe he could get some sleep while his clothes dried. With luck, Sylvie would find them in the morning and toss them in the direction of his bed.

As he rinsed and wrung the wet clothes, he pictured her sleeping in the darkness of the house, her eyes closed, her lips full and baby soft. Those lips had felt as soft as they looked. And her woman's body in that thin nightgown had roused him to the brink of serious temptation. But he'd sworn off touching her again, he reminded himself. And if he was going to control his actions he would also need to bridle his thoughts. Maybe in the future he could try to look on her as a younger sister, in need of tenderness and protection but nothing more. That might do the trick.

Or it might not. Maybe he should just be honest with her—lay the cards on the table and hope she'd be sensible enough to know that a man like him could ruin her life.

Right now, neither choice held much appeal. All he

really wanted was to crush her in his arms, carry her off to someplace warm and dark and lose himself in making love to that responsive young body.

*Damn!*

Shivering in the breeze, he carried the damp garments to the clothesline and began hanging them up to dry.

Daniel was snoring like a tired puppy, his head buried in the pillow and his limbs spread-eagle across Sylvie's narrow bed. Sylvie had long since given up hope of a comfortable night. She was braced half asleep on the outside edge of the mattress when she heard the familiar creak of the pump handle and the trickling sound of water.

Heart slamming, she leaped to her feet, flung on her wrapper and rushed to Ishmael's room next door. The room was empty, the bed undisturbed. Only then did she remember that he had gone to bury the dead man. It made sense that he would use the pump to wash up afterward. But heavens, what time was it? Before drifting off she'd lain awake for what seemed like hours, listening for the sound of his footsteps and the opening of the door. But she'd dozed off without ever hearing him return.

Her feet pattered across the floor as she tiptoed to the kitchen. The porthole window above the counter gave her a view of the pump—and the man standing next to it, splashing water over his magnificent male body.

Her throat jerked, almost choking off her breath.

Ishmael had turned away. Water streamed off his hair, flowing in silver rivulets down his back. Sylvie's captive eyes traced the curve of his spine, down to the dimpled V that separated his taut buttocks. True, she'd seen most of his body while he was sick. But not like this—gloriously bathed in water and moonlight. If the sea prince in her fairy tale had come to life, he would look like this man.

As if he'd sensed someone watching him, he glanced around. Sylvie drew back with a little gasp. Moments later, when she dared to venture another look, she saw that he'd wrapped his hips in the towel she'd hung out to dry that afternoon. He'd pumped some water into the tub and was wringing out his clothes.

For a guilty moment she let her gaze linger on his powerful body. This wasn't proper, Sylvie lectured herself. Tending the man while he was ill was one thing. Ogling his nakedness was quite another.

Not that it was Ishmael's fault. While his clothes were drying, he'd have nothing to wear, except maybe a sheet or blanket. Her father's clothes, even the shirts and stockings, were too small.

Then she remembered something.

Back in the bedroom, she rummaged through the chest, looking for a nightshirt she recalled putting there. It had come in a box of old clothes her father had picked up somewhere and brought home. Since the garment was too long for him, Sylvie had laundered it and put it aside, thinking she could cut up the warm cotton flannel and make something for Daniel. But she'd never gotten around to the project. Now, holding the nightshirt at arm's length, she calculated it would do nicely for a man of Ishmael's height.

Shaking it out, she folded it over her arm and hurried to the front door. With her hand on the latch, she hesitated. She'd vowed not to be alone with Ishmael again. But the reality was, he needed the nightshirt and Daniel was fast asleep. Waking the boy to act as a chaperone would be carrying her resolve too far.

Never mind, she could handle this small matter. She would be polite and natural and force herself to forget the way Ishmael's kiss had lit a bonfire inside her. That bonfire was out now. As far as she was concerned, that kiss had never happened.

Decision made, she lifted her chin, opened the door and stepped out onto the porch.

Ishmael was draping the last of his clothes over the line. At the slight creak of the door he jerked around, half crouched as if ready for combat. As Sylvie stepped into the moonlight, he exhaled and straightened. Something flickered in his eyes, a naked hunger she pretended not to see. He swiftly masked it with a scowl.

"You're supposed to be asleep."

Knees trembling beneath her wrapper, she held up the nightshirt. "It's chilly out here. I thought maybe you could use this. But of course if you'd rather be left alone…" She turned back toward the door.

The sound he made was somewhere between a moan and a growl. "Come back here and give me that. I'm not in the mood for games."

"Maybe you're the one who needs to be in bed."

She tossed him the nightshirt. "It's late. You must be tired."

"I'm fine." Turning away from her, he slipped the nightshirt over his head. The sleeves were short but it was otherwise roomy and hung past his knees.

"Where have you been for so long? Did you get that awful man buried?"

He nodded. "By the time it was done, I was so dirty that I went for a swim in the cove. Just hoping my clothes will dry by morning."

Sylvie glanced toward the sagging clothesline. "They'll dry faster if you use the clothespins. And that way you won't find your clothes blown all over the yard in the morning." Sylvie walked to the line, took the long drawers he'd doubled over the rope and pinned them by the waist. She could feel his eyes on her as she repositioned each garment and fastened it to dangle in the breeze. As the silence grew awkward, the yearning stirred in her body. What if she turned around and opened her arms? Would he hold her again? Would he kiss her?

Did she want him to?

Ishmael cleared the huskiness from his throat. "I can finish that. You should go back inside."

"Why?" She glanced back at him, her moon-silvered eyes glinting with challenge.

"Because if you stay, I might not be able to keep my hands off you."

Her fingers froze in midmotion. Silence crawled before she spoke, her voice as sharp and brittle as blown glass. "Don't worry, Ishmael. Your virtue is quite safe with me. I've no intention of letting you near me again."

He forced a chuckle. "Well, at least we understand each other."

"Do we?"

He sank onto the edge of the porch, resting his elbows on his knees. "You've treated me well, Sylvie. Probably better than I deserve. But I know I don't belong here. I'd leave at first light if I thought you and Daniel would be safe here alone."

"I killed one man tonight. I can do it again if I have to." Her chin was up, eyes glimmering with a hint of tears. "Besides, my father should be home soon. He's always taken care of us."

"We need to talk. Sit down." He motioned to a nearby spot on the porch. Sylvie had pinned the last stocking to the clothesline. After a moment's hesitation, she joined him, settling herself at a discreet distance. One hand smoothed her windblown hair back from her face.

"You're not responsible for our family," she said. "We got by before you came. After you're gone, we'll make do as we always have."

"That's pride talking, not common sense. The plain truth is your father's overdue, and you don't know what's happened to him."

Sylvie stared down at her hands. Ishmael could tell she was fighting tears. But he couldn't spare her the truth. She needed to hear what he had to say.

"One of those two men ran off. If he comes back

with more of his kind, you'll have more trouble than a lone woman can handle. Do I have to draw you a picture?"

She shook her head. "But why should they come back? They said my father owed them money. They know he isn't here. And if you look around the place, you'll see nothing worth taking for the debt."

"There's you. And there's Daniel. Think about it. If someone wanted to hurt your father or manipulate him into doing what they wanted, what would be the surest way?"

A shudder passed through her body. He resisted the urge to lay a hand on her shoulder and pull her close. "Think about it, Sylvie. Someone came all this way, most likely from San Francisco. When they didn't find your father, they tried to hurt you. And when I ran them off, they came back later. What did they really want?"

"I don't know." She was beginning to crumble.

"Did your father take anything special to sell? Anything that might draw attention—maybe cause people to suspect there was something more?"

"You mean, like part of a treasure? Heavens, no! He sold ordinary things—tools, ropes and canvas, lumber, sometimes a few extra goats. My father's a good person. I don't believe for a second that he cheated those men. That was just a story."

Agitated now, she stared at him. "What I don't understand is *your* part in this. Those men recognized you, Ishmael. They must have known you from somewhere—as an enemy…" She hesitated, drawing a deep breath. "Or as an ally."

"You're sure?"

"I know what I heard. Don't you remember anything about them?"

He shook his head. "I could swear on a stack of bibles that I'd never seen them before in my life. But right now that wouldn't be worth a damn. Hellfire, they could be my brothers, and I wouldn't know it."

"You don't remember anything at all?"

"Nothing of any use. Except…" He rubbed his tired eyes, willing himself to concentrate. "When I was swimming in the cove, I looked up at the cliff, and for a few seconds I felt as if I could remember the storm and the boat filling up with water. But the odd thing was, I recalled seeing a light atop the cliff. Tonight it was gone."

"A light?" Her eyes had gone wide. "But there *was* a light! I hung a lantern on the windlass at dusk, as the storm was blowing in! My father doesn't—" She broke off, staring down at her hands.

"What about your father, Sylvie?"

"My father…" She met his eyes, then dropped her gaze to her hands. "My father always says that the ships out there beyond the cove are in God's hands. If they run onto the rocks and go down, it's no fault of ours. They'd do the same if we weren't here to salvage the cargo. That's what he says, and in a way, I suppose he's right."

"But you hung the lantern."

"He wouldn't allow it if he knew. But when he's

away—if there's fog or storm, or when it's the dark of moon—yes, I hang the lantern at the top of the cliff. It's a small thing, but if it can guide a ship away from the rocks…"

"So you give God a little help." Ishmael forced the words past a surge of tenderness. Sylvie was a beauty with a heart as pure as a child's. A man could move the earth for such a woman.

But it wasn't his place to be that man.

"Sometimes I imagine having a real lighthouse here at the top of the cliff to guide the ships away," she said. "Papa could have the care of it—he'd do a fine job. We might not have much money, but we wouldn't have to live the way we do, like vultures feeding off other people's misfortune."

Ishmael studied the glow of moonlight on her wind-blown hair. The next words came without forethought. "This is most likely an empty promise. But if I get my memory back and discover that I know someone who can help you…"

"You'd do that for us?" Her starlit eyes were bright with excitement.

"Only if I could, and that's a long shot. But I'd say this place needs a lighthouse as much as any spot in California."

Sylvie's expression was so hopeful that Ishmael wanted to punch himself. What had made him think he could help her? He could be a wanted criminal or some no-account without a cent to his name. And here he was, dangling the moon in front of her pretty nose, filling her head with dreams. He deserved to be horse-whipped.

That aside, a lighthouse in this spot struck him as an excellent idea. Now that he thought about it, he remembered that the building of lighthouses was a congressional matter. To get anything done, he would need the ear of someone with connections in Washington, D.C.

So how in the devil had he known that? It was as if the wreck had shattered his memory into a hundred thousand fragments—fragments that drifted back to him randomly like dust motes after an explosion. Here a name. There a face, or a smell, or a phrase.

"Are you remembering something?" Sylvie was watching him intently.

"Nothing of any damn use." Ishmael stood, wishing he had a bottle and could drink himself senseless. He was a prisoner of his own forgetfulness, pounding his head against the bars.

"Your memory will come back. It's got to." She rose to stand beside him. Her touch on his arm was like the brush of a feather. "Think about Catriona. Her name was the one thing that stayed with you, the one thing you never lost. She's out there somewhere, Ishmael, waiting for you to remember her and come home."

"Stop it!" He swung toward her. "Don't you think I've tried? I know it has to mean something, but I've racked my brain for some link to that name. Is she my wife? My sweetheart? I don't know, and the answer won't come." He glared at her. "I know you think you're helping, but you're only tormenting me. So be quiet and go to bed. We could both use some rest."

Sylvie's chin went up. With a little huff, she stood and stalked toward the door. "Good night, Ishmael," she said in a chilly voice. "Your bed's ready when you want it. Don't worry, I won't trouble you again."

The door clicked shut behind her, leaving him alone.

*She wasn't going to cry!*

Fighting emotion, Sylvie stumbled through the darkness toward her bedroom door. Her toe stubbed the leg of a wooden chair, sending a shock of pain through her foot. She bit back a yelp. The last thing she wanted was Ishmael to hear her and come charging into the house.

Why hadn't she kept her silly mouth shut? Ishmael didn't need her badgering to help him remember. If anything, she was a hindrance, babbling away while he was trying to think, distracting him from what mattered most—getting back to the loved ones who needed him.

Her throat jerked as a new thought struck her.

What if she didn't want him to remember?

It was a hard question, but one that had to be faced. Finding Ishmael on the beach had plunged her whole life into confusion. When she was with him, every sense seemed heightened. Her blood sang through her veins. Colors seemed brighter, bird songs more musical, flowers more fragrant. When he'd kissed her it was as if, until that instant, she'd never known how it felt to be truly alive.

Did she love him?

But the answer to that question made no difference. Once Ishmael recovered his memory, he would have no reason to stay.

And if he never remembered?

But that, Sylvie knew, would be the cruelest outcome of all. Even if he stayed with her, Ishmael would be in torment all the days of his life, not knowing who he was, where he'd come from, or who was waiting for his return.

If she truly cared for him, she would pray for his recovery and prepare herself to let him go. Any other choice would be morally wrong—and in the long run, would break her heart.

Reaching the bedroom door, she paused. Daniel lay sprawled in a shaft of moonlight, his hair an inky spill against the pillow. His eyes were closed in innocent sleep.

She had more urgent concerns than romantic love, Sylvie reminded herself. The well-being of this small boy was in her hands. It was her responsibility to keep him safe and healthy and to raise him to young manhood. Nothing mattered as much, least of all her own selfish, fleeting happiness.

Moving carefully, she eased herself into the narrow space along the edge of the bed. Tomorrow she would keep her distance from the man she'd named Ishmael. She would immerse herself in her work and leave him alone, giving him time, perhaps, to remember. And if her resolve weakened, one thing would remind her to keep strong—the memory of a name.

Catriona.

* * *

Ishmael was drunk with exhaustion. But he remained on the porch until he was sure the house was quiet. He wasn't proud of the way he'd snapped at Sylvie, driving her away. But if she'd stayed any longer the temptation to yank her against him and silence her lovely mouth with kisses would've been too much to resist. Much as he wanted her, he wasn't free to let anything happen between them.

*Who was Catriona?* The question was eating him alive. Of all the names in the world, why had that been the one that surfaced in his mind? Was he bound to her in some way? Married? Engaged?

Until he knew, he had no right to touch Sylvie Cragun, or to offer her anything except his protection.

But what was he thinking? What else could he offer her? Love? Marriage? Or, more likely, a few stolen moments in the dark? Lord, she deserved better. She deserved a prince, like the one in her fairy tale, who'd sweep her away to the land of happily ever after. Not a man who didn't even know his own name.

Stumbling with weariness, he entered the house and slid the bolt behind him. The door to Sylvie's bedroom stood ajar, though not far enough to see inside. He could almost imagine her lying there, her eyes closed, her golden hair trailing over the pillow like the tendrils of a moonflower vine. What would happen if he stepped into the room, leaned over the bed and brushed a kiss on her lips? Would she be frightened? Angry? Or would she open her arms and draw him down to the warmth of her woman's body?

*Damn!*

He'd sworn off those kinds of thoughts, Ishmael lashed himself. He had no right to touch Sylvie, or even to go near her. But he did need to make sure she was safe. He would just look in for a moment. Then he'd stagger to bed and pass out for what remained of the night.

Easing the door open a few inches, he glanced into Sylvie's room. Still clad in her wrapper, she lay along the very edge of the bed with one arm flung across Daniel's sprawling form. Both of them were fast asleep.

An aching tenderness tightened Ishmael's chest. This wasn't what he'd expected to see, but he shouldn't have been surprised. It would be like Sylvie to comfort and protect her little brother on this dangerous night.

His eyes lingered on her sleeping face—the shadow of her long lashes against her cheek, the rose-petal softness of her parted lips. A man could spend the rest of his life looking at that face, he thought.

But not a man like him.

Weary in every bone, he backed out of the doorway, closed the door and made his way to bed. He'd feared he might be too troubled to sleep. But by the time his head settled on the pillow he was already spiraling into dreams.

*He could see every detail. The two-room house was no bigger than the bed of a hay wagon, with a sod roof and walls of crumbling sun-baked adobe. Most of the backyard was taken up by a vegetable garden, where potatoes, turnips and carrots waited to be dug and stored in the root cellar next to the back porch. Getting them there was a tedious job for a thirteen-year-old boy, especially on a warm autumn day. But it had to be done. Otherwise he, his ten-year-old sister and their ailing father would have little to eat in the cold months ahead.*

*As he bent to gather up the newly dug potatoes, his sister came prancing around the corner of the house, trailed by a neighbor boy about her own age. She was prettier than any child had a right to be, with a mop of ebony curls, a cherub's face and green eyes that could dance with mischief. They were dancing now.*

*"Jackie here says you're a coward," she announced. "But I know better. I bet him a penny that you wouldn't be scared to go down in the root cellar and catch one of those big cat-faced spiders that lives there."*

*He rested a foot on the shovel blade. "What if you lose the bet? I know for a fact you don't have a penny."*

*She shook her curls. "Maybe not. But if I lose, I promised to give him a kiss. Right on the mouth."*

*He thrust the shovel deeper. The big tan spiders that lurked in the root cellar, though not dangerous, were crawly and repulsive. He wouldn't enjoy going after one, but he couldn't have his little sister cheapen herself by kissing the neighborhood boys. Who could say where that might lead? He scowled down at her.*

*"So if I help you win, you get a penny. But what do I get?"*

*"I'll help you finish the garden. You can dig, and I'll put the vegetables in the basket. You'll get done sooner that way."*

He sighed, having known all along that she'd get her way. "All right. Here I go."

Wiping his sleeve across his sweaty forehead, he headed toward the root cellar. The wooden door lay open, anchored to the side of its frame by leather hinges. A ramp of packed earth led down to the space dug out under the house. The cellar was dark and dirty. He didn't like it much, but it shouldn't take long to snatch a spider off its web. After that, he planned to give his sister a stern talking-to. Betting kisses with grubby neighborhood boys was hardly a fitting pastime for a young lady of noble birth.

And his family was of noble birth. His father often talked about the estate in Ireland where he'd grown up and how, as the younger son of the family, he'd left for America to seek his fortune. Now he was too sick to work, and the only thing of value he owned was the sapphire-and-gold signet ring on his finger. He could have sold it to buy medicine, but it was all he had left to remind him of home—all he had to leave his children when he died.

Toward the back of the cellar, the spiderwebs hung like draperies. He could see the spiders, pale shapes suspended against the darkness. He would catch the biggest one he could find, he vowed, big enough to scare the starch out of his saucy little sister and her friend.

From the cellar's entrance, he could hear them whispering. Pesky kids. He should have kept on working and refused to be caught up in their mischief. After all, he was almost a man, too old for silly games. With *his father coughing blood and getting weaker by the day, it was left to him to take care of the family. He'd promised his father he'd stay in school, but maybe he could find work at night, or on Saturdays. That would at least give them enough to eat.*

*He'd chosen his spider and was reaching for it when he heard the creak of a rusty hinge. He jerked around in time to see the rising cellar door crest above his head. In the next instant it slammed downward, plunging him into darkness.*

*"What the heck?" He charged up the earthen ramp, intent on pushing the door open. But the click of the hasp and the sound of childish laughter told him it was too late. The little minx had locked him in.*

*"Open this door!" Dirt showered around him as he pounded on the rough planks. "You hear me, Catriona? If I tell Papa, you won't be able to sit down for a week!"*

*The silence was punctuated by a barely suppressed giggle.*

*"Open this door, Catriona!" he yelled. "Open it right now, or you're in big trouble!"*

*This time there was no response.*

*"Catriona!" he shouted. "Are you there? Blast it, when I get my hands on you—"*

The dream shattered as Ishmael jerked himself awake.

# *Chapter Nine*

*Catriona.*

Drenched in cold sweat, Ishmael stared up into the darkness. His thoughts roiled as he struggled to hang on to every detail of the dream—not just a dream, but an actual memory.

Everything in the dream had happened. He couldn't remember how long Catriona had left him in the cellar or what he'd done when she let him out. But he remembered the darkness, the smell of damp earth and the sound of impish laughter through the cellar door.

Catriona—his sister. The memory was a crystalline glimpse into the past. But the rest, whatever had happened before and after, was still shrouded in fog.

Sitting up, he rubbed his eyes. Maybe he was still dreaming. Nothing here seemed entirely real—not the odd little house, not the sound of the sea, or even the fairy-tale beauty who'd rescued him from the tide. For all he knew, when he awoke again it could be in another time and setting.

But the dream had come from deep inside him, a place so raw and honest that he couldn't doubt its truth.

Where would his sister be today? In the dream they'd been children. She'd be a grown woman by now, probably with a family of her own. Wherever she was, he needed to find her. She was the one sure link to the missing pieces of his life.

As for his father… Ishmael fingered the heavy signet ring. His father would have died, of course. Even in the dream, he'd been dying. But Ishmael had no memory of his death. He wasn't even sure where they'd been living when the scene in the dream took place.

Closing his eyes, he examined the dream in minute detail. If his sister had spoken his name, even once…

But that bit of information was still missing. Ishmael's dream had given him vital pieces of the puzzle. But it hadn't told him who he was.

Rising, he walked out onto the front porch. By now the sky was beginning to fade. Soon the animals would be stirring, and Sylvie would open her beautiful eyes. How much should he tell her? Would things be different between them now that he knew Catriona wasn't his wife?

Did he want them to be different? Or would knowing the truth only complicate things between them?

That impulsive kiss had seared them both. The idea that he was likely single would raise the temptation to take up where they'd left off. Unless he planned to marry the girl, which he was in no position to do, that would be cruel. He cared deeply for Sylvie. The last thing he wanted was to hurt her when he left.

And there was still the chance he might be married. Was that even possible? Ishmael pondered the question. Now that he knew where the ring had come from, and that Catriona was his sister, he didn't *feel* married. There was no memory of a name, a face, a voice. There was no one. The more he thought about it, the more certain he became.

But that didn't give him the right to trifle with Sylvie's affections. Perhaps he had no wife because he didn't earn enough to support a family. Perhaps he had a sweetheart and was planning to propose. There was no way of knowing, and Sylvie deserved better than to give her heart to a man who could offer so little certainty in return. For now, at least, he would keep his secret—and his distance.

In the time that remained here, he would look for work to do around the place. Sylvie could use the help, and keeping busy would be good for him. He would start by gathering in his dry clothes and getting dressed. Next he would do something about her dwindling woodpile.

As dawn broke he lingered on the porch, listening to the early-morning birdcalls and watching the sky fade from pewter to rose. The sea was a gentle murmur, his spirit at peace for the first time since the shipwreck. His memory was no longer a void. He knew something about his past; and in the days ahead, as more pieces emerged, he would come to know more and more.

Until he knew enough to leave.

Sylvie woke to the ring of an ax outside her bedroom window. Peering through the heavy porthole glass, she saw Ishmael splitting off pine knots for kindling. He worked with a skill no prince would have mastered, raising the heavy ax high and bringing it down on the wedge with a whack as precise as a surgeon's scalpel.

The clamor of the goats told her it was time to be up doing chores. Turning, she gave Daniel's shoulder a gentle shake. He yawned and opened his eyes.

"Time to get up, sleepyhead," Sylvie said. "There's work to be done before breakfast."

Daniel groaned and snuggled deeper under the covers. "Just a little longer," he begged.

"You aren't sick, are you?" Sylvie laid a hand on his forehead. The boy was no warmer than usual, but it wasn't like him to linger in bed.

"Not sick. Just tired." He drew up his knees, curling into a stubborn little ball.

Sylvie pulled back the covers. "Come on, now. You'll feel fine once you're up and dressed. Ishmael's already outside working. After you've gathered the eggs, you might ask him if he needs some help."

The mention of Ishmael seemed to animate the boy. He sat up, wriggled his toes and stretched his feet to the floor. Sylvie smoothed his rumpled hair. "Run upstairs and get dressed, now. It's going to be a beautiful day."

He tottered to the ladder that led to his sleeping loft,

only to pause with his foot on the first rung. "Do you think Papa will get home today?"

Something jabbed at Sylvie's heart. "Let's hope so. Hurry, now."

After he'd gone, Sylvie dressed hastily, splashed her face and brushed back her hair. With so much going on yesterday, she'd had scant time to worry about her father. But it seemed that Daniel had done enough worrying for both of them. With every day, the possibility loomed larger that something had gone wrong— something bad enough to keep Aaron Cragun from returning to his children.

Ishmael was right, she had to start making plans. Given the danger and their limited supplies, she and Daniel couldn't remain here much longer. But where would they go? How would they live?

Pushing the thought aside for now, she hurried outside. From around the corner of the house she could hear Ishmael chopping wood. She was about to go and greet him, when she remembered her resolution to give him some distance. Chopping wood was a good chore for thinking, and he needed to think. She would leave him alone until breakfast time.

Daniel had let the goats out to graze. Catching the nearest nanny, Sylvie led the animal to the milking shed and began filling the pail. She needed to churn a batch of butter from the cream this morning. Maybe there'd be enough milk leftover to make some cheese later on.

Unfortunately, milking was also a good chore for thinking. As Sylvie pulled on the teats, her thoughts wandered again and again to Ishmael and the kiss that had roused a world of new sensations. Oh, she knew she'd be foolish to put too much stock in it. According to what she'd read, men were apt to kiss girls whenever the chance arose. Usually it meant no more than whirling a partner in a dance—there and gone.

A handsome man like Ishmael had probably kissed dozens of women. And if perchance he was married… But that thought was better left unfinished. She knew what married people did together. And she hadn't forgotten about Catriona, who might be his wife.

When it came to kissing Ishmael, she could be certain of just two things. First, it had been the most thrilling experience she'd ever known. Second, she'd be a fool to ever think of doing it again.

With the milking done, Sylvie went back into the house and started on breakfast. The basket Daniel had left in the kitchen held five fresh brown eggs. Too bad there was no bacon to go with them. Sylvie had been counting on her father to bring back a side in the wagon, but the meat was the least of her worries. She just wanted him to come home. Right now there was nothing she wouldn't give to hear the creak of wagon wheels and the wheezing bray of her father's cranky old mule.

As she stirred the boiling oatmeal, she could hear Daniel outside talking to Ishmael. A glance out the window confirmed that they were working together, Ishmael chopping the wood, the boy stacking the pieces. Daniel was getting far too attached to the stranger, but there was no easy way to keep them apart.

A few minutes later she called the two of them in to breakfast. They washed at the pump and stomped the dirt off their feet before they trailed into the kitchen.

"Smells good." Ishmael's manner was so impersonal he could have been speaking to the wall.

"You two worked up an appetite this morning. Eat hearty." Sylvie set the eggs, fresh biscuits and bowls of oatmeal on the table, along with a pitcher of milk. At that moment, she would have given anything to erase last night.

They took their places. Daniel, when asked, mouthed a few words of grace. Sylvie passed around the hot biscuits. Ishmael took two. Daniel took one and left it on the edge of his plate.

Ishmael broke one biscuit open, dabbed it with chokecherry jelly and took a bite. "Good," he muttered. "I was looking at your springhouse. Appears to me it could use a new roof. I could split enough shingles in a few hours, and probably have them nailed on in the next couple of days. Do you have any nails?"

"You'll find a keg of nails in the shed. And thank you." Sylvie poured milk into her barley coffee. Daniel had punctured the yolk of his fried egg with his fork, but Sylvie had yet to see him take a bite.

"Is something the matter with your food, Daniel?" she asked. "You usually wolf down your breakfast."

"Just not hungry." He put his fork down on his plate.

"Are you sure you're not sick?" Alarmed, she laid a hand on his forehead. He was warm, but not alarmingly so.

"Uh-uh. Just tired, like I said," he muttered. "My head hurts."

"Bad? Do you want to lie down?"

He shook his head. "I want to help Ishmael. He said I could."

Sylvie cast Ishmael an anxious glance across the table. She saw the concern on his face. "I don't think—" she began.

"I'll keep an eye on him," Ishmael said. "If he shows any sign of getting sick I'll bring him right in."

Sylvie hesitated, then sighed and nodded. Unless her brother was truly ill, he'd be whiny and miserable in the house. "All right. But you'll have to eat some breakfast first, Daniel. And after lunch you're to stay in and work on your lessons."

The boy picked at his food, nibbling at his biscuit and dabbing it in his egg. By the time Ishmael had cleaned his plate, Daniel had eaten enough to redeem himself.

Sylvie watched as her little brother trailed his new hero outside. Daniel had always been a healthy child. With no neighbor children to expose him to the usual childhood maladies, he'd scarcely had a sick day in his life. Now, the thought of him being seriously ill raised a knot of fear in her chest. In an isolated spot such as this, a hundred miles from the nearest doctor, a sick child could easily die.

*Stop fussing,* she lectured herself as she cleared the table. The boy had most likely eaten something that upset his stomach. Surely he'd feel better as the day wore on.

As she went ahead with her work, however, the fear remained. She had her thumb-worn medical book, but she was no doctor. And apart from a few common herbal remedies, she had no medicine and no medical instruments. In the face of a serious illness, she would be all but helpless.

What would she do if something happened to her little brother?

Outside, she could hear the tap and splinter of Ishmael splitting short pine logs into shingles. It was a tedious job, requiring more than a measure of skill. Glancing out the window, she saw him bent over his task. He seemed so good with his hands, but he appeared well educated, too. What kind of work had he done in that other life—the life he couldn't recall?

She remembered the pistol she'd found in the wrecked boat and the way he'd dealt with the two thugs who came onto the property. They had recognized him. They'd even seemed afraid of him.

All her instincts told her that Ishmael was no common man. But who was he? *What* was he?

Sylvie was still weighing the question when the front door crashed open and Ishmael stumbled across the threshold. His face wore an expression of stunned anguish.

Daniel's limp body lay in his arms.

Sylvie's hands froze. The saucer she'd been wiping crashed to the floor. Her lips formed the silent question.

*What happened?*

Ishmael shook his head. "Lord, I don't know what went wrong. He seemed fine, picking up the shingles and chattering away like he usually does. Then he clutched his head and doubled over. When I lifted him, I could feel the fever. He's burning up."

"We've got to cool him. Wait—I'll put a clean sheet on the table." Sylvie's face reflected shock, but she moved with efficiency, returning from the bedroom with a sheet, which she flung over the tabletop. Without being told, Ishmael lowered the boy and began unfastening his clothes. From the top of his head to his leathery little feet, Daniel was as hot as burning sand.

A bucket of water stood on the counter. Sylvie soaked a towel, wrung it out and laid it over the small, fevered body. With another wet cloth she sponged his face and hair. Daniel's eyelids fluttered opened. His coppery eyes were glazed with pain. "Hurt…" he mumbled. "Hurt all over."

"It's all right, love, I'm here." Leaning close, Sylvie brushed a kiss across the bridge of his nose. Watching her tenderness, Ishmael ached. It would kill her to lose this lively little boy who was more like her child than her brother.

Nothing in his fogged memory suggested that he might be a doctor. But it didn't take a medical expert to see that Daniel was gravely ill. Children died from fevers like this one. Here, with their limited resources, all he and Sylvie could do was keep the boy comfortable as best they could, and pray.

Sylvie was a whirlwind of energy, filling the kettle,

stoking the fire, rummaging through her store of herbs and setting some aside. Only her wide eyes showed how terrified she was. "Willow bark," she muttered. "Maybe sage or pine gum… Dear heaven, he's so hot. If only we had something stronger."

"What can I do to help?" Ishmael asked.

She dropped a handful of herbs into the kettle. "For now, just hold him and talk to him. Try to keep his mind off the pain."

Soaking the cloth in the bucket again, she twisted out the excess water and began wetting down Daniel's black hair. On the stove, the kettle had begun to simmer. Ishmael knew about the tea. It had eased his own fever and aching head. But it would take time to steep before it was ready. Meanwhile, the boy was clearly in pain. He whimpered every time he moved.

Ishmael tried to soothe him, while Sylvie sponged his head. She was wiping behind his ear when she gave a little gasp. "Oh, no," she whispered. "Look!"

Turning the boy's head slightly, she pulled back his hair. Buried in the groove behind his ear was a dark, flat lump, the size of a small nail head.

Ishmael recognized it at once. It was a wood tick, imbedded so deeply in Daniel's skin that it had probably been there for days. Something flickered in his memory.

"Tick fevers—how much do you know about them?" he asked.

"Only what I've read in my medical book. There's more than one kind. The worst can be—" she choked on the word "—fatal. Especially for children." Her frantic eyes met his. "The symptoms match—fever, headache, pain in the limbs. Before we do anything else we've got to get that tick out."

"I'll do it. I've done it before." This time the memory was clear and sure—the coffee-brown tick against the white flesh of his sister's ankle. He'd used the point of his penknife—the only thing he had—to make the creature let go. Afterward, when they'd told their father, he'd lectured them about how dangerous a tick could be, and how important it was to get it out in one piece, without squeezing it or breaking off its fragile head.

Strange, what he could remember when he needed to.

"Do you have tweezers?" he asked her.

She shook her head. Ishmael could almost feel her thoughts scrambling. "Would a darning needle work? Or a knife?" she suggested.

"I'll take both. Make that knife the smallest, sharpest one you can find."

She tore herself away from her brother and rushed off to fetch what he needed. Ishmael watched her go. She was quaking with fear. But he sensed that she was strong enough to do whatever needed to be done.

Daniel whimpered and opened bloodshot eyes. "It's all right, son," Ishmael murmured, stroking the boy's fevered cheek. "You're in a bad way, but we'll do all we can to make you better." He glanced toward the stove where the herbs were steeping in the kettle. "Your sister's brewing some tea to help the fever. And something else—there's a tick behind your ear, making you sick. We'll need to get it out. It'll hurt a little. Can you be brave?"

Daniel nodded in complete trust. Ishmael felt the swell of emotion in his throat. Given the power, he wouldn't have hesitated for an instant to trade places with the precious little boy.

Minutes later Sylvie returned with a long needle and a small-bladed penknife, freshly washed and wrapped in a clean handkerchief. Faint tear trails stained her cheeks. Ishmael resisted the urge to take her in his arms and comfort her. Now, while they were fighting for Daniel's life, was not the time for emotion.

"Get him on his side. Then push back his hair and lift his ear out of the way." Ishmael selected the needle and held it against the stove top to heat the tip. He'd heard somewhere that a hot jab sometimes caused the tick to let go.

"Ready?" he asked, turning back to the table.

Sylvie leaned over and murmured something to Daniel. Cradling his head to expose the back of his ear, she glanced at Ishmael and nodded.

Shifting the table to get maximum light from the window, Ishmael bent over the trembling child. He held his breath as he worked the hot tip of the needle under the tick's flat body. The wiry legs moved, but the head remained buried. He was going to need the knife.

Praying he wouldn't hurt the boy, he pressed the flat of the blade against the stove. Catriona's tick had barely fastened onto her skin. This one had dug in deep. He could only hope the hot knife could get it out without causing Daniel too much pain.

Sylvie's eyes met his as he bent over her brother. In their silvery depths, he read fear, hope and trust. He owed her his best. He could only pray it would be enough. If things were different he would fall on his knees and offer these two people a lifetime of protection, shelter and love. But right now all he could do was ply the blade with a steady hand.

"Hold still, Daniel," he muttered as he worked the point under the tick. "This won't take a…second." He slid the knife all the way beneath the flat body and saw it lift free, head and all. "Got it!" He opened the stove and shook the awful creature off the knife, into the fire.

Sylvie was pressing a cloth against the tiny wound. When she spoke, there were tears in her voice. "You were so brave, Daniel. I'm so proud of you."

"Will I get better now?" the boy asked.

Sylvie glanced at Ishmael. The tick was gone, but the sickness it had brought was still raging. The battle for Daniel's life had just begun.

"You won't get better right away," Ishmael said. "Your body needs to get rid of the sickness, and that won't be easy. You'll have to be strong and brave and take all the medicine your sister gives you."

"All right…" Daniel's teeth were chattering. He'd begun to chill. Sylvie removed the damp towel and covered him with the afghan from the back of the rocker while she dabbed her pine salve behind his ear.

"I'm going to put you to bed now," she said, scooping him up in her arms. "Then I'll bring you some tea. It won't taste good, but you need to drink every drop. Understand?"

He hung over her shoulder, his head drooping listlessly. "Will you stay with me?" His mouth muddled the words. "Promise?"

"I promise. If I leave it will only be to get things you need."

"And when your sister can't stay, I'll be with you," Ishmael said. "You won't be alone."

Sylvie gave him a swift glance. "I'll need some of the tea in a cup. Cool it with a little water before you bring it in."

When Ishmael entered the bedroom with the tea, Daniel's teeth were still chattering. Sylvie knelt beside the bed, cradling him in her arms as she tried to keep him covered. When she looked up he saw the tears.

He held out the mug. "He's apt to thrash when you try to give him this. It'll be easier if I hold him."

Nodding, she moved aside and took the mug from his hand. Ishmael seated himself behind the boy, where he could hold him in a sitting position. The little body was shaking with chills. Lord, he was so small and so helpless—and so loved.

"It's all right, Daniel," he murmured. "Sylvie has some tea for you. If you drink it all, it should help you feel better." Ishmael could only hope he was telling the truth. He knew next to nothing about this kind of fever. Maybe later, if there was time, Sylvie would let him look through the medical book she'd mentioned. Meanwhile, she was the closest thing to a doctor they had.

Ishmael steadied the boy's head while Sylvie tipped the cup to his lips. At the first taste, Daniel, sick as he was, choked, clenched his teeth and began to struggle. Ishmael held him tighter. "Swallow it like a man," he whispered. "No matter how bad it tastes, you've got to get it down."

The feverish little body strained with effort as Daniel opened his mouth and allowed a sip of the tea. More than once he gagged, but with Sylvie's persistence, he managed to empty the mug. It was a tiny victory.

Sylvie hugged him, her eyes streaming tears. It was all Ishmael could do to keep from gathering them both into his arms. He would give anything, he thought, to keep them well, safe and happy. But whatever happened in the hours ahead was out of his hands. Beyond a pitiful measure of support, there was little he could do.

"Lie back now." Sylvie tucked the blankets around her brother as Ishmael moved out of the way. "Try to sleep. The tea should help you rest."

Daniel's eyelids fluttered open. "Will you sing to me, Sylvie?"

She almost broke then. Ishmael watched as she fought for control. Softly, in a shaking voice, she began to sing. "'Hush-a-bye… Go to sleep…'" A sob broke the flow of the song. Gulping it back she continued, "'Angels watching over you, keep you safe till dawn breaks through… Sleep my little one, sleep…'"

Listening, Ishmael swallowed the ache in his throat. Heaven help him, he might not know his own name. But he knew he loved her.

# *Chapter Ten*

By the time Sylvie finished the fourth chorus of her lullaby, the willow bark seemed to be working. Daniel was still hot with fever, but the chills and pain appeared to have eased some. He lay in a drowsy stupor, drifting between sleep and whimpering agitation.

Heartsick, Sylvie hovered over him. The tea might have eased her brother's symptoms, but she had nothing to fight the malady the tick had pumped into his blood. She had never felt so helpless in her life.

Ishmael stood against the wall, his face etched with worry. "Go and do whatever you need to," he said. "I can stay here with the boy."

"Maybe later. For now, I don't want to leave him." She brushed the damp locks back from his forehead. "Why didn't I realize sooner how sick he was? I should have suspected something when he didn't want to eat."

"Don't blame yourself. It wouldn't have made any difference." His hand brushed her shoulder as if to settle there, then pulled away. "What do you remember reading about the fever? You said there was more than one kind. How can you tell them apart?"

Sylvie tried to visualize the page of the book she'd read so many times. "You can't until later on. For the first few days the symptoms are almost the same. Then, if it's the worst kind, he'll get a blistery red rash that starts on his hands and feet and works its way along his limbs to his body. That's when we'll know. After that, he'll keep getting worse until—" She choked, unable to go on.

"And if it's the less serious kind?" he asked gently.

"He may get a rash, but it will be lighter. Then he'll start getting better, although he may have relapses. Either way, there's no cure we can give him. All we can do is try to keep him comfortable. And wait. And pray."

Ishmael stirred restlessly. Like most men, Sylvie guessed, he didn't take well to waiting. "You're going to need plenty of willow bark for the tea," he said. "There's a clump of willows down by the creek. I could cut some and peel you a good supply."

"That would be helpful," she said, knowing it would be a mercy to send him off with something to do. "I'll call for you if we need anything."

"I won't be far." He turned to leave the room. As he reached the doorway, Sylvie was struck by a sudden thought.

"Ishmael, wait."

He glanced back toward her.

"I was wondering," she said. "When you offered to

get the tick off, you said you'd done it before. Was that something you remembered?"

For an instant he looked hesitant. Then his dark eyes met hers. "Yes, just a flash. Years ago, when I was a boy—I can't even remember where or how it happened—I pulled a tick off my sister's ankle."

"Your sister?" Sylvie asked, intrigued.

"My younger sister." He took a quick breath. "Catriona."

Ishmael sliced off the willows at the base, selecting only those thick enough to have mature bark. He would carry an armful back to the porch, where he could peel the bark away and cut it into pieces.

His thoughts churned as he worked. He hadn't planned to tell Sylvie about his sister, but when confronted with the question, he'd known he couldn't lie to her.

He'd told her about the ring, as well. Then he'd excused himself and left before she could question him. At a time like this, the issue of his marital status was probably the last concern on Sylvie's mind—as it should be the last thing on his. Nothing could be settled between them while Daniel's life hung in the balance.

*And what if the balance swung the wrong way?*

Ishmael gathered up the willows he'd cut and strode back through the trees, toward the porch. The possibility had to be faced. Graveyards were filled with the markers of children who died from fevers. But losing the child she'd raised with so much love would destroy Sylvie. She might never recover from her grief.

Right now, for Ishmael, only one thing was certain. He loved Sylvie. Whatever fate had in store for them, he would be there for her, if not as her husband, then as her friend. He would never walk away and leave her alone and helpless.

Seating himself on the porch steps, he began peeling the bark off the willow he'd cut. From inside the house, there was no sound. He could only hope Daniel was resting peacefully with his sister keeping watch. He remembered Sylvie seated with the lamplight on her hair, cradling the boy in her arms while her voice wove the tale of the prince from the sea. Such a beautiful pair. He could hardly imagine one of them without the other.

And he could no longer imagine his own life without them. But as things stood, it was as if the three of them were walking on quicksand, with every step more uncertain than the last.

What could he do? Nothing—that was the hell of it. While he stood by helplessly watching, the boy could die in his sister's arms.

Ishmael had no memory of religious belief. He couldn't recall ever having gone to church. But some instinct in him reached out to the one source of help that remained. Without knowing how to begin or what to say, he prayed.

Sylvie jerked as a hand shook her shoulder. Gritty with exhaustion, she blinked her eyes open. Through the bedroom window, the sky was as gray as lead. It was morning—the fourth morning of Daniel's illness.

She hadn't meant to drop off. But sometime before dawn, her head had sagged onto the bed. She'd passed into dreamless sleep with one arm over her brother's feverish body. Now she could feel the labored rise and fall of his chest. At least he was still alive.

Ishmael stood over her, red-eyed and unshaven, his clothes rumpled from sleep. They'd fallen into a routine of trading off every few hours, one of them keeping watch while the other worked or snatched some rest on the double bed in the other room. By now they were both worn out, and Daniel was as sick as ever.

"I can take over now," Ishmael said. "Go on, lie down and get some real sleep."

"Daniel's going to need more tea." She staggered to her feet, headed for the kitchen.

He stopped her with a touch on her arm. "Leave him for now. I'll put the tea on and give it to him as soon as it's light. I'll sponge him off, too. That might make him feel better." He guided her toward the door. "Go on, now, and get some rest. I'll call you if there's any change."

Sylvie stumbled into her father's bedroom, still upset with herself for nodding off. What if Daniel had needed her? What if he'd taken a turn for the worse while she slept? But it was all right now, she reminded herself. Ishmael was there. She could count on him to keep watch while she got some much-needed rest.

Over the course of her brother's illness, Sylvie had come to depend more and more on Ishmael. He'd become skilled at every aspect of the boy's care, from brewing the tea to judging the heat of the fever. He'd taken on the outside chores and even used his spare time to study the useful pages in her medical book. Although she knew he was exhausted, he remained patient and soft-spoken. What would she have done without him?

What would she do when he left?

As her head settled onto the pillow, the memory of what he'd revealed rose in her mind. *Catriona wasn't his wife. She wasn't his sweetheart. She was his sister. And the ring was a legacy from his father—he'd told her that, too. It had been in his family for generations.*

Did that mean Ishmael was free? Did it mean that it wasn't a sin for her to love him?

But how could she even ask such questions when her little brother lay at death's door getting weaker by the day? She'd been taught to believe that if Daniel died he'd go straight to heaven, into the waiting arms of Pilar, his mother. But even if that was true how could she go on without him? She'd be lost without the warmth of his small, wiry body in her arms, the smell of his hair, the shine of his coppery eyes and the patter of his tough little feet. Without Daniel, who would hear her songs and stories? What would she have left to live for?

Tears welled in her burning eyes. What a wicked creature she must be, to think of her own needs when an innocent child was suffering. Why couldn't that awful tick have bitten her instead? Why couldn't she be the one lying in that bed, whimpering in fevered pain? She should have thought to warn the boy about wood ticks. She should have checked him more closely, every inch of him, every single night.

Turning over, she closed her eyes and willed herself to sleep. But her mind, weary beyond exhaustion, pitched like a ship in a storm, giving her no release.

Then, from the bedroom came the low murmur of Ishmael's voice. He'd fallen into the habit of talking to Daniel when he was in the room, whether the boy could hear him or not. The thin wall muffled his words. But the low timbre of his voice was like peaceful water. He was there. He was taking care of things. It was all right for her to rest, to sleep.

She felt the tempest calming. With a long breath, she let go.

"Sylvie, wake up!" Ishmael's voice echoed down a long tunnel of sleep. Sylvie's eyes jerked open. The sun was streaming through the porthole window, filling the bedroom with blinding light.

She focused her gaze on Ishmael's haggard face. What time was it? How many hours had he let her sleep? A jolt of dread clenched her stomach. What if—

"Lord, no, it's not that." He'd read her fear. "Come on, there's something you need to see." He seized her hand, pulling her to her feet. Still unsteady, she followed him into the next room.

Daniel lay uncovered in the bed, his eyes open, his body glistening with sweat. His nightshirt had been unbuttoned, exposing the fine, light rash on his torso. "I'm no doctor," Ishmael said softly, "but I'd like to think he's getting better."

Sylvie dropped to her knees beside the bed and laid a hand on Daniel's forehead. It was cool and damp. The fever had broken.

"How do you feel, Daniel?" she asked.

"Tired," he murmured. "But I don't hurt so much. Am I going to die, Sylvie?"

"No." Choking back a sob, she squeezed his small hands. "You're not going to die. We won't let you. Are you hungry?"

"Thirsty."

"I'll bring him some water." Ishmael stepped out of the room.

"And I'll warm some broth. He'll need nourishment." She paused in the doorway to glance back toward the bed. "Rest, Daniel. Don't you dare try to get up. We'll be right back."

Sylvie paused again, then rushed back to kiss his damp forehead. Glancing upward she mouthed a silent prayer. *Thank you...*

Hurrying now, she dashed out the front door, headed for the springhouse where she'd stored a crock of chicken soup. Chilled by the stream than ran through the cool box, the broth should still be good.

Ishmael had gone outside first. As she came out onto the porch, Sylvie saw him refilling the bucket at the pump. He finished, straightened and turned. Their eyes met. How weary he looked, and how relieved, she thought. Ishmael had been here the whole time for her and Daniel, working, watching and comforting. No father could have been more devoted or more protective to Daniel—and no husband could have been more caring or supportive to her. She owed him more than she could ever repay.

Her tears welled, clouding her vision with the iridescence of rainbows. For a moment he didn't move. Then he lowered the bucket, strode the distance between them and caught her in his arms.

Sylvie broke against him with a low sob. Her arms crept around his rib cage. She clasped him tight and hard, as if she could mold him to her and make him hers forever. Even then, she knew better. But she'd been yearning to hold him, and to be held like this, ever since the first time he'd touched her.

The breath eased out of him, as if he'd been holding it painfully in for days. Wordless lips caressed her hair, her temples, her tear-dampened eyelids. When she raised her seeking lips, he took them in a tender, hungry kiss that flooded her with need. She strained upward, deepening the contact of their mouths and bodies until he sighed and eased her gently away. Even then, his gaze clung to her.

"We'd better get back to Daniel," he muttered thickly. "Go on, now. We'll deal with this later."

With a quick nod, she spun away from him and dashed toward the springhouse. The ground was rough, but she scarcely felt the sharp stones beneath her bare feet. Her head buzzed with a heady mix of emotion and exhaustion. Her brother was getting well, and Ishmael had kissed her the way a man would kiss the woman he loved. She felt as if she'd sprouted wings.

Dared she hope that Ishmael really loved her? But that would be foolish, she lectured herself. Ishmael didn't know his own name, let alone his own mind. Tomorrow his memory could awaken, and everything he'd ever felt for her could become a forgotten dream.

But Ishmael was everything she'd ever dreamed of in a man—handsome, intelligent, brave, kind and giving. She loved him to the depths of her soul.

Oh, she'd read enough to know how love could deceive and betray the unwary heart. But how could she let the fear of being hurt keep her from the only happiness she might ever know?

Sylvie returned to the house with the broth and put it on the stove to heat. By then Ishmael had taken a cup of water into Daniel's room. She could hear them talking, Daniel's voice becoming more animated by the minute. The boy still had a long recovery ahead of him. Fevers like this one tended to relapse until the body gained strength enough to fight off the sickness. It would be an ongoing struggle to keep her active little brother quiet until he was fully recovered. But the fact that recovery now seemed likely was enough to make her heart sing.

Sylvie spooned warm broth into a bowl and carried it into the bedroom. Ishmael stood to move out of her way. Her breast brushed his arm as she passed him, delivering a flash of wet heat to the core of her body. Color flamed in her cheeks. Was that all it took? Just an accidental touch? Had he noticed?

Ishmael cleared his throat. "I'll see to the chores," he muttered, and ducked out of the room. No, he couldn't have missed her reaction. She was as transparent as a silly schoolgirl.

Daniel was sitting up, propped against the pillows. "How are you feeling?" she asked him.

"Better." He gave her a wan smile.

"I've got some broth here. It'll get your stomach used to food again." She dipped a bit into the spoon and held it to his mouth. He hesitated, then took a taste and swallowed.

"I'm not a baby," he said. "I can feed myself."

"Maybe next time. You're still shaky. I don't want you spilling."

He acquiesced, taking the next spoonful of broth without complaint. "Is Papa home yet?" he asked.

Sylvie felt her heart drop. "Not yet. We're still waiting." Should she prepare the boy? she wondered. Should she raise the possibility that their father might not be coming back at all?

Not now, she decided. Not until he was stronger.

"Papa will be back soon," Daniel said. "I know because I saw him in my dream. He brought us presents."

"You saw him in your dream?" Sylvie had read about people who emerged from sickness or injury with the gift of second sight. But Daniel was just a child, hardly more than a baby. Surely he was just imagining. "What else did you see?" she asked.

Daniel took another spoonful of broth. "He brought me some toy soldiers. And he brought you a book and a pretty bracelet. I asked him why he took so long to get home, and he said he had to hide from some bad men."

"What else did you dream about?" Sylvie gazed at him, surprised at the detail he remembered.

"Nothing. Just that." Daniel opened his mouth for another spoonful of broth.

"Well, let's hope your dream comes true," Sylvie said. "Meanwhile, you need to rest and get well. If you'll finish the broth and rest while I get some work done, I'll come back later and read you a story."

"A long one?"

She gave him a smile. "As long as you like."

"Will you leave the door open so I can look out? And can Ebenezer come in and visit me?"

"Ebenezer's going to need a bath first. Then we'll see." Sylvie thought about the little spotted goat. The animals roamed freely during the day. It was possible that Daniel's tick had come from his pet. It would be wise to check all the goats for ticks. Sylvie added that, and the bath, to her mental list of things to be done that day.

She took a moment to splash her face and smooth her hair. Then she hurried into the kitchen to start breakfast.

After lunch, Ishmael volunteered to bathe Daniel's pet goat. Catching the little beast was a mission in itself. Most of the time Ebenezer was a pest, always sticking his nose where he wasn't wanted. Today he sensed that something was afoot. He led a merry chase around the yard, keeping inches beyond Ishmael's fingertips the whole time.

Churning butter on the porch, Sylvie convulsed in

helpless laughter. Had he ever heard her laugh? Ishmael couldn't recall. But the sound was as sweet as any music he'd ever heard. If he had his way, he would make her laugh far more often. He wanted to hear every sound of happiness and pleasure she could make. Especially at night.

The morning had passed in a whirlwind of activity, caring for Daniel and catching up on all the chores that had been put off during the boy's illness. There'd been no time to talk about private matters, or to follow through on that heart-stopping kiss. But he planned to.

Sweating and cursing, he managed to corner Ebenezer inside the milk shed. He emerged with the thrashing, bleating goat clutched in his arms.

"Remember to check him for ticks," Sylvie called.

"Soon as I get the little beggar in the water." Ishmael carried his burden toward the washtub, grateful that he'd thought to fill it first. Ebenezer squealed as his legs sank into the cool water, but a gentle rubbing with soap relaxed him enough to finish the job. A lump in the thick hair at the base of his neck proved to be a tick, engorged with blood. Ishmael used his knife to pry the creature loose and kill it. Deer, dogs, sheep and other free-roaming mammals often carried ticks. But as far as he knew, only humans got sick from the bites.

Where there was one tick there were liable to be others. Ishmael checked every inch before he wrapped the little goat in a towel and carried him inside to see Daniel.

* * *

The boy's eyes lit as he saw his pet, soft and clean and wrapped like a baby in the towel. Sylvie stood in the doorway, watching as Ishmael sat on the edge of the bed, holding the little goat where Daniel could stroke it. What a wonderful father he would make, she thought.

For a moment she allowed herself to enjoy the fantasy—building a life with this man, sharing his bed, raising his children along with Daniel. That, she knew, would be too much to expect. But here and for now he could be hers—all she would ever know of him.

Did she have the courage to make the most of this sliver of time? Or would she look back at the end of her life and regret what she'd missed?

They waited until after an early supper to pen the other goats and check them for ticks. It took both Sylvie and Ishmael, working together, to do the job. Bundled in blankets, Daniel watched from the rocker on the porch as they cornered the animals, one by one. Ishmael held each goat still while Sylvie inspected every inch of its body. Any ticks she found were removed with the knife tip and dispatched with a stroke of the blade.

By the time they finished, it was nearly dusk. Fog was drifting up from the cove, blanketing the woods and the clearing in soft blue-gray. Crickets chirped in the twilight. Sylvie followed Ishmael out of the pen and fastened the gate. Her hair and skin crawled with the memory of the ticks they'd found. She knew she wouldn't feel safe until she'd washed herself from head to toe. It would be the same for Ishmael.

Abandoning modesty, she stripped off her dress, shoes and stockings and dropped them at the foot of the steps. Clad only in her chemise and petticoat, she mounted the porch and lifted Daniel in her arms. Ishmael read her intent at once. "I'll fill the washtub while you tuck our patient in," he said. "You can go first."

Thanking him, she carried Daniel into her room and lowered him to the bed. He was dressed in a fresh nightshirt. His hair was clean, his skin cool and fresh-smelling from the sponge bath Ishmael had given him.

"Did you get all the ticks off the goats?" he asked.

"As many as we could. But they're bound to get more from the brush. We'll need to check ourselves every night. Can you help me remember to do that?"

He nodded, snuggling into the pillow. "Maybe Papa will come home tomorrow," he murmured.

"Maybe. We'll see." Sylvie kissed his forehead. "Now, go to sleep. We'll be close by. Just call if you need anything. All right?"

She waited for an answer, but her brother was already drifting into slumber.

Sylvie found a clean nightgown for herself and gathered up Ishmael's nightshirt from the other bedroom, along with a bar of soap and two towels. When she came outside, she saw that Ishmael had put the tub on the porch and used the bucket to fill it halfway with clean water.

"Sorry, it'll be cold." He was standing below the porch, his gaze politely averted.

"There's a kettle of hot water on the stove. That should warm it up a bit. I'll heat some more for you." She was aware of her scanty dress, and the way her nipples stood out through the thin muslin. But she felt strangely comfortable standing before him. *Look at me, I'm yours,* she wanted to say. But the words refused to leave her mouth.

"Since I don't want to carry any six-legged passengers inside, I'll take a walk till you're finished. That'll give you some privacy. If you need anything, shout. I'll stay close enough to hear." Turning, he moved off toward the cliff and vanished into the fog.

"Be careful," she called after him.

The only answer was the rush of the incoming tide below the cliff.

Back inside, she took the kettle off the stove and poured steaming water into the tub. After putting more water on to heat, she stripped off her clothes and inspected her body for ticks. Finding none, she picked up the soap and lowered herself into the lukewarm water.

The night breeze raised goose bumps on her wet skin. She soaped her head and body, then used the dipper of fresh water she'd put aside to rinse her hair. By the time she'd stepped out of the tub, toweled herself dry and slipped into her nightgown, she could hear the kettle simmering on the stove.

"Ishmael," she called softly. "Can you hear me? Your bath is ready."

There was a moment of silence. Then he came walking around the corner of the house. She should have known he'd stay close, to protect her.

"There's more hot water. I'll get it." She flitted into the kitchen and came back with the kettle. By then he was standing on the porch, stripping off his shirt and the undershirt beneath. His hands slid over his chest and down his arms, checking for ticks.

"Here, let me help." Sylvie put the kettle next to the tub. "Sit down on the step. I'll check your back and your hair."

"Good idea." He sank onto the step. The moon, shining through the fog, gave some light, but not enough to see well. She would need to check with her hands.

She started with his head, making furrows in his thick, dark hair. She loved the feel of him, the contour of his bones and the way his hair curled around her fingers. She loved the shape of his ears; her fingertips caressed them lightly as she checked every curve and hollow where a tick could hide.

Finding nothing, she moved lower, to the back of his neck. He exhaled with a soft groan as she rubbed the taut ridge of muscle that connected to his shoulders. Sylvie's legs were trembling. This was becoming something far different than a tick hunt.

"How's Daniel?" His voice was a husky growl.

"Fine. He went right to sleep. But he keeps asking about our father. I don't know what to tell him."

"There's nothing you can tell him. All you can do is wait and hope." He took a deep breath. "Sylvie—"

"Raise your arms." Sylvie cut him off. She was in no

mood for a litany of the reasons he couldn't stay with her. She knew them and had come to accept them. All she wanted now was some time with him, something to remember when he was gone.

All she wanted was for him to be still and love her. But where were the words to tell him? How could she even know where to begin?

He raised his arms. Reaching from behind, she checked his armpits, weaving her way through the thick tufts of hair with careful fingers.

"Sylvie," he began again.

"Hush." Her lips brushed the nape of his neck. "Not tonight. We can talk tomorrow."

Her hands slid down his back, thumbs tracing the muscular furrow along his spine. Reaching his belt, they fluttered and stopped. How much courage did she have?

As if sensing her hesitation, he stood and turned to face her. "I can finish this myself. You go on inside before you catch a chill with that damp hair. You're right, it's best if we talk in the morning, after we've both had a good night's rest."

Cupping her face between his two hands, he lifted her chin and planted a tender, exquisitely restrained kiss on her lips. "Good night," he murmured. "Sleep well."

Sylvie could have wept.

Back inside the house, she tiptoed to her own bedroom and opened the door. Daniel was sleeping like an angel, one arm flung above his head in the usual way. His forehead felt cool and damp, his breathing unlabored. All was well.

For a moment she gazed down at the bed, thinking. She was tired enough to sleep anywhere, and there was room for her to stretch out along the outer edge of the mattress. That was surely what Ishmael had in mind when he'd bidden her a chaste good-night.

Was she willing to settle for that?

Emotions churning, she walked back toward the kitchen. Wisps of fog drifted past the porthole windows. From the porch she could hear the faint splash of water as Ishmael bathed.

Turning back toward the bedrooms, she faced two doors. Behind the door on the left lay the safety of life as she had known it. Behind the door on the right lay risk, uncertainty and probable heartbreak.

Taking a deep breath, Sylvie made her choice.

# Chapter Eleven

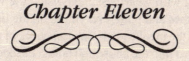

Ishmael finished bathing, stepped out of the washtub and toweled himself dry. Shivering in the cool night air, he donned the flannel nightshirt and dropped his dirty garments into the bathwater. Given the fog, they'd probably still be damp come morning. Damn, what he wouldn't give for a decent change of clothes!

Finding a broom on the porch, he used the handle to stir the clothes in the soapy water. Any ticks hiding in the folds would be forced to swim or drown.

The house was dark and quiet. Sylvie had probably gone to bed. A freshet of warmth stole through his body as he remembered the feel of her hands on his bare skin. Hellfire, how he'd wanted her! The worse of it was, she'd seemed so willing. If he'd waited any longer to send her away, he'd have lost all control. He'd have caught her up in his arms and taken her right there on the porch, consequences be damned.

Only her trust had stopped him.

She'd been right about one thing. They needed to talk in the morning when they were clear-eyed and rested. He would never intentionally hurt her, but given his memory loss, she needed to understand the risks. Until he knew who he was, all he could promise her was his love. Sylvie would have to decide whether that would be enough.

Aching with weariness, he twisted the water out of his clothes and hung everything on the line. After emptying the tub, he made one last check of the clearing, trudged into the house and bolted the door behind him.

As had become his habit, he opened the door of Sylvie's bedroom to look in on Daniel. Sylvie's brother was sleeping like a baby, his eyes closed, his breathing relaxed and even. A wave of tenderness washed over Ishmael as he stood in the doorway. He had no recollection of having been a father, but it would be easy to love this lively little boy as his own.

Seconds passed before the realization struck his tired mind. Daniel was sleeping alone. Where was Sylvie?

Closing the door behind him, he turned toward the other bedroom. If Sylvie had left the house he would have seen her. She might have gone up to the loft, although she'd mentioned that Daniel's pallet was too small for her. If she wasn't there, that left one possibility. Pulse hammering, he opened the bedroom door.

Sylvie lay in a spill of moonlight on the double bed. Curled between fresh, smooth sheets, she'd left ample room on the near side of the mattress. The covers were turned down in open invitation.

As Ishmael stepped into the room, her eyes opened. She smiled, turned onto her back and held out her arms—an innocent temptress in a muslin gown she'd unfastened all the way to her belly.

He knew what would happen if he got into that bed. She had to know it, too. But he needed to be sure she understood the consequences.

"Sylvie—" he began.

"Hush. We'll talk in the morning. Wasn't that what we agreed?"

He groaned.

"I love you, Ishmael." Her voice quivered, not quite breaking. "I know it might not be forever, but if this is all I can have, it's what I want." Her hand reached out and caught his wrist. "I'm a big girl. No regrets, and no nasty scenes when it's over, I promise. Now, stop being noble and come to bed."

With a half-muttered groan, he slid beneath the covers and gathered her in his arms. She was trembling like a fawn. He could imagine the courage—and the love—it had taken for her to offer herself like this. In mere seconds his body had become aroused and ready. But Ishmael knew better than to rush. This time would be for her.

Ishmael's skin was cool through the flannel night-shirt. His damp hair smelled of homemade soap. Sylvie wrapped her arms around him, filling her senses with his nearness as she warmed him. She'd pondered the idea of leaving her nightgown off and welcoming him naked, to make certain he knew what she had in mind. In the end she'd been too shy, but he seemed to have gotten the message.

His lips found hers in the darkness. This time, his kiss was even longer and deeper than the one he'd given her on the porch. Sylvie felt her mouth soften against his, felt the natural urge to open and let him in. The brush of his tongue against hers trickled heat along her sensitive nerves. A whimper of need stirred in her throat.

"Are you all right?" He drew back a little.

"Very much so." Sylvie tried to sound clever, but her voice shook. "I want to please you, Ishmael, but I don't know what to do."

His laugh rumbled low in his throat. "Don't worry, love," he muttered. "I'll enjoy teaching you. But there's one rule you need to understand. If anything I do frightens or hurts you, tell me and I'll stop."

"You could never frighten me...or hurt me." Her hands caught his head, pulling him down to her for another kiss. Her mouth opened to the full thrust of his tongue. The sensation was strange but deliciously intimate. Far more intimate than anything she'd read about in Jane Austen.

She'd left her nightgown undone on purpose, wanting him to touch her as she'd yearned to be touched. She sighed as his hand slid around the naked curve of her waist. Her body vibrated with pleasure, like the strings of a new fiddle being played for the first time.

"Oh..." she whispered, then *"Oh!"* as his palm

cupped her breast. As he stroked her, a whirlwind of sensations rushed through her body. This was Ishmael touching her, Ishmael loving her. "Yes…" she murmured, dizzy with the wonder of it.

"Yes?" His finger teased her nipple, circling the soft areola until the puckering made her ache inside. "Yes, what?"

"Yes…more."

"More of this?" He shifted upward, his mouth capturing the raspberry nub. His tongue skimmed the tip; then he began to suckle her softly, almost playfully. The tingling tremors crept lower. She felt her womb contract, pulsing in the dark, moist depths of her body. Instinctively her hips rose against him. Her wildly seeking hands clutched at his flannel nightshirt.

"Take it off," she gasped. "Let me touch you."

He rose, stripping off the nightshirt and flinging it aside. For the space of a breath he stood over her, beautiful in the moonlight. Sylvie had seen him naked once before, but not like this, standing over her, his arousal jutting so huge and hard that her mouth went dry at the sight.

"Do I frighten you, Sylvie?" he asked.

"No…" She groped for the right word. "You *astonish* me. I've never seen…" Her words trailed off.

"Do you still want to touch me?"

"More than ever."

He lowered himself into bed beside her. "Then touch me here," he growled, guiding her hand down along his belly to the nest of crisp curls that framed his shaft. He withdrew his hand, leaving her free to pull away if she chose to. But Sylvie willed herself to be bold. Her trembling fingers touched him, stroked him. Softness over tempered steel—skin like a baby's and beneath it...merciful heaven, the size of him!

There was a diagram in her medical book showing exactly how a man and woman's parts fit together. Sylvie had studied it, but she couldn't imagine how it would feel to have a man inside her. And saints save her, Ishmael seemed as big as a stallion. What if she was too small? What if she failed him?

As if he'd read her mind, he bent and kissed her gently. "Lie still, love. Tell me when you want me."

His caressing hand moved down her belly to rest on her soft mound. Her breath caught as it hovered there, skimming, lingering. He kissed her again, his stubbled chin grazing her mouth, her throat. She moaned and lifted her hips beneath his hand, intensifying the contact. Heat simmered between her legs.

Tenderly, as if he was separating the petals of a rose, he deepened his touch. His finger found her moistness and slicked it up and down along her cleft. The sensation was so exquisite that she gasped.

"Ishmael, what are you doing?" she whispered.

"Do you want me to stop?"

"No...don't stop..." She arched against his touch, rising to meet the pressure that was driving her wild with desire. Her legs opened. Her hips thrust upward in a pulsing rhythm that seemed to be born in her. She was made for this, she thought, made for him and no one else.

When he found the sensitive nub at her center, it

was all she could do to keep from crying out. Moisture drenched her as he stroked the spot, muttering half-heard endearments between kisses. The urges that rose in her were like a warm spring flood, surging and swelling, demanding release.

His finger penetrated gently, touching off a throb of need. She pushed against his hand, her fears forgotten. All she wanted was to have him inside her, filling the empty, aching place that had been waiting for him.

*"Now,"* she whispered urgently. "I want you, Ishmael."

She heard the sharp intake of his breath as he shifted above her. Sylvie had read that there might be pain the first time, but as his shaft glided through on her moisture, she felt only a slight tearing sensation. Then his full length was buried deep inside her, fitting as if they'd been made for each other.

Heaven.

His eyes locked with hers in the moonlight. "Sylvie, I—"

"Hush." Her finger touched the scar at the corner of his mouth. "No promises. This is for now."

She pulled his head down to hers in a lingering kiss. Her hips pushed upward, meeting his thrust again, then again and again as she lost herself in loving him. Then it was as if they were flying through a sky full of shooting stars, soaring, spiraling upward together. She heard him gasp as they burst, shattered and drifted blissfully back to earth.

Sylvie cradled him in her arms, holding him close.

Inside Ishmael was a man she had never known, with a life she couldn't share. But for now he was hers. Her prince. Her love.

Sylvie reached up to pin Ishmael's clean shirt to the clothesline. The breeze was warm, the sunlight a wash of transparent gold. A cloud of snowy gulls soared above the cliff. On a day like this, the laundry should dry in no time.

From the rear of the cabin, she could hear the sound of Ishmael's hammer blows, accompanied by Daniel's happy chatter. The two of them were reinforcing the goat pen, adding walls to the overhanging roof that served as a shelter. Daniel, who'd bounced back from the fever with his usual boyish energy, followed his hero around like a puppy, eager to help and proud to be learning a man's work.

Over the past week Sylvie had found time to sew some sturdy denim into a set of work clothes for Ishmael. She'd also knitted him a pair of much-needed wool stockings. True, the homemade costume wasn't something a gentleman might wear in San Francisco. But at least the shirt and trousers would save wear on his regular clothes.

She paused to savor the sounds of the man and boy working together. The hammering and the low murmur of voices told her that, except for her missing father, all was well in her small world. Daniel was healthy; the strangers who'd terrorized them seemed to be gone; and Ishmael's loving had brought her a sensual contentment that Sylvie would never have believed possible.

By day she reveled in his presence—the flash of his smile, the catch in his voice and the lingering tenderness in his touch. By night he was her lover, and she was shamelessly his. Her hunger to be joined with him blazed every time he touched her. For the first time in her life, she understood what it meant to be a woman.

There were times, like today, when she could almost believe it would last. But that kind of thinking was dangerous, Sylvie knew. Her prince belonged to another world, and one day, when he remembered it, he would go home. The thought that he might take her and Daniel with him was nothing but a dream.

Her best real hope was that Ishmael might leave her with child—a small piece of him for her to love, and a playmate for Daniel. It wouldn't be easy, managing a baby on her own. But she could do it. Women made do under all sorts of circumstances, and these weren't the worst. At least, for now, she had a home.

Her gaze wandered to the parting in the trees where the road led down the mountain. She could almost imagine the creak of wagon wheels and the homecoming bray of her father's mule as they rounded the last bend. A tear welled in her eye and trickled down her cheek. Daniel still insisted his father was coming home soon. But how long could she let the boy go on believing?

How could things be so good, and yet, at the same time, so worrisome?

Where was that blasted goat? Ishmael tramped through the woods that bordered the landward side of the clearing. Ebenezer had taken to wandering of late, and now the harebrained creature was gone again. While the older goats seemed to sense the risk in straying from the safety of the yard, Daniel's young pet had no such instincts. Alone in the forest, he'd be easy prey for a coyote or bobcat, or even a passing bear or cougar. It would serve the little pest right, Ishmael groused. But Daniel would be heartbroken if Ebenezer vanished for good, and that made finding him a matter of high urgency.

"Ebenezer, come here, you little renegade!" Ishmael whistled softly. How did you call a damn goat, anyway? Daniel had wanted to search with him, but the forest could be a dangerous place, especially toward evening when predators were awakening. Sylvie had agreed that the boy should stay close to the cabin. Ishmael had left them in the kitchen, Daniel doing his sums while Sylvie prepared supper.

"Don't worry," Ishmael had promised the boy. "I won't come back till I find him."

Now he was beginning to wonder if he'd promised too hastily. A glance at the sky told him he had less than an hour of daylight left and a lot of ground to cover in that time. If he failed to find the goat… Ishmael shook his head. There was no need to weigh the odds of a small, bleating animal surviving a night in the forest.

As he searched, Ishmael's thoughts wandered to Sylvie and what came next. That he loved her and wanted a life with her was beyond question. The happiness he'd found in her arms was beyond anything he'd ever known—even with so little memory he felt sure of that. And he'd fallen under the spell of this peaceful spot beside the sea, so much so that he felt he could be content here forever. If he could get permission and funding to build a lighthouse, he could make Sylvie's dream come true. They would have a livelihood and a place to raise their family for as long as they wanted to stay.

But without his name he was powerless to make anything happen. He had no legal right to offer himself to Sylvie as a husband or to petition the government for a lighthouse. Without his name he was nobody.

As he shaded his eyes, the sunlight glinted on his sapphire ring. He had a name, a noble one, Ishmael reminded himself. He had a history, maybe even a home. But unless his memory came back like a thunderclap, he wasn't likely to discover anything here. There was only one way to find out who he was. He needed to go to the one place where somebody might know him.

He needed to go back to San Francisco.

But how was he supposed to manage that, with no horse or wagon and not a cent to his name? He could always walk, and live off the land. But how could he leave Sylvie and Daniel here alone and possibly in danger?

A faint sound broke into his thoughts. He froze, ears straining in the stillness. For the space of a breath he heard nothing. Then, as faint as the flutter of a leaf, it came again—the frantic bleat of a small, frightened animal.

Ishmael followed the sound into the trees, so far that he lost sight of the clearing with its house and sheds. Here the forest was a tangle of deadfalls and prickly undergrowth. Layers of white fungus sprouted from the bark of a rotting stump. A raven scolded from a scraggly pine.

Holding his breath, he listened for the bleat. There it was again, closer this time. Thorns caught at his clothes as he moved toward the sound.

At his approach, a low, furry shape flashed into the underbrush. A coyote. Ishmael swore under his breath. He could only hope he hadn't arrived too late. Ignoring the brambles, he plunged ahead.

Relief surged through him as he spotted Ebenezer in a clump of sumac. The little goat appeared to be trapped. Eyes wild with terror, he was struggling to get free from what looked like a snare. Bending close, Ishmael saw that it was indeed a snare, fashioned from thin, flexible wire. It had tangled around Ebenezer's hind leg and was digging into his flesh as he kicked and twisted.

"Hold still, you four-legged disaster!" Clasping the goat around the middle, Ishmael used his free hand to loosen the wire and free the leg. Sylvie, he knew, set clever snares in her garden. Any rabbit foolish enough to raid her vegetables was liable to wind up in a stew. But this wasn't one of Sylvie's snares. She used string, not wire. And she would never set a snare this far from the house.

Somebody else was out here in the woods.

Gripping Ebenezer under one arm, Ishmael inspected

the earth around the snare. The ground was covered with pine needles and leaf litter. The only tracks recent enough to leave an impression were his own. Even when he brushed down to bare soil, there was nothing to be found.

So the snare could be an older one. But someone had set it—someone who'd been here long enough to need fresh meat. Had it been the men who'd threatened them earlier, or maybe just the one who ran off? Was someone out there now, waiting for Ishmael to leave so they could take possession of Aaron Cragun's house and his children?

Maybe there was nothing to worry about. But that was a chance Ishmael couldn't afford to take. He needed to warn Sylvie to keep Daniel close and to keep the gun handy. And he needed to devise some ways to protect the place.

Keeping a tight grip on Ebenezer, he strode through the woods and back to the house. Daniel came bounding out onto the porch. He was overjoyed to see his pet, but Sylvie insisted on a thorough tick inspection before he could go near the little goat. While Ishmael checked Ebenezer's body and ears, she dashed to the cupboard for her pine salve to rub on the goat's sore leg.

As she dabbed salve on the raw lines, her eyes met Ishmael's. In their silvery depths, he read the understanding that she'd sensed trouble. But he knew better than to bring up his worries in front of Daniel. *Later,* her expression told him. After the boy was asleep they would talk.

* * *

Sylvie lay next to Ishmael in the darkness, her head nested against the hollow of his shoulder. The night was so peaceful they could hear the murmur of the sea below the cliff. *How dare they?* she thought as he told her what he'd found in the woods. How dare anyone invade the blissful world she'd found with this man?

"Are you sure there's somebody out there?" she asked, wishing she could disbelieve him.

"That snare didn't set itself. Is there any chance your father might have done it when he was here?"

She shook her head. "He wouldn't have set one so far from the cabin."

"Then it had to be somebody else. We've no choice except to assume they're still around and take precautions. You'll need to stay close to the house and we'll need to keep Daniel in sight. No more letting that goat wander off. And it might be a good idea for you to carry a gun, too."

"I can take the pocket pistol." She shuddered, remembering the dark night and the man she'd killed with that tiny gun. "What about you?"

"I'll take the shotgun and keep an eye on the yard, maybe rig up some kind of warning system with that string you use for snares. Let's hope we won't need it."

Turning, she kissed the hollow of his throat. "I'm sorry," she whispered. "I know you never bargained for this."

He pulled her against him. "I've no idea what I did bargain for. But fate carried me here to you, and I wouldn't change that for the world."

"What's going to become of us, Ishmael?"

"I don't know, sweetheart. But whatever happens, know that I love you, and I want to be here for you and Daniel." His lips brushed her hairline. She could feel the hard ridge of his arousal against her belly, and she knew what would happen next. Words were just words, she knew. When Ishmael came back to himself—and he would—nothing he said now could bind him. But for now, in this time and this place, he was hers to love.

She would love him with all she had.

The next day dawned with a sky like the pearlescent heart of a seashell. Striding out early to milk the goats, Sylvie found herself wondering how anyone could feel gloom on such a beautiful morning. Yet she did. She'd awakened with a sense of dark foreboding that no amount of reason could shake. There was change in the air—and not a change for the better.

Sometime in the night she'd remembered the pistol she'd found in the wreck. So many things had happened since the day she'd hidden it in the cliffside that she'd almost forgotten about it. But now, with danger threatening, Ishmael would need the weapon along with the powder and caps she'd found with it.

After breakfast, while he and Daniel were busy rebuilding the goat shed, she would walk down the trail and get the gun for him. It might be awkward, explaining why she'd stashed it in the first place. But surely Ishmael would understand and forgive her.

In the house, Sylvie did her best to dismiss the dark premonition. For breakfast, she made flapjacks with elderberry jam, Daniel's favorite. She and Ishmael had decided not to frighten him with tales of hidden bogeymen in the woods. But they planned to keep him close by, so they could get him into the house at the first sign of danger.

The boy chatted happily over breakfast as Sylvie and Ishmael exchanged glances. Maybe the day would be fine. Whoever might be out there in the woods hadn't bothered them yet. Maybe they were waiting for Ishmael to leave, or for Sylvie's father to return. Or it was possible that whoever had set the snare was long gone.

After breakfast, Ishmael took Daniel outside with him to work. Ebenezer was nibbling grass close by, tethered to the fence by a thin rope knotted around his neck.

After Sylvie had cleaned up the kitchen and set some sourdough to rise, she struck out for the cliff trail. She'd debated whether to tell Ishmael about her errand, then decided against it. First, she would need to explain her reason for going. Then he'd probably insist on going with her. That meant they'd be taking Daniel as well, and Daniel would be whining to go down to the cove. All in all, it would be simpler and faster just to walk down the trail and get the things she'd hidden.

She stuck the loaded pocket pistol into her apron. Not that she'd need it. The narrow cliffside trail was open all the way with no place an intruder could hide. But she'd promised Ishmael she'd keep the tiny gun with her. That was the least she could do to please him.

As if in defiance of Sylvie's dark-edged mood, the

morning had brightened into a beautiful day. Far below in the cove, sunlight shimmered on a moiré of rippled waves. The foam that curled onto the beach was like lace along the hem of a billowing gown.

By now the ravages of sand and tide had reduced Ishmael's boat to half-buried timbers. Weeks from now it would be gone without a trace.

*Would Ishmael be gone as well by then? Would her father be home? What was going to become of them all?* The useless questions pecked at her mind like a flock of blackbirds. Impatient with herself, she shooed them away.

The niche that had served as a hiding place was about halfway down the cliff trail. Finding it, Sylvie reached up and pulled out the concealing moss, only now beginning to wonder what exactly she would find. She'd assumed there was no seepage in the deep crack. But what if she was wrong? Water could have damaged the pistol, powder flask and caps beyond repair.

A sigh of relief escaped her as she drew out the bundle. The apron she'd used to wrap the items was clean and dry. Everything appeared just as she'd left it. But she would check to make sure. Returning Ishmael's property could be a delicate matter. She wanted no surprises.

Crouching at a wide bend in the trail, she laid the bundle on the ground and unfolded the apron. The gun belt and holster were mildewed but still useful. The pistol had a few spots of rust that could be cleaned off with oil. The powder flask, which had been sealed with wax, was still tight. When she shook it, she could hear the shifting dry powder inside.

The pouch had suffered the most damage. The leather was stiff and moldy, the twisted rawhide string dried in the shape of its knot. Sylvie struggled to loosen it. If she'd opened the pouch when she found it, she could have poured out the percussion caps and knotted them into a dry corner of her apron. Now she was paying for her haste. She could only hope the caps would still be usable.

The stiffened drawstring broke in her hands. Caps and lead balls spilled and scattered. Most fell onto the apron, but a few bounced onto the trail. Sylvie scrambled to pick up the strays and pile them together. Only as she was scooping them back into the pouch did she realize there was something else inside.

Gingerly she reached into the pouch and lifted out a folded, mildewed sheet of notepaper. Her pulse leaped. What if it held some clue to Ishmael's identity?

The paper was slightly damp and had to be unfolded one delicate layer at a time. At last it lay flat before her. Sylvie stared at the faded, bleeding pen lines. Her mouth went dry.

She was looking at a hastily sketched map—a map of the northern California coastline. The area with the cove and the cliff was clearly marked and circled.

"No," she whispered. "It can't be true." But it was. The evidence was right in front of her.

The night the storm struck, Ishmael had been on his way here, with a gun.

# Chapter Twelve

Ishmael was hammering a board onto the goat shed when Sylvie burst around the corner of the house. One arm clutched a wrapped bundle against her chest. She looked as if she'd just seen the devil.

Ishmael lowered the hammer. Not wanting to alarm Daniel, he masked his apprehension. "What is it?"

"I need to talk to you." She met his eyes, then glanced toward Daniel. Clearly this was something she didn't want her brother to hear.

Ishmael stood. "We'll be on the front porch, Daniel," he said. "You stay here and take care of Ebenezer. Don't go anywhere until I come back, all right?"

"All right." Daniel scratched the young goat's ears. "Can I hammer in some nails?"

"Go ahead. Watch your fingers." Ishmael followed Sylvie around the house to the front porch. From behind him came the ring of childish hammer blows.

Sylvie stopped in the shadow of the porch and

turned back to face him. By now Ishmael could read her well. She was quivering with tension.

"What is it, love?"

She drew herself fully erect, as if she were facing an enemy. "I've been keeping something from you. Until today I didn't know how much."

As Sylvie began her story, Ishmael remembered how he'd watched her from the cliff top as she took something from the wrecked boat and hid it along the trail. He'd even gone down to look for it later, but he'd evidently missed her hiding place.

As she finished, he was dimly aware that Daniel's hammering had stopped.

"Why didn't you tell me before this?" he demanded.

She gripped the bundle tighter, as if reluctant to give it to him. "At the time I didn't know anything about you or the state of your mind. I didn't think it would be wise to give you a weapon. Later on, with those men coming here and Daniel being so sick, I simply forgot. I didn't remember until last night, after you told me there still might be someone in the woods."

Hooking a finger beneath her jaw, he lifted her face. "So what's upset you now, Sylvie? Your hiding the gun was perfectly understandable. Did you think I'd be angry?"

"Perhaps. But no, that's not it. There's more." She thrust the bundle toward him. "Take this. It's yours."

Laying the bundle on the porch, he unrolled it to find a .36 Navy Colt, slightly rusted but still in usable condition, a sealed flask of powder and a moldy leather pouch, which held a handful of percussion caps and a tin of lead balls. The items would doubtless come in handy. But Ishmael had no memory of having owned any of them. He shook his head.

"They were in the forward compartment of the boat," Sylvie said. "They must be yours. Don't you remember?"

"I don't remember a thing." He shot her a scowl. "And I still can't figure out what's got you in such a lather. Is it something I've done?"

Without a reply, Sylvie reached into her apron pocket and drew out a lightly folded sheet of damp, moldy paper. Ishmael opened it, stared at the faded lines. Nothing came to mind.

"You don't recognize it?" she asked.

He shook his head.

"I found it in the pouch. It's a map, with the cove marked and circled. You didn't wash up here by accident, Ishmael. When that storm struck, *this* place was where you were headed." She pointed to the spot on the map. "Right here. With a gun. Maybe it's time you start remembering."

Had she spoken too hastily? Sylvie hadn't meant to imply that Ishmael had been deceiving her all along. But now that she'd said as much, it made a certain amount of sense. What if he'd had something to do with her father's disappearance? What if he'd come here, pretending amnesia, bent on some dark scheme she couldn't even imagine?

His eyes had gone cold. "Lord, is that what you think? That I came here on purpose, wrecked in a storm and then faked losing my memory? That makes about as much sense as one of your fairy tales."

"Whether your memory loss is real or not, you had *something* in mind when you headed this way. Something involving my home, and a gun. Can you explain the map any other way?"

"No, damn it. I'd give anything to know where that map came from and what it was doing—what *I* was doing—in the boat. But I can't answer your question. Lord help me, *I don't remember!*"

She gazed up at him, seeing the rage in his sapphire eyes, the seething frustration. Was this the man who'd claimed her heart and her body? Or was this someone she didn't even know?

"Do you believe anything I've told you?" he demanded. "Do you believe me when I say I love you, Sylvie?"

She felt something crack apart inside her, like ice shattering a glass jar. "I don't know," she said. "I need time to think about all this. For now, please go back to Daniel and send him inside. It's time for his lessons."

Without waiting for a reply, she wheeled away from him, stumbled into the house and closed the door behind her. Only when she was safely out of his sight did Sylvie begin to crumble. Her knees sagged under her. She sank onto a kitchen chair and buried her face in her trembling hands. The burning desolation in Ishmael's eyes haunted her. She loved him so much, and she wanted to believe him. But the trust they'd shared was gone, maybe for good.

Why hadn't she waited to tell him about the map?

She could have thought about what she'd learned, taken time to test her suspicions. Instead, she'd gone storming up the trail to confront him, without a plan in her silly head. What an emotional fool she'd been!

Forcing herself to rise, she went to the bookshelf, retrieved Daniel's slate and books and carried them to the kitchen table. Any second her little brother would be coming inside. It wouldn't do to let him see her so upset.

She was arranging the lesson materials on the table when the door opened. Expecting to see Daniel, she turned.

Ishmael stood braced in the doorway. He was out of breath, his face so haggard that he looked ill.

"Daniel's missing," he rasped. "The goat, too. I can't find them anywhere."

Ishmael had come around the house to find the boy gone. The rope that had tethered the goat was still tied to the fence, the loop lying empty on the ground, as if it had slipped off Ebenezer's sleek head.

Not wanting to alarm Sylvie, Ishmael had made a frantic circle of the cabin, searching in all directions. He'd checked the privy and the sheds and examined the ground for tracks—the latter a waste of time, since there were tracks all over the yard. After that, sick with worry, he'd gone to tell Sylvie.

The sight of her stricken face knifed his heart. Wordlessly she followed him around the house to where Daniel had last been seen. The hammer and a few nails lay on the ground next to the rope.

"The goat must've gotten loose, and Daniel went after it," Ishmael said. He didn't have the heart to bring up the darker possibility, that someone had snatched the boy and his pet. But he could imagine what was going through Sylvie's mind.

"Daniel!" Sylvie raced out into the yard. "Come back here! Leave the goat. We'll get him for you!"

She stood listening, but there was no reply. When she turned back to Ishmael, her eyes were welling with tears. "This is my fault. If I hadn't taken you away from him—"

"Stop that! It's nobody's fault. The boy's wandered off, that's all." Ishmael paused, thinking. "Would he go down to the beach?"

Her eyes lit with hope. "He might. He's not supposed to go alone, but—"

"Come on!" He raced toward the cliff trail, with Sylvie on his heels. They'd reached the windlass when they heard it—a thin cry coming from somewhere below the edge of the cliff.

Sylvie froze. "Daniel?" she called.

The cry came again, distinctly human, followed by the sound of a falling, bouncing rock.

From where they stood, they were unable to see below the cliff's edge. Telling Sylvie to stay put, Ishmael moved down the trail, far enough to get a view of the cliffside. That was when he saw Daniel.

The boy was several yards off the trail, hanging by his hands from a tree root that curled outward from the side of the cliff. A few feet beyond him, Ebenezer stood on a narrow lip of rock, looking as if he didn't have a care in the world.

It was plain to see what had happened. One way or another, the little goat had gotten loose and wandered down the cliff. Daniel, frantic to rescue his pet, had left the trail and tried to get to him. The ledge had crumbled beneath Daniel's feet, leaving the boy hanging with the barest of footholds. If his small hands lost their strength, he would tumble to his death on the rocks below.

"Daniel, I'm here," Ishmael said in a quiet voice. "Hang on and don't move. I'm going to swing over and get you." Glancing up, he shouted to Sylvie, "Throw down some rope from the windlass. When I tell you I'm tied in, keep it tight and steady."

As if Sylvie had anticipated his plan, the rope dropped at once. Ishmael took an instant to wrap a length around his body and tie a secure knot.

Daniel watched him with huge, frightened eyes. "What about Ebenezer?" he asked.

"He's a blasted goat. He'll be fine." Even as Ishmael spoke, Ebenezer, his hooves finding minuscule footholds, scampered up the cliff to safety.

Ishmael shouted a signal to Sylvie. The windlass cranked the rope tight. "Listen to me, Daniel," he said. "I'm going to swing over and catch you. It may take a few tries, so don't let go until I have you. When I do, wrap your arms around my neck and hang on. Whatever happens, don't let go. Ready?"

The boy nodded. His white lips tightened as the meager ledge under his feet crumbled in a shower of rocks. Now he was dangling in midair, his full weight hanging from his hands.

With a prayer on his lips, Ishmael backed up and swung himself off the trail, into space. The rope yanked tight, grinding against him as it took his weight. Straining for distance, he felt his momentum slow and stop short of Daniel. His heart sank as the rope swung backward. How long could a child's hands hold on?

Pushing hard off the cliff, he launched himself forward again. This time the miracle happened. His hand stretched out, caught Daniel's waist and pulled him loose from his grip on the tree root. Ishmael felt the solid little body against him, felt the tension of the added weight on the rope. A relief that bordered on giddiness swept over him. It would be all right, he thought as Daniel's thin arms locked around his neck. If Sylvie couldn't pull them up, she could lower them to the trail. As long as the rope held—and it was a stout one, designed to haul far heavier items—everything would be fine.

The rope was still swinging backward in a weighted arc, toward the trail side of the cliff. Hanging on to the boy with one arm and the rope with the other, Ishmael was paying no attention to his momentum or to the jutting cliff face directly behind him.

His backside slammed into the rock, knocking the breath out of his lungs. Lights flashed in Ishmael's head, lights that flickered and went out like torches hurled into black water.

Flynn O'Rourke opened his eyes. He was dangling at the end of a rope, with the sea rushing below him and a small boy clinging like a monkey to his neck. For the space of a breath, none of this made sense to him. Then he remembered.

He remembered everything.

He remembered that Catriona was dead, strangled in an alley by a thieving vulture named Aaron Cragun. He remembered setting out for Cragun's hideout and wrecking his boat in a storm.

And he remembered falling in love with Cragun's beautiful, innocent daughter.

Lord almighty, what a mess he'd made of it!

"Ishmael, what's happened? Are you all right?" Sylvie's voice called from the top of the cliff.

Flynn winced at the sound of the name she'd given him. How long had he blacked out? It couldn't have been more than a few seconds. But it was as if a locked door had burst open. "All's well," he called back. "I've got Daniel. We're both safe. Can you haul us up, or will you need to lower us to the rocks?"

"I'll lift you to the top of the trail. Don't worry, I've helped my father plenty of times."

He heard the creak of the windlass and felt the tension on the rope. Slowly he and the boy began to rise.

Daniel's arms tightened around his neck. His face was pressed against Flynn's shoulder. Flynn felt an unexpected surge of tenderness. "How are you feeling, son?" he asked. "Were you scared?"

The boy nodded. "Is Ebenezer all right?"

"He's fine. Goats can climb anywhere. If he ever does that again, just let him get back by himself. All right?"

Once more the boy nodded. His hair was warm against Flynn's throat, his arms tight and trusting. Aaron Cragun's son. And Sylvie, his loving Sylvie, was the murdering bastard's daughter.

What in hell's name was he going to do?

Should he let them know his memory had returned? Everything hinged on that question. Aaron Cragun could already be dead. If he was, there'd be no need for his children to know about their father's crime and no reason for Flynn to hide his identity.

But what if Cragun was alive? What if he was on his way home? As long as there was any chance of that, Flynn knew he had to keep his secret. Otherwise, Cragun's children would act to protect their father.

Flynn had always hated lies and lying. But sometimes a lie was necessary. This was one of those times. For now he would continue to wear the mask of Ishmael, the man with no memory.

The lie was liable to cost him Sylvie's love. But his own selfish needs no longer counted. Catriona, his vibrant, beloved sister, had been heartlessly strangled. Her killer had to be brought to justice.

Was Aaron Cragun that killer? The things he'd learned about the man would argue against it. Wisdom cautioned him to reserve judgment until he knew the full story.

But there was one certainty. If Cragun was alive, and if the evidence proved he'd murdered Catriona, he would have to pay.

Sylvie felt the rope go slack as Ishmael set foot on solid ground. A moment later he strode into sight, still carrying Daniel against his shoulder. There was something about the way the sun glinted in his eyes, something sharper, harder than she remembered...

But what was she thinking? The man she loved had just saved her little brother. Laughing with relief, she dropped the rope and ran to meet them.

"Take this little renegade and ask him what he's learned about goats." Ishmael thrust Daniel into her arms. Sylvie caught the boy close, holding him fiercely.

"I'm sorry, Sylvie." His face was streaked with dirt and tears. "Please don't be mad at me."

"What were you doing?" she demanded. "Ishmael told you to stay by the fence."

Daniel's eyes would have melted granite. "No, he told me to take care of Ebenezer. That's what I was doing."

"Did you untie him?"

"Ebenezer didn't like the rope, so I took it off him. I told him to stay with me, but he ran away."

Sylvie suppressed the urge to shake him. "You could have fallen and died! Don't you ever do that again! Will you promise?"

He nodded solemnly. Sylvie sighed. "Ishmael said you learned something about goats. What was it?"

Daniel glanced over her shoulder at Ishmael. "I found out Ebenezer could climb up by himself. I didn't need to save him."

Ishmael cleared his throat. "Right now we need to put Ebenezer in his pen. Ask your sister if you can help catch him before you go in for your lessons."

"Can I, Sylvie?" Daniel was bright-eyed once more.

"All right. But you're to come inside as soon as that goat's penned up. We'll be starting on times tables today."

Sylvie watched them cross the yard, Ishmael shortening his stride so Daniel could keep pace. Now that the crisis was over, it was all she could do to keep her knees from buckling. What if Ishmael hadn't been here? She could never have saved her brother alone. She hadn't even thanked Ishmael. But then he'd barely spoken to her when he brought the boy back. What little he had to say, he'd passed through Daniel.

True, they'd argued before Daniel went missing. She'd confronted him with the map she'd found, and implied some ugly suspicions that she should have kept to herself. But in the light of Daniel's rescue their quarrel seemed trivial, even silly. Surely Ishmael would see that.

She would *make* him see it.

Tonight would be a celebration—a special supper with potatoes and gravy, fresh sourdough rolls with butter, young carrots from the garden and wild berry cobbler with fresh cream. And after Daniel was asleep...

Heat crept into Sylvie's face as she thought of the night ahead. When it came to lovemaking, she wasn't a sophisticated woman. But she was learning. If Ishmael had any doubt that she loved him, she would erase that doubt in bed.

Gazing across the yard, she saw Daniel and Ishmael trying to corner the small goat. They were laughing and dodging, making a game of it. A smile teased

Sylvie's lips as she lingered to watch them. They were her world. She loved them both so much.

Reminding herself of the work she had to do, she turned away and headed for the house.

Flynn surveyed the carefully set table, the gingham cloth, the matching, folded napkins, the little vase of lovingly arranged wildflowers. Sylvie had outdone herself tonight, and all for him. The hell of it was her efforts only made him writhe with guilt. The fact that he still loved her—and that he knew she loved him— made everything worse. With every word he spoke, he was deceiving her. And if her father returned and proved guilty, the thing he'd sworn to do would break her heart.

As they bowed their heads in grace, he glimpsed her across the table. She was as beautiful as a Madonna, the lamplight framing her like a halo as her eyes closed in prayer. Filling his gaze with her, he ached in silence.

"We thank thee for this food, and for the gift of Daniel's life," she said. "And we thank thee for our friend Ishmael, who saved him and who blesses us with his presence. We pray for the safety of our father. Keep him in thy care, Lord, and bring him home to us soon… Amen."

"Amen," Daniel murmured and opened his eyes. "Yum! Let's eat!"

It was all Flynn could to do keep from groaning out loud. They were so precious, these two, so trusting and innocent. They'd become part of him in a way that no one ever had, not even his beloved sister. And now, with Catriona gone, they'd become the closest thing he had to family.

What would they do if he had to take their father?

Sylvie passed him the platter of succulent chicken she'd roasted. He'd been working all day and should have been ravenous. But guilt had taken the edge off his appetite. He would have to force down every mouthful.

Leave at first light—that would be the reasonable thing to do. Aaron Cragun was overdue and probably dead. Even if the man was alive, why wait for him here? He could just as easily meet him on the road or look for him in San Francisco. That way, the man's children would never have to know what happened to their father or why—surely a blessing in disguise.

The idea was tempting. But Flynn couldn't leave Sylvie and Daniel here unprotected. He would stay, continuing to lie like a medicine drummer, until he knew it was safe for them to be here alone.

"Have some more bread." Sylvie reached for another warm sourdough roll to lay on his plate.

"I'm saving room for dessert." Flynn waved the offering away. "But you're a wonder, Miss Sylvie Cragun. Knowing what little you had on hand, I can't imagine how you whipped up a feast like this one. If you ever decide to move to a town, you could earn your living as a cook."

"Really?" Her silver eyes brightened. "You're not just saying that to be nice?"

Flynn shook his head, glad he could be truthful for once. "I wouldn't say it if it wasn't so. People everywhere appreciate good food, and you have a gift. If not that, you could teach school. I've seen the way you work with Daniel on his lessons. Think about it."

A shadow passed across her face. Flynn could guess what she was thinking. Sooner or later, if her father didn't come home, she and Daniel would have to leave. They would need a way out of here, a place to stay and some way to earn a living. For a young woman as sheltered as Sylvie, the prospect would be frightening. But she needed to face it. He was forcing her to face it.

Maybe he could find a way to help her. He had connections in San Francisco, including people who would give her a room and a job. And he had enough money to hire a wagon and driver for the move. That much would be easy if Aaron Cragun was already dead. But Sylvie would never accept help from the man who'd brought down her beloved father.

And that wasn't all. Much as he loved her, Flynn had to face another truth. Sylvie and Daniel were the offspring of the man who'd likely killed his sister. If he made Sylvie his wife, the memory of that crime would haunt him every time he looked into their innocent faces. He couldn't let that happen. He couldn't marry her.

And if he couldn't marry her, he shouldn't sleep with her. That would be the most hurtful pretense of all. But what was he supposed to tell her?

"How about some cobbler?" Sylvie rose, her smile artificially bright, almost as if she'd read his thoughts. As she dished up the flaky pastry, with its juicy dark red filling, she chatted away about Daniel's lessons, and how he'd already learned his two-times tables.

"Smart boy. You've taught him well," Flynn said. "He should do fine when he gets in school."

"Yes, I know." She flashed him an uncertain smile. Her eyes glimmered with tears. "One day Daniel's going to make us all proud."

After supper, Ishmael and Daniel helped Sylvie clean up. She'd promised Daniel a story if they finished before bedtime. The boy pitched in eagerly, drying the knives, forks and spoons and putting them in the drawer.

As Sylvie washed, Ishmael fished the dishes out of the rinse water, wiped them and stacked them on the shelves. Never a talkative man, he was unusually quiet tonight. Sylvie felt the tension in him—not unlike the strangeness she'd sensed earlier, when he'd brought Daniel up the cliff. At the time, she'd dismissed it as something she could fix with good food and lovemaking. She hadn't understood. Now she did.

He was going to leave them.

He'd told her as much over supper, when he'd suggested she find employment as a cook or teacher. As his future wife, she wouldn't need a job. But Ishmael had made it clear that she and Daniel were to be on their own.

The man had made her no promises, Sylvie reminded herself. She had given him her body of her own free will, knowing all along how things might end between them. She would accept his decision with as much grace and dignity as she could muster; and she would hold back her tears until he was gone.

It was as much as her pride would allow.

The twilight had deepened into darkness around the cabin. Rising above the pines, the moon silvered ghostly tendrils of fog that crept along the ground. Below the cliff, the incoming tide whispered against the rocks.

Inside, the cabin glowed with light and warmth. Scrubbed, combed and dressed in a clean nightshirt, Daniel snuggled on Sylvie's lap, waiting for his bed-time story.

Seated in the opposite chair, Flynn filled his eyes with the sight of them. Such a beautiful pair. If he'd been an artist, he'd have painted them just like this, dark head against fair, surrounded by a golden aura of love. He ached to be a part of that love. But it wasn't going to happen. As soon as he could resolve the issue of safety for Sylvie and Daniel, he needed to leave.

"So what story would you like to hear tonight?" Sylvie asked her little brother.

"You never finished the story about the prince from the sea," Daniel said. "I want to hear the end of it."

"And so you shall!" She nestled him closer. "So where did we leave off?"

"The prince was walking on land with his new legs, and he fell in love with the girl. But you said there was a problem."

"Oh, yes. And I asked you what you thought it was."

"You did?"

Sylvie laughed. "I did, but you didn't answer because you were asleep. The problem was, the prince was only visiting on land. He knew that soon he would have to go back to the sea. The girl knew it, too."

"Couldn't she go with him?"

"She wanted to. But what do you think would happen if she tried to live in the ocean?"

"She couldn't breathe under the water," Daniel said. "She'd drown. But this is just a story. Can't we have some magic happen so she could be all right?"

Sylvie glanced up, her eyes meeting Flynn's. For the space of a heartbeat, their gazes held. Then she looked away.

"Stories don't always end the way we want them to," she said. "The girl loved the prince with all her heart. But she knew they couldn't be together. So she told him to go back to the sea and be happy."

Daniel's forehead creased in thought. "Did he go?"

"Yes, he did. As soon as he dived into the waves, his legs became a tail again. He swam home, married a beautiful sea princess and they lived happily ever after. But he never forgot his visit to the land or the girl who'd loved him enough to send him back where he belonged."

Flynn swallowed a surge of emotion. He had never loved Sylvie more than at this moment. But there was no way he could tell her the truth.

"What happened to the girl?" Daniel asked.

"She was sad. But she knew she'd done the right thing. She went on to travel the world and have wonderful adventures. But she never forgot her first love, the prince from the sea."

"Did she ever get married?"

Sylvie kissed the top of his dark head. "That's a story for another time. It's getting late. Say good-night to Ishmael, and I'll tuck you in."

Slipping out of the chair, the boy pattered over to where Flynn sat. "Good night, Ishmael," he said, shaking Flynn's hand like a little man. "Thank you for saving me."

"Anytime, pal." Flynn spoke past the knot in his throat. "Sleep tight. I'll see you in the morning."

Flashing a boyish grin, Daniel scampered off to Sylvie's room, where he'd continued to sleep since his illness. Although Sylvie shared Flynn's bed now, she always took care to be up and dressed before her brother woke. The boy seemed to accept the situation as natural.

But nothing about tonight felt natural. Getting around what had happened to him would be awkward as hell.

As Sylvia vanished into the bedroom, he rose, took the shotgun down from its rack above the door and stepped out onto the porch. He had some heavy thinking to do, and he needed to do it alone.

# *Chapter Thirteen*

Flynn stood on the porch listening to the dark. The muffled crash of waves, the mutter of drowsing goats, the windlass creaking in the night breeze—all were familiar sounds now. Yet he seemed to be hearing them with new ears, knowing for the first time who he was and why he'd come here.

Sylvie would likely be in bed by now, waiting for him to join her. When he thought about that lush, willing body, his for the taking…hellfire, he'd break through solid iron to have her. But he wouldn't give in to temptation. As Ishmael, he'd already done enough damage. To take her again, knowing what he knew, would be a cruel betrayal of her innocent love.

It would be the most despicable thing he'd ever done.

Mouthing a curse, he lowered himself to the rocking chair and laid the shotgun across his knees. Was anyone out there in the shadows? It didn't seem likely on such a peaceful night. But somebody had set the snare he'd found, and he was tired of waiting for them to show up.

Tomorrow he would clean, oil and load the .36 Navy Colt revolver Sylvie had returned to him. Well armed, he would scour the woods around the clearing. If the bastards were out there, he would track them down, find out what they wanted and make sure they never threatened Sylvie again. Or, if he discovered no recent traces, he could at least conclude they were gone.

Maybe then he'd feel free to leave and search for Aaron Cragun.

"Ishmael?" Sylvie's voice was a breath behind him. Flynn willed himself not to turn around.

"Are you all right?" She moved to stand at the back of the chair. Her fingers came to rest on his shoulders, massaging the knotted muscles. He battled the urge to reach up, pull her head down to him and lose himself in kissing her.

"I'm fine," he lied. "There's no way I couldn't be fine after a supper like that one."

She was silent for a moment, her fingers kneading away the tightness. "Aren't you coming to bed?" she asked.

He exhaled, thinking how blessedly simple it would be to get up and follow her inside. "You go on," he said. "Something tells me I need to be out here, keeping watch."

"You aren't still angry about this morning, are you?"

"I could never be angry with you, Sylvie."

Her fingers stilled, resting in place. "You know I won't hold you to anything, don't you?" she said.

"Daniel and I managed fine before you came. We'll manage the same when you're gone. You should feel free to leave anytime you choose."

"Sylvie—" Something inside him seemed to be breaking apart. At that moment Flynn would have given anything to be Ishmael again, to take her hand, lead her to the bedroom and spend the rest of the night loving her as she was made to be loved.

As Ishmael, he could stay with her and the boy. He could be the man they needed, with no memories to pull him away. He wouldn't have to remember the sight of his sister's rain-soaked body lying in that garbage-strewn alley behind the theater. He wouldn't have to remember the purple bruises around her throat or feel the fury when he thought of the wretched little man who'd killed her for the emerald necklace and matching bracelet she'd worn that night.

How could anyone walk away from a memory like that?

"What is it, Ishmael?" Sylvie had been waiting for him to finish what he'd begun to say to her. Whatever it was, his wandering thoughts had blotted it from his mind.

"I'm sorry," he said. That much, at least, was true. And it was true that he loved her to the depths of his soul. But telling her now would only make things more painful between them.

"It's all right." Leaning over his shoulder, she brushed a kiss along his cheekbone. Her lips were soft and moist, making him yearn for more. Lord, if he could only make things right with her. But no power under heaven could undo what had been done or change what he'd pledged himself to do.

"Good night," she said. "I'll leave the door unlocked."

"Thank you." Flynn knew he wouldn't be opening that door tonight. One step across the threshold would be enough to crumble his resolve. "Good night, Sylvie," he said. "Sleep well."

He heard her footsteps and the closing of the door. Then he was alone with the night.

She wouldn't cry until he was gone. Sylvie reminded herself of that as she lay alone in the bed, staring up into the darkness. She'd planned a far different ending to the evening's celebration. But something had gone wrong, and she didn't know how to fix it.

In the quiet house, she could hear the patter of a squirrel running across the roof. She could hear the snap of dying embers in the belly of the stove and the flutter of a moth against the windowpane. The one sound she wanted to hear was the opening of the front door. But she knew better than to hope. Ishmael was a troubled man tonight. Whatever the reason, he'd made it clear that he wanted to be alone.

Restless, she sat up, swung her feet to the floor and sauntered into the kitchen. A bolder woman might have flung open the front door, strode onto the porch and demanded that Ishmael stop brooding and come to bed—or at least tell her what was wrong. But Sylvie knew better than to try. What she knew of Ishmael was only a small part of the man. As for the rest, he was a stranger, no more hers than the wide-winged birds that circled the cove and flew back out to sea. She didn't own him and couldn't even pretend to understand him. She only knew that she loved him.

He would leave, of course. Maybe that was what weighed on him now—how and when to go and what to say to her and Daniel. If she loved him, she would make it easy for him. That was what she'd tried to do tonight, with her story. But that didn't mean she wasn't hurting. When he walked away for the last time a part of her would die. She could almost feel it dying now.

It felt like her heart.

Flynn had prowled the dark yard, checking the outbuildings and the brushy thickets that ringed the clearing. He was going through the motions, nothing more. Nobody was going to show up, especially given that he was armed and in plain sight. But the night was getting chilly, and walking was less likely to get him into trouble than shivering on the porch, yearning to be nestled against Sylvie's warm, satiny curves.

And walking could help a man remember. He was remembering now as he followed the path to the windlass and stood looking down into the fog-shrouded cove. The sea was quiet now, the ebbing tide a lapping of foam along the beach.

As a lawman, Flynn had learned the skill of careful recollection. He drew on that skill now, using it to gather his scattered thoughts and focus his mind. He would start by going over the events that had brought him here, examining every detail, looking for anything that might give him some answers. He knew what had happened. But he had yet to understand how and why.

On the night of Catriona's murder Flynn had planned to attend the opening night of her musical review at the Tivoli Theater. Dressed in evening clothes, he'd been leaving his rooms when a runner from the police station had caught up with him. A suspect in the slaying of three Barbary Coast prostitutes had just been brought in. Since the case was Flynn's, and the need to solve it was urgent, he'd put off his own plans and set out for the police station to question the man.

Flynn had hoped to be at the theater for the second half of Catriona's show. But at the station, one thing had led to another. By the time the drunken dockworker had made a full confession, it was after ten.

Laden with flowers and apologies, Flynn had rushed to the Tivoli, hoping to catch his sister before she left the theater by way of the backstage door. Only then had he seen the crowd swarming outside the police-cordoned entrance to the alley.

Now he stared into the darkness, letting the grief trickle through his frozen soul. Catriona had been beautiful, gifted and full of life. She'd been all the family he had. Seeing her dead had slammed a shock through Flynn that hurt like a shotgun blast in the gut. He felt it every time he thought about her. He would feel it until he brought her killer to justice, maybe longer. Maybe forever.

No one in the crowd had seen Catriona die. But the first witnesses on the scene had described a small, ragged man crouching over her, removing her emerald

necklace and bracelet before fleeing into the shadows.
Two of the men had identified him as Aaron Cragun.
A police informant had known where Cragun lived.
He had sketched a map of the sea route.

Catriona's funeral, held two days later, had over-
flowed St. Mary's Church. Many of the mourners
had been men. A few of the wealthy ones had been
her lovers. Catriona had basked in their attention and
enjoyed the expensive gifts they'd lavished on her. But
her heart was like a wild bird, refusing to be caged. If
his sister had ever been in love, Flynn hadn't known
about it.

The front pews of the church had held some of the
most powerful men in San Francisco. Flynn had been
too grief-stricken to pay close attention, but now their
profiles, as he'd seen them lined up along the row,
flashed through his mind—Thurlow Stevens, the ship-
ping magnate, Archie Sutton, who'd made a fortune in
gold, and Slade Quincy, the owner of the theater where
Catriona had given her last performance.

Seated next to Quincy, fighting tears, was Jacob
Hawn, who owned the city's biggest construction firm.
It was Hawn who'd given Catriona the emerald jewelry.
He was devastated by the idea that his gift might have
led to her death. A florid, handsome man, expensively
dressed, he'd cornered Flynn after the service. "Your
sister had consented to become my wife," he said. "We
were to have been married next month. If you find the
little bastard who murdered her, bring him back to me
so I can rip him apart with my bare hands!"

Within an hour of his sister's burial, Flynn had

boarded the boat and was sailing north with the map he'd been given. He'd planned to arrive ahead of Cragun and wait for the man to show up. He hadn't counted on the storm or the loss of his memory. And he certainly hadn't counted on falling in love with Aaron Cragun's daughter.

So many questions and so few answers. Jacob Hawn was a powerful man with a small army of people on his payroll. His hirelings could have nabbed Cragun in San Francisco and brought him to their boss. The thugs who'd shown up here could also have been working for Hawn. But something about the two possibilities didn't mesh. If Hawn already had Cragun, why would he send those two bruisers to look for him here?

Only one man had the answers Flynn needed. That man, if he was still alive, was Aaron Cragun.

Turning away from the cliff, Flynn gazed down the wooded slope to where the road wound upward through the pines. "Where are you, you little bastard?" he muttered. "How much do you know, and what the devil has become of you?"

Yawning with weariness, Flynn walked back to the porch. He was about to slump into the chair when a new thought struck him. Jerking wide awake, he swore out loud.

How could he have missed it? The answer was right under his nose.

Sylvie awoke to the dazzle of sunlight. For a moment she lay staring at the ceiling. Sometime after midnight she'd fallen into exhausted slumber. If she'd dreamed, she remembered none of it. The time was simply gone. Now, with chores to be done, she'd overslept. The goats and chickens would be clamoring. Daniel and Ishmael would be needing breakfast.

*Ishmael.*

She sat bolt upright. Ishmael had been outside when she went to sleep. If he'd come in, she hadn't heard him. What if something had gone wrong?

She sprang out of bed. After a pause to check on the slumbering Daniel, she rushed to the front door and flung it open.

The porch and yard were empty. There was no sign of Ishmael anywhere. Heart pounding, she glanced around the room. The shotgun had been replaced on its rack above the door. But the pistol she'd recovered from the boat, along with the powder and caps, was missing from the shelf where he'd left it.

She'd told him he was free to go. But how could he go like this, without even saying goodbye? Fighting hurt and anger, she turned back toward the bedroom, where she'd left her clothes. Only then did she see the note, scrawled on Daniel's slate and left on the kitchen table.

*Gone hunting. Stay close.*

Sylvie sank onto a chair. At least he'd left her a note. But she'd reacted like a fool, letting his absence throw her into a panic. Sooner or later, Ishmael would leave her for good. When the time came, she couldn't let herself crumble the way she had this morning. She was a grown woman, capable and strong. She would prepare herself, starting now, so that when he walked away...

"Sylvie, are you all right?" Daniel stood in the bedroom doorway. He was dressed in his baggy nightshirt, his eyes muzzy, his hair standing on end. "Where's Ishmael?"

Blinking back tears, Sylvie held out her arms. "Come here, little man," she said. "Your big sister needs a hug."

Flynn moved through the underbrush, his footsteps as quiet as an Indian's. The weight of the Colt revolver in his hand was familiar, almost comforting. He'd managed to clean and load the gun earlier without waking Sylvie—all to the good. The less explaining he had to do, the better.

So far he'd found nothing. But he'd set up a search pattern, starting with a semicircle around the edge of the clearing, then widening the curve with each pass like a spider building a web. If anyone was out here, he would find them.

His reflexes clenched as a young spike buck scrambled out of a thicket and bounded away through the trees. The venison would have made a welcome addition to Sylvie's larder. But Flynn couldn't bother with meat today. The sound of a shot would reach every ear in a half mile of forest.

His eyes studied the ground as he walked. Flynn had learned to track from an old army scout his father had befriended. Over the years, he'd honed his skills. A footprint in the earth, an overturned pebble, a grass blade out of line; there was little his keen eyes missed. But after covering everything within a quarter mile of the house, he had yet to see any sign of his quarry.

It was the smell that caught his attention. Faint on the breeze at first, it grew stronger as he walked upwind. After seven years of police work, there was no mistaking the putrid odor of a decomposing body. It would likely be an animal, maybe a bear or cougar kill. With that in mind, Flynn approached cautiously, pistol cocked, finger resting on the trigger.

The scent was overpowering now. As Flynn rounded a deadfall, two ravens squawked and flapped skyward. His stomach tightened as he saw they'd been feeding on a man. The face had been picked down to bone, but Flynn recognized the clothes, especially the greasy red bandanna still knotted around the bony neck. It was the taller of the two thugs who'd attacked Sylvie, the one who'd run off after his partner was killed. Judging from the condition of the body, he'd likely been dead for three or four days.

Digging a grave was out of the question. Flynn had neither the tools nor the time. To cover the awful sight and give the wretch a shred of dignity, he piled fallen limbs and brush over the remains. The man's identity was no mystery. But his death was. He hadn't appeared to be wounded the night he'd fled the clearing. So that meant something had killed him after that.

Something or someone.

Senses prickling, Flynn continued his methodical outward-search pattern. He'd made two more wide sweeps when his nostrils caught a faint whiff of smoke on the breeze. Smoke and coffee. A camp.

Scarcely breathing, he crept closer. Now, through the trees, he could hear the snorting, wheezing bray of a mule.

It had to be Aaron Cragun's mule.

If Flynn's hunch was right, Cragun had been out here in the woods for heaven knows how long, keeping an eye on his family and property. Odds were, Cragun had killed the thug who'd threatened his children. The little man might be a murderer, but Flynn had seen plenty of evidence that he was a devoted father.

So why had he kept out of sight? But Flynn had already guessed the answer to that question. Most likely Cragun would have seen him around the cabin. He'd stayed hidden, uncertain whether it would be safe to show himself to a stranger.

Now, at last, the waiting was about to come to an end. Flynn's pulse lurched to a gallop as he edged toward the camp. He'd caught a lot of criminals in his career, but this was personal. Ahead of him the trees thinned. He could make out a small, grassy clearing. Next to a fallen log was a bedroll and the smoking embers of a campfire. Aside from that, the clearing was empty. Pistol cocked, Flynn crept closer.

"Drop that gun, mister." The nasal voice crackled behind him. "Drop it now or I'll blow a hole right through your back."

The jab of a cold steel barrel against his spine told Flynn the threat wasn't an idle one. Cursing his inattention, he dropped the pistol into the grass at his feet.

"Kick it away. Out of reach. Go on."

Flynn did as he was told. He knew better than to look around, but then he didn't have to. "You're Aaron Cragun," he said.

"And you're the son of a bitch who's been sleeping with my daughter."

Flynn thought fast. Cragun didn't seem to know who he was or why he'd come here. If he wanted to put the man at ease, maybe catch him off guard, it would be safer to remain Ishmael, the man with no memory.

"So why haven't you already shot me, Cragun?" he asked.

"Because, from what I've seen, my daughter loves you. And that sparkler on your finger tells me you're not a common trail bum. I've been worried about how my girl and her brother would fare if something were to happen to me. Having a good man in the picture would do a lot to ease my mind—providing you have something to offer her, and decent intentions, of course."

"I do on both counts. But Sylvie might have a few things to say about that." Flynn released his breath. As long as Cragun believed him to be a promising suitor for his daughter, the man wasn't likely to pull the trigger. He didn't relish the pretense, especially since, whatever happened, Sylvie was bound to be hurt. But right now Flynn had little choice except to play along. Cragun nudged him forward with the gun, taking time to pick up Flynn's pistol. "She's a headstrong girl, my Sylvie. But she's sensible. As long as you're willing to do right by her, she'll say yes. And my boy, he likes you, too. I've seen that. But first, we need to clear up a few things."

Flynn sighed. If he managed to arrest Cragun, Daniel would be hurt as much as Sylvie. And what would the two of them do without their father? He would change things if he could. But for now, all evidence suggested that this man had strangled his sister, stolen her jewels and left her lying dead in the rain.

Catriona deserved justice. Flynn had sworn to get it for her.

"As long as we understand each other, maybe it's time you took that gun out of my back," he said.

"Not until I hear your story. What brought you here in the first place? You wouldn't be working for a dirty snake named Jacob Hawn, would you?" The cold muzzle pressed harder into Flynn's back. "If my gut tells me you're lying, you're a dead man. I already killed one of Hawn's thugs to protect my family. Don't think I won't do it again."

"Was he a skinny buzzard with a red neckerchief?" Flynn asked, already knowing the answer.

"Yup. You know him?"

"Two men came onto the property last week, bent on some mischief. Your daughter shot one of them. I just found his pal lying in that thick stand of trees. Not much left of him except that red bandanna."

"Then you know I mean business," Cragun snapped. "And you still haven't answered my first question. What are you doing here with my children?"

"I washed up on your beach with my memory gone.

Sylvie and Daniel found me and saved my life. That's all I can tell you."

"Amnesia?"

"I believe that's what it's called. Your daughter named me Ishmael."

"And Hawn? You know him?"

"If I ever did I don't remember. In my condition, he could be my best friend and I wouldn't recognize him. Hell, I don't even remember my real name." It was Flynn's first lie, a necessary one.

"So you could be working for the bastard and not even know it?"

"That's right." Flynn suppressed the urge to start asking questions. The less he said, the less apt he'd be to arouse Cragun's suspicion.

"Well, isn't this a fine kettle of fish!" Cragun lowered the barrel of his gun. Flynn turned around slowly, getting his first good look at Sylvie and Daniel's father.

Aaron Cragun was short and wiry, not much over five feet four. His foxlike features were accented by an aquiline nose and crowned by a thatch of gray-streaked red hair that matched his scraggly beard. His hazel eyes were sharp and intelligent. He didn't look like a murderer; but then, how many people did?

His hands balanced a long-barreled rifle—one of the new Colt revolving carbines that could fire multiple rounds, Flynn noted. The man had made a shrewd trade somewhere. It was a truly enviable weapon.

Looking down at Cragun, Flynn felt the clash of warring emotions. This man had raised two superb children and fashioned a home that was a wonder of engineering. He could also be a murderer and a thief, the lowest of the low. If he was guilty, he deserved no less than hanging by the neck until dead. Flynn was determined to see that happen—after a fair trial. Gone was the need to avenge Catriona's death with his own hand. He wouldn't—couldn't—do that now. But justice still had to be served. Eventually. For now, Cragun was the one holding the gun.

"It's time we headed back to the house," Cragun said. "I've been missing my children and the comforts of home. After I hear what Sylvie has to say about you, I'll decide whether to let you live." He glanced toward the camp spot. "Pick up that bedroll and kick some dirt on the campfire. Then we'll be on our way."

Flynn did as he was told. Sooner or later the time would come to make his move. But the longer he kept quiet, the more he was likely to learn.

He was wondering about the braying sound he'd heard, when Cragun gave a sharp whistle. The bushes rustled as a lop-eared mule trotted into the clearing pulling a narrow wagon loaded with supplies. "Had to drive this rig across some rough country," Cragun said. "Bastards might've trailed me on the road. Being we're this close to home, we may as well walk. You go ahead, where I can keep an eye on you."

They trekked back toward the house, Flynn leading the way and the mule following Cragun like a hound. Where would Sylvie be when she first saw them? Flynn wondered. How would she react when he took her father into custody? Despite being taken prisoner himself for the moment, Flynn felt confident he could manage to get the upper hand. All he needed to do was bide his time until Cragun dropped his guard, then wait for the right moment.

But Lord, it wouldn't be easy. Sylvie had given him her innocence and her love. She and Daniel trusted him. What he planned to do would destroy them both.

Sylvie was sweeping the porch when they came through the trees and into the clearing. She froze, dropping the broom as she recognized her father. Shouting for Daniel, she plunged off the porch and raced toward them.

Glancing back, Flynn saw that Cragun had lowered the rifle. To his children, it would appear that he and Flynn had simply met in the woods and come home together. However, he still had Flynn's pistol, tucked into his belt under his jacket.

"Papa!" Sylvie flung herself into her father's arms, her face wreathed in joy. Cragun staggered backward under the impact. Dropping the rifle, he embraced her, half laughing, half weeping. Unprepared for such an emotional scene, Flynn stood at a distance like a lurking specter of doom.

Taking this man away from his children would be the most monstrous thing he'd ever done. Sylvie and Daniel would hate him forever. But some things couldn't be changed. This was one of them.

"Papa! Papa!" Daniel had come outside. Like a small, dark projectile he hurtled across the yard and wrapped himself around his father's legs. "I knew you'd come home! I never gave up!"

"We were worried about you, Papa." Sylvie drew back a little. "Where were you for so long?"

Cragun shot Flynn a sidelong glance. "Close by, keeping an eye on the place. I've got some bad hombres after me, including the pair that showed up. When I spotted your friend here, I thought he might be one of them."

"Ishmael?" Sylvie's eyes widened. "Oh, no, Papa, he'd never hurt us. He's done a lot of work on the place, and he even saved Daniel from falling down the cliff. I can't imagine what we'd have done without him!"

Flynn's throat clenched as Cragun turned toward him with a gap-toothed smile. "Well, my girl's say-so is good enough for me. And if you saved my boy's life, I owe you." He extended his right hand. Flynn forced himself to accept the handshake.

Cragun reached under his jacket, withdrew Flynn's pistol and handed it back to him. "Reckon I can trust you with this. We'll have more to talk about later. For now, what do you say we unhitch the mule and unload the supplies? Then we'll go inside and have Sylvie rustle us up some breakfast."

Untangling himself from his father's legs, Daniel tugged at the hem of his jacket. "Did you bring us any presents, Papa?"

Cragun chuckled. "I was wondering when we'd get around to that. Don't worry, I didn't forget you."

Fishing in his pockets, Cragun brought out a tin box and something wrapped in a knotted handkerchief. He handed the box to his son. "Open it. Take a look."

Daniel's small hands worked the lid open. His eyes

lit. "Toy soldiers! Just what I wanted! Thank you, Papa!" Clutching the box, he scampered off to the porch to examine his treasure.

"And this is for you." He presented the weighted handkerchief to Sylvie. "I hope the gift will make up for the sorry wrapping. I wanted you to have something special."

*Something special.*

Flynn felt a sick weight in his stomach as Sylvie labored with the knot. Even before the ends loosened, he sensed what would be wrapped in that handkerchief.

"Oh, Papa, this is too much!" Sylvie held up the glittering object. Faceted green stones caught the sunlight, casting a rainbow on her beautiful face.

It was Catriona's emerald bracelet.

# *Chapter Fourteen*

F lynn's hard-won self-control snapped. His hand flashed to his holstered pistol. In the next instant the muzzle was jammed against Aaron Cragun's side.

"Lieutenant Flynn O'Rourke, San Francisco Police Department," he snarled. "Aaron Cragun, you're under arrest for the murder of Catriona O'Rourke…" He paused, the words burning like lye in his throat. *"My sister."*

He heard Sylvie gasp. Cragun's mouth worked as he struggled to speak.

"Papa, is it true?" Sylvie whispered.

"Tell her, you bastard." Flynn thrust the gun harder against the man's ribs. "Tell her how you strangled a woman and stole her jewelry! Tell her where you got that emerald bracelet!"

In the silence that followed, the bracelet dropped from Sylvie's fingers. Flynn heard it strike the ground, but he couldn't bear to meet her wounded eyes.

*"Tell her!"*

Cragun coughed. "I stole the jewels, all right," he said. "But I didn't kill that woman. So help me God, by the time I got to her, she was already dead."

Realization washed through Flynn. There it was— the missing piece of the puzzle that brought everything else in line. He hadn't understood how the papa that Sylvie and Daniel loved so much could kill a woman in cold blood. But if Cragun had only been near Catriona's body so that he could rob it—a repulsive act, but not nearly as out of character as murder—then that changed everything. But was the man telling the truth? It sounded right—but was that just because Flynn wanted to believe him?

"So you robbed her," he sneered, hoping to frighten and intimidate the man into telling him the truth. "Just like you rob the poor souls who wash up on your beach."

"We need money to live on. And I wanted my girl to have something fine—as fine as she deserves." Cragun's voice shook. "I pawned the necklace before I left town. But I swear on my dear wife's grave, I didn't murder your sister. I couldn't have done it, especially not that way."

Flynn glared down at the man. "What do you mean, you couldn't have done it? Why should I believe a vulture who lives by robbing the dead?"

"I can prove it," Cragun insisted. "Sylvie, since this man has me at a disadvantage, please help me with my jacket."

Sylvie moved like a sleepwalker, slipping her

father's ragged woolen jacket off his shoulders and down his arms. Flynn sensed that she was in a state of shock. Later on she would hate him for this. Right now her overpowering emotion was disbelief.

Flynn ached for her. He would have given anything he owned to spare her this pain; but there could be no returning to the time when he had no memory. Ishmael, the gentle stranger she'd loved, was gone. In his place was a cold and angry man who loved her more than ever but was duty bound not to show his feelings.

With his jacket off, Cragun unbuttoned the left cuff of his shirt and began rolling up the sleeve. Flynn stared as the withered arm was revealed, an arm that was little more than shriveled skin and crooked bone. "Crushed it years ago in a rockslide," Cragun said. "Doctor saved the arm, but the muscle's gone. I can only raise it partway, and my hand can barely hold a nail in place, let alone choke a body to death."

The pistol sagged in Flynn's hand as the truth sank home. Catriona had been a robust woman, half a head taller than Aaron Cragun. With his weakened arm, there was no way the small man could have overpowered her. Flynn recalled the distinct finger-shaped bruises on both sides of his sister's neck. Those bruises couldn't have been made with just one hand. Cragun might be a thief, but he was no murderer. *Thank God.*

"As you see, I couldn't have strangled your sister," Cragun said. "But I know who did. I saw it happen. That's why I'm on the run."

Flynn felt the final piece of the puzzle slam into place. Suddenly everything made sense. "It was Jacob

Hawn, wasn't it? That's why his hired killers are after you, because you saw him." He was overcome by rage, relief and an odd flicker of hope. Maybe this nightmare would come out right after all.

Sylvie stood like a ghost behind her father, anguish etched on her lovely, pale features. Flynn crushed the urge to gather her into his arms. But he felt sure that right now, that was the last thing she would want.

Cragun shrugged, as if dropping a heavy weight from his shoulders. "Put that gun away, O'Rourke, and I'll tell you everything."

Ever cautious, Flynn took a moment to move Cragun's rifle out of reach before holstering his pistol. "Go ahead. I'm listening."

"There's not that much to tell. I'd enjoyed some late-night socializing and was on my way back to where I'd left the wagon. I passed the alley and heard a man and woman arguing. Being a curious sort, I stopped to listen."

"Was it my sister and Hawn?"

Cragun nodded. "I didn't know them right off. It was too dark to see their faces. But the man was a big lunker, and he was as mad as a bull. Kept going on about how she'd promised to marry him and then, after he'd spent a bundle of money on her, she'd changed her mind. The woman—a pretty one with lots of dark hair—started to laugh, called him a pompous old fool. The more she laughed the madder he got. Then all at once he was choking her."

Cragun shook his head. "It happened faster than I could think. Next thing I knew, he'd dropped her and run off. I got to her quick as I could, meaning to help her, but she was already dead."

"So you stole her jewelry." Flynn's tone was flat with disgust.

"Can't say I'm proud of that. But if not me, somebody else would've done it."

"How did you know it was Hawn? And how did he know you'd seen him?"

"He came back a minute later. I'm guessing it was to get the emeralds, or to make sure she was really dead. I was just pocketing the jewels when I saw him at the end of the alley. This time the light from a window fell on his face and I got a good look at him. It was Hawn, all right. I'd met him before, when I sold some timber to his foreman."

"So he knew you, too."

Cragun nodded. "By then people were swarming to the street end of the alley. Somebody was shouting for the police. Hawn ran out the back and I ran the same way, managed to lose him in the dark. But I was the one people saw, and I knew I'd be blamed. I pawned the necklace at a place I knew, bought a new rifle and got out of town. I've been hiding ever since."

Silence hung on the sunlit air as Flynn weighed what he'd heard. There were no holes in the man's story. Everything he'd said rang true.

"You're still in trouble, Cragun," he said at last. "But if you'll testify against Hawn, I can promise to make the theft charge go away."

"I'll do anything to put this right," Cragun said.

As if by some unspoken signal, both men turned

toward Sylvie. She stood like a stone pillar, her face pale, her gaze as flat and lifeless as slate. Catriona's emerald bracelet lay in the dirt at her feet.

"How long have you been lying to me, Flynn O'Rourke?" she asked.

Flynn had grasped at the fleeting hope that, with her father proven innocent, they might have a chance. But now, looking into those stricken eyes, he knew better. There was no way to undo what his betrayal had done to her.

"My memory came back when I hit my head while I was snatching Daniel off the cliff. After that, I did what I had to. I'm sorry, Sylvie. You can't know how sorry I am. But there's one thing you need to know."

Her chin lifted in defiance.

"I never lied about loving you," Flynn said. "And I'm not lying now."

"Listen to him, girl." Cragun took a step toward his daughter. "Neither of us meant for you to be hurt. But now, all's well that ends well. The best thing you can do now is forgive and forget."

Sylvie's gray eyes glimmered like frost. She paused a moment. Then, with slow deliberation, she turned her back on them both and stalked toward the house.

On the porch, Daniel was lining up his toy soldiers in parade formation. He looked so blissful that Sylvie passed him and went inside without saying a word. Why spoil this fleeting happiness for the boy?

Only with the door safely closed behind her did she give way to emotion. Legs trembling, she sank onto a kitchen chair and pressed her balled fists to her eyes. There were no tears. She was too angry to weep.

All her life she'd willed herself to do what was right and good. She'd raised Daniel from babyhood and cared for her father's house and possessions with scarcely a thought for herself. She'd never lied, never cheated, never tasted liquor or sworn an unladylike oath.

If she had one black mark on her heavenly slate, it was giving herself to a man without a proper wedding. But even that she'd done with a full and honest heart. She had truly loved Ishmael—except, as it turned out, he wasn't Ishmael. He was a lawman, a lying, flinty-eyed stranger she scarcely knew.

And the father she'd respected—he was no better than a grave robber, stealing a bracelet from a murdered corpse and presenting it as a gift to his daughter. How many other things in this house had he stolen directly from the dead? The very idea sent a shudder of revulsion through her body.

She could beat her chest, demand to know why she'd been so wronged and betrayed; but crying over spilled milk had never been her strong suit. What was done was done. All that remained was deciding what to do next, then doing it.

As Sylvie pondered her choices, one reality emerged. She couldn't remain here, living off the misfortunes of others in this lonely place. Neither could her little brother. They needed a normal life with neighbors around them. Daniel needed friends. He needed to go to a real school, and to church.

The more she thought about leaving, the more urgent the need became. She would do it, she resolved. She would gather some essentials, take the mule, the wagon and the shotgun, and set out today before her will had time to weaken.

If their father wanted to join them later, she would leave that door open. But Aaron Cragun would have to find another way to make a living, and she wasn't going to wait around for that to happen.

Their departure would be hard on Daniel. But she couldn't leave him here to learn his father's unsavory trade. She would tell him they were going on an adventure, to see new places and meet new people. Given a little time, she could bring him around.

All that remained to be decided was where to go. San Francisco was big, bewildering and far away. But her father had mentioned logging camps and new settlements cropping up along the road. Maybe she could find a place that needed a cook or a teacher. She was confident she could do that sort of work. Ishmael had told her so—when she still believed him to be Ishmael.

His real name was Flynn O'Rourke, she reminded herself. It was a lyrical sort of name, one she might even like if she could abide the man. But how could he have lied to her, pretending to still have amnesia while he waited to arrest her father? Why hadn't he told her the truth when his memory came back?

Why hadn't he trusted her to understand?

As Ishmael, she had loved him with every beat of her heart. But Flynn O'Rourke was a very different man.

She never wanted to see his lying face again.

* * *

"Give her some time to cool off." Cragun hefted a grain sack with his strong right arm, hoisted it to his shoulder and lugged it into the shed. "My Sylvie's a sensible girl. She'll come around."

"I wouldn't lay odds on that." Flynn swung a bag of oats off the wagon bed. "This isn't just female pique. I might've had my reasons for lying to Sylvie, but justified or not, I hurt her badly. And I take it she's not too happy with you, either. We both let her down. If she's furious, you can't blame her."

It was ironic, Flynn mused. Less than an hour ago, he'd nearly arrested this man for murder. Now here they were, talking like friends. In the balance, weighing his unsavory ways against his innocence and good intentions, Aaron Cragun wasn't a difficult fellow to like.

"So, do you love my girl?" Cragun asked.

"More than my life," Flynn replied without hesitation.

"And you'd make her an honest woman?"

"Sylvie's the most honest woman I've ever known. If you mean would I marry her, yes. I'd be honored to. But after what I've done to her, I can't imagine she'd have me."

"Have you asked her?"

Flynn lowered the bag of oats into the grain bin. "Never had the chance. And now I figure it's too late."

"Don't be so sure. Women can surprise you." Cragun's hand rested on the back of the mule, who was standing in the traces, enjoying a feed bag of oats.

"There's a story I've never told anybody, including my children. But you need to hear it. I'm trusting you to keep it to yourself, all right?"

At Flynn's nod, Cragun began.

"Years ago, in Indiana, I had a job clerking in a store. The owner had a daughter about my age, as beautiful as an angel. When she came into the store the earth quivered under my feet. I worshipped her, but of course she never gave me a second look. I was nothing but the homely little clerk who bunked in a storeroom on the second floor.

"One day my employer called me into his office. His daughter, he told me, had gotten involved with an unscrupulous man who'd run off and left her in a family way. To atone for her so-called sin and save her family from disgrace, she'd agreed to marry any man her father chose." Cragun's voice broke slightly. "He chose me—offered me a house and a handsome raise in the bargain. I accepted, of course. But I had no illusions that my bride would ever love me.

"We were married the next day. Lord, she was so beautiful I could scarcely look at her. I promised myself then and there I'd treat her like the queen she was. We spent our wedding night on opposite sides of the bed. For the first few weeks we barely had a word to say to each other. But over time she became accustomed to this ugly little man. She even grew to care for me. By the time her baby was born we'd become a family." Cragun wiped away a tear. "I couldn't have loved that little girl more if I'd fathered her myself."

Flynn remembered the family portrait he'd seen, the

beautiful mother, the beautiful child. "Sylvie doesn't know?"

Cragun shook his head. "I was there when she was born. I'm the only father she's ever had. If that isn't enough, think how the truth would reflect on her mother—and on her."

"She'll never hear it from me. You have my word," Flynn replied as a new realization hit him like a gut punch. As Ishmael, he'd made love to Sylvie so many times that he'd lost count. Worse, in his muddled state, he'd done it without any kind of protection. What were the odds that he'd left her with child?

Whatever had happened to drive them apart, he'd be damned if he'd walk away and leave her to her mother's fate. Pregnant or not, he intended to make Sylvie his bride. And he wouldn't take no for an answer.

Cragun's story had hit home. Given time and patience, love could grow, and maybe forgiveness, too.

Meanwhile, Flynn couldn't forget his duty to the law and to Catriona. Jacob Hawn had to be brought to justice. Cragun's eyewitness testimony could send him to the hangman. But nothing about the situation was simple. To arrest, try and convict Hawn, Flynn needed to be in San Francisco with Aaron Cragun close at hand. He would also need to keep Cragun and his family safe from Hawn's hired thugs, who could be anywhere. To complicate matters, they had no horses. Their only transportation was a beat-up wagon and an aging mule. And what could they do about looking after the property and the animals?

The logistics were enough to give a man a splitting headache.

Flynn and Cragun had finished unloading the wagon and driven up to the shed when Sylvie came out onto the porch. She was wearing her boots, a light jacket and a straw hat. Her face was fixed in a look of grim determination.

"Don't unhitch the mule," she said. "I'm going to need the wagon."

"What the devil for?" Cragun stared at her, dumbfounded.

"I'm leaving, Papa, and taking Daniel. We can't live like this anymore, scavenging off the dead, no friends, no neighbors, never knowing whether you'll make it safely home…" Her voice trailed off, but she didn't break.

"But why now?" Cragun croaked. "Where'll you go? And what the devil makes you think you can take the wagon?"

"I'm leaving now because we'll need plenty of daylight, and because I can't stand to stay here another minute," Sylvie replied. "Where we're going is down the road, till we find a place with decent people who'll take us in and give me work. And if you don't let me take the wagon, I swear to heaven I'll walk every step of the way. If Daniel gets tired, I'll carry him, and if we can't find shelter we'll sleep on the ground. Don't try to stop me, Papa. I won't be stopped."

She stood like a torch, blazing defiance. Cragun was no match for her. Flynn saw him begin to crumble. "Will I ever see you again?" he asked brokenly.

She hesitated. In that moment Flynn glimpsed her fear, her vulnerability. Drawing herself up, she spoke. "When we're settled somewhere I'll let you know, and you can come get the wagon. You'll be welcome to visit us. But I don't want to come back here. I don't want to be reminded of the awful things you did to provide for us."

Cragun stared down at his boots. The face he raised had the sagging expression of a beaten man. "If your mind's made up, girl, then listen. About fifteen miles down the road there's a lumber camp. A few of the men have families there. They're good people, and they know me. I can't say they'll have any work, but at least they'll give you shelter. Promise me you'll stay there long enough to think things over."

"No promises. But I'll do whatever's best for Daniel."

"Can we help you load the wagon?" Cragun offered.

She shook her head. "Don't bother. I might as well learn to do it by myself."

In his work, Flynn had learned not to interfere in family matters, but this was urgent. He stepped forward.

"Don't let anger make you reckless, Sylvie. If you have to go, at least wait till we know it's safe out there, or let me go with you as far as the lumber camp."

The glare she gave him would have frozen the fires of hell.

"I'll be taking the shotgun, and I know how to use it," she snapped. "As for you, Flynn O'Rourke, I never want to hear your lying words again!"

She began bustling in and out of the house, carrying clothes, bedding and provisions stuffed into flour and feed sacks and placing them in the wagon bed. Without asking, Cragun fetched a piece of canvas sail from the shed and used it to cover everything. The poor man appeared beside himself with grief. But Sylvie's fury had burst through lifelong layers of forbearance, with a force too explosive to be contained.

Daniel had come out onto the porch, dressed for travel. His small face wore a look of confusion. Lord, Flynn wondered, how were these two innocents going to manage? Daniel had never been away from home; and what little Sylvie knew of the outside world, she'd acquired from childhood memories and books. She had no money for food, lodging and other necessities. If she couldn't find work, the two of them could end up homeless and hungry, or worse, at the mercy of people who wouldn't hesitate to exploit them.

In a few weeks' time, after the business of his sister's murder was resolved and Sylvie had a chance to think things over, Flynn planned to find her and kneel at her feet. But now, even though she might not accept his help, he couldn't let her go without something to sustain her.

The emerald bracelet, which he'd slipped into his pocket, was evidence in a murder case. Even if he could offer it to her, he knew Sylvie wouldn't touch it. But as he watched Daniel trudge back toward the goat pen, presumably to say goodbye to Ebenezer, a solution—the only one that made sense—struck Flynn like a lightning bolt.

Glancing back to make sure Sylvie and her father were busy, he followed the boy around the corner of the house.

*Don't look back.*

How many times in the past hour had Sylvie said those three words to herself? She had driven the wagon out of the yard and down the road, willing herself not to even glance at the two men who'd watched her go. Seeing her father's stricken face would have made a shambles of her resolve. And meeting Flynn's eyes would have reduced her to tears.

Flynn had lied to her, with cold intent, she reminded herself. All he'd cared about was finding his sister's killer. If he'd crushed her heart in the process, the man had scarcely given it a second thought. She bit back a moan as the memory of their nights swept over her. Her body would hold the imprint of his loving forever; but it was her tender Ishmael, not Flynn, who'd won and loved her. Now it was almost as if Ishmael had died, and she was in mourning.

*Don't look back.*

Squaring her shoulders, Sylvie gazed ahead, between the mule's lopsided ears. The road was little more than a rambling path, bordered on both sides by towering walls of pine. Sunlight fell along it in a bright, narrow ribbon. Far above, the sky was a deep, clear blue—as blue as the sapphire on Flynn's finger, as blue as his eyes.

Daniel stirred against her arm. He had waved from the back of the wagon until his home vanished from view. Now he sat beside her on the bench, a silent bundle of melancholy. Was she doing the right thing, separating him from everything he had known and loved? Certainly the boy needed a normal life. He needed to learn how to live in the world and interact with people around him. But to tear him away from familiar surroundings so suddenly, with no time to prepare... It was a cruel and selfish thing to do to a child who'd had no say in the matter. But she would make it right for him, Sylvie vowed. Someday, when he'd grown up to be well educated and successful, her brother would thank her for this.

"Look, Daniel! A rabbit!" She pointed to the furry shape that bounded across the road. The boy didn't respond.

"Don't be so gloomy," she chided him. "We're off on a grand adventure! We're going to see new places, meet new people! It'll be exciting!"

"I miss Ebenezer," he said. "I miss Papa and the chickens and the goats. I miss Ishmael."

Sylvie felt her chest contract. "Ishmael was a make-believe name we gave him, Daniel. His real name is Flynn O'Rourke. He's a policeman, but you might as well know he's not a nice person."

"But he's still Ishmael to me. And he is nice. He gave me something and said it was for you." Daniel reached into the pocket of his jacket, fumbled a moment and came up with something knotted into the white handkerchief Sylvie had given him earlier. She felt the weight as he dropped it into her hand.

Passing the reins to her brother, she worked at the

tight knot. What if it was the bracelet—the hated emerald bracelet her father had stolen off a dead woman?
That would be the crowning indignity. She would fling
it as hard as she could into the trees.

At last the knot loosened and parted. As the handkerchief fell open in her palm, Sylvie's lips formed a
silent O.

Reflected sunlight gleamed from the depths of a
sapphire mounted in heavy gold. It was Flynn's ring—
the ring that linked him to his past and to his family
heritage. He had given her his most precious possession.

Daniel touched the ring with a fingertip. "Ishmael
said we could sell it if we needed money. He told me
it was worth at least five hundred dollars, maybe even
a thousand, so we shouldn't let anybody cheat us."

"He said we could sell this?" A lump rose in Sylvie's throat. Flynn—gruff, steely eyed Flynn O'Rourke
who'd lied and schemed against her family—had cared
enough about her and Daniel to sacrifice his greatest
treasure.

The boy nodded. "He told me to keep it safe."

"Then we'd best do that." Sylvie ripped a thin strip
off the hem of her petticoat, passed it through the
ring, knotted it around Daniel's neck and tucked it
beneath his shirt. Hopefully, a thief bent on robbing
them wouldn't take time to search a ragged little boy.

"You're in charge of this ring," she told her brother.
"Whatever you do, keep it hidden. Don't even take it
out to look at it."

Daniel squared his shoulders, clearly proud to be

given such a vital responsibility. "You can count on me," he said.

Taking the reins again, she urged the plodding mule to a faster walk. The mule was old and tired, and Sylvie knew better than to push it too hard. The poor beast probably wished it was back home rolling in the grass and munching oats.

Daniel, too, wished he was home, Sylvie reminded herself. It wasn't as if she'd given him any choice. She'd simply told him they were leaving. Given his say, he would never have chosen this adventure.

She thought of the hardships ahead, the grueling days and dangerous nights. She'd told herself she wanted a better future for the boy. But could she provide that future? What if they broke down or fell into bad company? What if Daniel got a relapse of tick fever or some other illness? What if they lost the ring? What if she couldn't find work?

What would her father do without his children?

And what would she do without the man she loved?

She'd promised herself she wouldn't think about Flynn O'Rourke. But the truth was, she'd never really stopped thinking about him.

What a fool she'd been.

Not only had Flynn told her he loved her, he'd shown her how much. A treasure beyond price was hanging on a strip of muslin around her brother's neck. Flynn had given it away without a thought for himself. And here she was, widening the distance between them with each turn of the wagon wheels.

All she wanted was to be in his arms.

"Whoa." She gave the reins a gentle tug, halting the mule. The morning seemed frozen in silence. A raven flapped from the top of a pine.

Daniel looked up at her. "Let's go back home, Sylvie," he said.

As she nodded, Sylvie felt the tears start. Eyes blurring, she backed the wagon to the side of the road and swung it around in the opposite direction.

Her heart crawled into her throat.

Lined up across the road, a stone's throw ahead, were three mounted men.

Reaching down, she picked up the shotgun and laid it across her knees. "We've no business with you," she called out. "Let us pass."

The man in the middle, older, taller and more expensively dressed than the others, laughed. "I know that rig, honey," he said. "It belongs to a filthy, murdering polecat named Aaron Cragun. And if the rig belongs to Cragun, I'm guessing the two of you belong to him, too. I'd call this one fine stroke of luck!"

# *Chapter Fifteen*

"I don't like this." Flynn gazed toward the empty road, shading his eyes against the midday glare. "We shouldn't have let her go."

Aaron Cragun stooped to pick up a piece of kindling wood. "How would you have stopped her? Knocked her out? Tied her up? Sylvie's of age, and she's a headstrong girl. She'd have found a way." He mounted the porch and added the kindling to the wood box. "I wish she hadn't taken the boy. But they've never been apart. She's like a mother to him. All we can do is hope she comes to her senses and turns around."

"You say there's a lumber camp down the road?"

Cragun nodded. "If she keeps a good pace, she'll make it there before dark. Decent folks. Always good for a meal and a bed."

*If she keeps a good pace. And if not? If something goes wrong?*

Flynn's fists balled in frustration. Damn it, what he

wouldn't give for a horse! If he had one, he'd gallop after Sylvie now, and he wouldn't leave her side until he knew she was safe.

The two thugs who'd shown up earlier would almost certainly have brought horses from San Francisco. But Flynn had seen no trace of their mounts and neither had Cragun. Either the animals had run off, fallen prey to bears or wolves, or been claimed by someone else.

Horses or no horses, he couldn't stand this helpless waiting any longer. Cragun might not be worried, but Flynn's danger instincts were screaming. Sylvie and Daniel could be in trouble out there. He had to reach them any way he could.

"I'm going after them on foot," he said. "Slow as that old mule is, I should be able to catch up with them in a few hours, or at least find them at the lumber camp. Might there be any horses there?"

"A few." Cragun nodded his understanding. "I've got cash left over from selling the necklace. I can give you enough to buy one."

"Give me enough for two horses. We'll need them to get to San Francisco."

"Fine. And if Sylvie's still set on a new start, maybe you could talk her into coming with us."

"We'll see." Flynn picked up a spare canteen from the porch. Carrying it to the pump, he began filling it with water.

"You don't want to walk that far on an empty stomach," Cragun said. "Come on inside. I'll heat you some coffee and make you a sandwich."

Flynn hesitated, thinking he should just leave. But

Cragun was right. He had miles to go, and he'd hold up better on the road if he wasn't weak from hunger. He followed Cragun inside, closing the door behind him. "Make it fast," he said.

While Cragun reheated the coffee and sliced Sylvie's fresh bread, Flynn checked the loads in his revolver, holstered the weapon and tied the pouch of extra caps, balls and powder to his gun belt. He hoped to hell there'd be no call to use them, but he'd learned to be prepared for anything.

He was just sitting down to eat, when, without warning, a rifle blast shattered the front window. Flynn dropped to the floor, pulling Cragun down with him, as a familiar voice bawled across the clearing.

"Aaron Cragun! Come on out, you murdering little buzzard. We got some friends here who want to talk to their papa!"

Cragun lurched upward. Flynn yanked him down again. "It's a trap," he hissed. "Once they get you, it's all over."

Together they crept toward the window and peered over the sill, screened by the broken glass along the edge. Flynn knew what to expect and was braced for it. Still, when he saw Daniel and Sylvie, flanked at gunpoint by two rough-looking men, his stomach clenched.

Sylvie stood erect with her hands tied behind her back. Her head was high, her chin defiant. But even at a distance Flynn could sense the fear in her eyes. Daniel clung to her legs, his face half hidden by her skirt. He didn't appear to be bound, but it was clear he wasn't about to leave her.

For the space of a breath Flynn willed his love to reach out to her. *Be brave, my dearest,* he thought. *Know that I'm here and that I'm coming for you.*

It was as close to a prayer as he could manage.

Behind them, partly shielded by their bodies, Jacob Hawn sat on his tall black horse. With his flawlessly trimmed beard and pearl-gray suit, he looked more as if he was dressed for a parade than for a killing. But knowing Hawn as he did, Flynn would have expected the man to stay clear and avoid soiling his hands.

Those huge hands had probably been wearing custom-made kid gloves the night they'd strangled Catriona.

"Cragun!" Hawn bellowed again. "Come out with your hands up. If you don't, the blood of these two fine young folks will be on your head."

Once more Cragun lurched upward. Again Flynn seized his shoulders and pulled him down below the windowsill. "Damn it, Cragun, I know you'd die to save your children. But giving yourself up won't help. Sylvie and Daniel have seen too much. Walk out that door, and all three of you will be dead in the time it takes to drop a feather."

Cragun was shaking. "Lord, we've got to do something. We can't just let them die."

"As I see it, we've got one chance," Flynn said. "Since the last two butchers he sent never made it back, I'm guessing Hawn and his friends don't know I'm here. If you can keep their attention on you, I'll go out the rear window, circle around through the woods and come in from behind." He touched Cragun's arm. "Can you do it?"

Still quivering, Cragun nodded. "I've never been a brave man. But I love my children. I can do it. Now, go."

Cragun had brought his carbine inside earlier. Passing it to him, Flynn ducked low and headed for the bedroom.

Sylvie had surrendered the shotgun without a fight. She'd been about to fire when she'd realized there was no way to hit all three men. She might blast one, but when the others returned fire, Daniel could be hit. Their best chance of survival lay in keeping quiet and waiting for a chance to get away.

"Stay as close to me as you can," she'd whispered to Daniel. "If I tell you to run, get away as fast as you can."

"What if you can't talk?" It would be like her little brother to ask such a question.

"Then I'll signal—three fast taps or three nudges, any way I can. You hear or feel *one, two, three,* then you go. Whatever you do, don't look back."

He'd glanced up at her, touching the slight bulge beneath his shirt. "Maybe if we gave them the ring they'd let us go," he'd whispered.

"Hush. They'd just take it. Now, keep still." She'd sat in silence as one of the men climbed into the wagon, took the shotgun and tied her hands behind her back. It had been easy guessing that the big man in the suit was Jacob Hawn, who'd murdered Flynn's sister, and that he'd brought his cruel-looking companions to silence her father for good. They would use her and Daniel as hostages to lure him outside and kill him.

Flynn was there, too, she'd reminded herself. He was the best hope they had. But he was only one man, and the odds were against him. The odds were against them all.

Daniel had clung to her in the wagon as Hawn's men led the mule back to the clearing. She was thankful, at least, that they'd lacked enough rope to tie the boy. But he was old enough to remember what happened here and to talk about it. There was no way their captors would let him go when all this was over. If he was going to live, he'd have to run. Whatever it cost her, Sylvie vowed, she would save him.

This was all her fault. If she hadn't been so headstrong she and Daniel would have been in the house with their father and Flynn. Together, they might've had a chance of fighting off Hawn and his men. Instead, the two of them would be used as bait to lure their father to his death.

The wagon had halted in the trees, just short of the clearing. Sylvie had prayed silently all the way. But why should God listen to her, when her own self-righteous pride had brought down this tragedy? She could only hope Daniel was praying, too, and that his childish prayer would be heard.

Brutal hands had dragged her and Daniel into the open. Now they stood at the edge of the clearing, opposite the house. The two men, their pistols drawn, stood on either side of them. Hawn, mounted and holding the rifle he'd fired at the window, was behind them.

Sylvie listened, straining against her bonds as Hawn bawled out his challenge. She saw a flicker of movement at the broken window, but the front door remained closed. At least her father knew better than to come out onto the porch.

Hawn took a moment to reload his weapon. "I know you're in there, Cragun!" he shouted again. "Come on out, you thieving coward!"

"I may be a coward," her father called, "but at least I'm not hiding behind innocent people. Get your fat butt off that horse, Hawn. Walk out in the open and face me like a man!"

"You're wasting time!" Hawn yelled.

"I've got all the time in the world, you bastard. What d'you think happened to those first two skunks you sent? I took care of them and I can take care of you." There was a pause. "Tell me, how do you sleep at night, Hawn? Do you have dreams about the woman you murdered—the woman I saw you kill in that alley?"

Sylvie struggled against the rope that bound her wrists together. What was her father doing? He seemed to be goading Hawn, like a man waving a flag in front of a bull. Surely he'd have his rifle. But she knew for a fact that his eyes were going bad. He wouldn't fire across the clearing for fear of hitting her or Daniel.

Where was Flynn? Was he somewhere close, moving in to surprise Hawn and save them? That had to be what her father was trying to do, buy time until Flynn could make his move.

Meanwhile, it was up to her to get free. Her hands pulled and twisted. She could feel a trickle of blood as the rough hemp cut into her wrists, but the knots seemed to be loosening a little. She kept trying.

"That's enough stalling, Cragun!" Hawn shouted. "Who do you want me to shoot first, your daughter or your son?"

Sylvie felt Daniel's arms tighten around her legs. She had to get the boy out of harm's way before it was too late. An old memory stirred in her mind—a cousin back in Indiana who'd been tragically ill. Strange that she'd remember now, unless it was for a reason.

"You don't have the *cojones* to shoot a rabbit!" Sylvie's father shouted back. "Let my children go. Once they're safe, I'm yours. You can do anything with me you damn well please."

"It doesn't work that way, Cragun. As I see it, I've got two of your kids here. I can kill one and still have the other to bargain with. So, which one can you spare?"

*Now,* Sylvie thought. *Now!*

Daniel was pressing against her leg. She gave him three furious nudges with her knee—the signal to run.

As she felt him break away, Sylvie gave a high, bird-like cry. She pitched to the ground, slavering and jerking in her best imitation of her poor, afflicted cousin.

"She's havin' a fit!" One of the men dropped to his knees beside her.

"Never mind her!" Hawn roared. "Get the damn boy!"

Sylvie heard the sound of scrambling, followed by

the whine of a pistol shot. Sick fear washed over her.
Was Daniel hit? Was he alive? She couldn't risk a look.
She had no choice except to continue the feigned sei-
zure, buying time as she prayed that Flynn was close
enough to help her brother.

A bone-jarring slap on the side of her head knocked
her almost senseless. Sylvie opened her eyes. Jacob
Hawn had dismounted and was sneering down at her.
"So, are you finished playacting, missy?" he snarled.
"Let's see how you and your papa like this kind of
play." Standing, he raised his rifle and nodded to the
two men. "She's all yours. Have your fun. I'll keep
watch."

One man seized Sylvie's shoulders, holding her to
the ground. The other pinioned her legs with his knees
and began unbuckling his belt. She knew what was
going to happen and why. There was no way Aaron
Cragun would stay inside the house and watch his
daughter being raped.

"No, Papa!" She screamed a warning. "Stay—!"

A vicious blow cut off the rest of her words.

Lungs burning, Flynn plunged through the trees.
Ahead, he could see the empty wagon with the mule
still hitched. Two saddle horses were tethered nearby.
He'd made it around the clearing. But had he made it
in time?

As he paused to draw and cock his pistol, he heard
a whimper in the undergrowth. An animal, he thought,
and was about to move forward, when a small, whispered voice halted him in his tracks.

"Ishmael!"

His hand parted the brush. Daniel lay huddled in a tight ball. His face was streaked with tears.

"Are you all right?" Flynn asked.

The boy nodded. "They shot at me, but I ducked. They've still got Sylvie. Hurry."

"Stay right here." Flynn moved forward silently, knowing that his one advantage lay in surprise. He'd heard most of the exchange between Cragun and Hawn, as well as the shot that had missed Daniel, but the brush and trees that screened his movements had also cut off his view. He had only a general idea of what was going on. But Cragun had done a fine job of keeping Hawn engaged. The rest would be up to Flynn.

*Damn!* he cursed silently as he edged closer. Hawn had dismounted, leaving his horse behind him. The animal's massive body was squarely in the way of a shot. He would have to move to one side.

Only as he shifted to the right did he see Sylvie. She was lying on the ground, her face obscured by her hair. One of Hawn's men held her shoulders. The other knelt between her legs, fumbling with his trousers. Hawn stood back a few paces, his rifle at the ready.

Fury surging, Flynn raised his pistol. But he wasn't fast enough to prevent all hell from breaking loose. With a shriek of rage, Aaron Cragun had burst out of the house, firing his rifle as he charged across the yard. His first shot hit the man who was about to rape Sylvie. The man toppled backward, clutching his throat. Cragun's second shot went wild as Hawn's bullet struck his chest. He staggered and pitched facedown, dropping the rifle as he fell.

The man who'd been holding Sylvie's shoulders sprang up. Seeing Flynn, he wheeled and raced for his horse. Flynn let him go. His business was with Jacob Hawn.

Sylvie had managed to free her hands. With a cry, she scrambled to her feet and ran to where her father lay. As Hawn raised his rifle, Flynn stepped behind him and jammed the pistol against his back. "Throw down the gun and put your hands up, Hawn," he rasped. "It's over."

Hawn chuckled as he tossed the weapon to the ground and raised his hands. "Flynn O'Rourke. I was wondering where you'd gone to after Catriona's funeral."

"I went to find the man who'd murdered my sister. And it appears I've just found him."

"You mean me?" Hawn laughed again. "You're out of your mind, O'Rourke. You don't have a shred of evidence linking me to the crime. Take me back to San Francisco, and the judge will throw the case out of court."

"Aaron Cragun saw you do it. He told me. That's why you shot him."

"Hell, who'd believe that little gutter rat? I'm betting he strangled Catriona himself. Anyway, I shot him in self-defense. The man was coming at me with a rifle. You saw what happened."

"Maybe I ought to just pull this trigger," Flynn growled.

"You could do that. But you won't. I'm unarmed, and innocent until proven guilty. As a lawman, it's your sworn duty to protect upstanding citizens like me." Lowering his hands, he turned around to face Flynn. "What do you say we just shake hands and forget this mess? Keep it out of the courts and I can make you a wealthy man. Better for both of—"

With surprising speed, his hand flashed for the pocket pistol tucked into the back of his belt. As he was raising it to fire at Flynn, a shot rang out from behind him. Hawn reeled and clutched his chest, a red tide seeping through the fingers that had closed around Catriona's throat. His mouth moved, but no sound emerged before he crumpled at Flynn's feet.

Flynn looked up. Sylvie stood over her father's body, the carbine in her hands. A thread of smoke trailed from the muzzle.

Plunging across the clearing, Flynn caught her in his arms. Trembling and sobbing, she clung to him. Minutes crawled past before she could speak. "I'm sorry, so sorry," she murmured. "This is all my fault."

He kissed her tears. "Was it your fault Hawn killed my sister? Was it your fault your father took her jewels? What happened happened, love. All we can do is put this to rest and go on."

"But how, Flynn? Look around you. My father's dead, and two men with him. This isn't going to just go away."

His arms tightened around her. "Don't worry, I'll take care of everything. It may take some time, but understand one thing—I'll always be here for you and Daniel. I'll never leave you again."

They took a few moments to wrap Cragun's body in canvas and move it out of sight. After dragging the other bodies into the trees for later burial, they went looking for Daniel. They found him huddled in the bushes, where Flynn had told him to stay. The boy asked no questions. His father's absence seemed to tell him enough for now.

Flynn cradled the two of them in his arms—the woman he loved and the child who was already like his son. Together they embraced and grieved. The days ahead would be filled with pain, sorrow and the need for understanding. But somehow they would make this work. They would be a family.

He held them close. They were his now, these two precious ones. His to cherish and protect. His to love. Forever.

# *Epilogue*

*June 1863*

A waning crescent moon hung above the cove. Veiled by wisps of cloud, it cast a silvery gleam on the tide pools among the rocks, where silent starfish waited for the morning sea. Moon-shimmered waves lapped along the beach.

At the top of the cliff, where Aaron Cragun's windlasses had once stood, a lighthouse rose against the stars. Its rotating beacon pierced the night, warning ships away from the rocks below.

Standing on the porch of her cozy house, Sylvie took the pins out of her hair and dropped them into her apron pocket. The cool night wind caught her hair, blowing it back from her face. She smiled with the pleasure of it. The day had been long and busy, teaching school in town and caring for her family at home.

She was grateful for the night, when her children were asleep and she could be alone with her husband.

Moving back inside, she tiptoed down the hall to the bedrooms. Daniel, who was almost twelve and big enough to have his own room, was sleeping soundly after a day of chores, school and play. In the next room, Kathleen, four, and Bridget, almost three, curled in their beds like slumbering kittens. Blowing them a kiss, Sylvie stole back outside, where she selected a lily from the flower bed next to the porch. She carried it with her as she set out on the path to the cliff top.

On the way, she passed the goat pen, where Ebenezer, now a majestic billy, ruled over his harem of nannies. The goats had become a thriving business, providing milk, butter, cheese and animals to the town in the valley below—the town which had sprung up when the lighthouse was built. Now her family had neighbors, friends, schools, stores and even a church. And they hadn't even needed to move from their peaceful home.

Where the path branched, Sylvie took the narrower one to the little knoll where her father was buried. Bending, she laid the flower on his grave. "I have a secret, Papa," she whispered. "One I haven't even told Flynn. I'm going to have another baby. If it's a boy, and I have a feeling it is, we're going to name him after you. Aaron O'Rourke… How does that strike you?"

Something on the soft sea wind told her the news had been well received.

The weeks following her father's death had been difficult. But with Flynn's guidance, the inquest had cleared Aaron Cragun of murder and named Hawn as the killer. It had also established that Sylvie had shot Hawn to save Flynn's life. That time was behind them now, all but forgotten.

She turned away from the grave, her feet skimming down the path to the lighthouse. Flynn always claimed he liked to tinker with the workings of the great lamp at night, when it was lit. Sylvie suspected he simply enjoyed being at the top of the lighthouse in the dark, as she also did. The view was glorious.

After the tragic events of five years ago, Flynn had had enough of law enforcement. He'd used his connections to get authorization and funding for a lighthouse above the cove. After supervising the construction, he had become its keeper. No more ships foundered on the perilous rocks. No more wreckage washed ashore.

As she climbed the winding stairs, Sylvie's heart sang with anticipation. Flynn had hung a lantern near the top to light her way. She could see him now as he leaned over the railing to wave down at her. Laughing, she quickened her step, mounting the top and almost leaping into his arms.

He kissed her with a passionate tenderness that spoke of everything they shared. Maybe she would tell him about the baby tonight. The time seemed right.

"Come on outside." He led her through the door onto the iron-railed catwalk that circled the structure below the light. The first few times she'd come out here the height had made Sylvie nervous. Now she loved it. She leaned back in his arms, filling her senses with starlight and wind and the sound of the waves below. "I love you," she whispered.

"And I love you." His lips nuzzled her hair. In silence they watched the progress of a lighted ship as it vanished over the horizon.

"Someday we'll go, when our children are grown," he said. "I'd like to see the whole world with you."

Sylvie smiled, remembering her girlhood dreams of travel and adventure. "That would be lovely," she said. "But right now, everything I want is right here."

* * * * *

# HISTORICAL

Where Love is Timeless™

## HARLEQUIN® HISTORICAL

### COMING NEXT MONTH
**AVAILABLE MARCH 27, 2012**

**A COWBOY WORTH CLAIMING**
*The Worths of Red Ridge*
**Charlene Sands**
(Western)

**MARRIED TO A STRANGER**
*Danger & Desire*
**Louise Allen**
(Regency)

**LADY DRUSILLA'S ROAD TO RUIN**
*Ladies in Disgrace*
**Christine Merrill**
**Three delectably disgraceful ladies, breaking every one of society's rules, each in need of a rake to tame them!**
(Regency)

**TALL, DARK AND DISREPUTABLE**
**Deb Marlowe**
(Regency)

# REQUEST YOUR FREE BOOKS!

HARLEQUIN® HISTORICAL:
Where love is timeless

## 2 FREE NOVELS PLUS 2 FREE GIFTS!

**YES!** Please send me 2 FREE Harlequin® Historical novels and my 2 FREE gifts (gifts are worth about $10). After receiving them, if I don't wish to receive any more books, I can return the shipping statement marked "cancel." If I don't cancel, I will receive 6 brand-new novels every month and be billed just $5.19 per book in the U.S. or $5.74 per book in Canada. That's a savings of at least 17% off the cover price! It's quite a bargain! Shipping and handling is just 50¢ per book in the U.S. and 75¢ per book in Canada.* I understand that accepting the 2 free books and gifts places me under no obligation to buy anything. I can always return a shipment and cancel at any time. Even if I never buy another book, the two free books and gifts are mine to keep forever.

246/349 HDN FEQQ

Name _____ (PLEASE PRINT) _____

Address _____ Apt. # _____

City _____ State/Prov. _____ Zip/Postal Code _____

Signature (if under 18, a parent or guardian must sign) _____

**Mail to the Reader Service:**
**IN U.S.A.:** P.O. Box 1867, Buffalo, NY 14240-1867
**IN CANADA:** P.O. Box 609, Fort Erie, Ontario L2A 5X3

Not valid for current subscribers to Harlequin Historical books.

**Want to try two free books from another line?**
**Call 1-800-873-8635 or visit www.ReaderService.com.**

* Terms and prices subject to change without notice. Prices do not include applicable taxes. Sales tax applicable in N.Y. Canadian residents will be charged applicable taxes. Offer not valid in Quebec. This offer is limited to one order per household. All orders subject to credit approval. Credit or debit balances in a customer's account(s) may be offset by any other outstanding balance owed by or to the customer. Please allow 4 to 6 weeks for delivery. Offer available while quantities last.

**Your Privacy**—The Reader Service is committed to protecting your privacy. Our Privacy Policy is available online at www.ReaderService.com or upon request from the Reader Service.

We make a portion of our mailing list available to reputable third parties that offer products we believe may interest you. If you prefer that we not exchange your name with third parties, or if you wish to clarify or modify your communication preferences, please visit us at www.ReaderService.com/consumerschoice or write to us at Reader Service Preference Service, P.O. Box 9062, Buffalo, NY 14269. Include your complete name and address.

HH11B

*Taft Bowman knew he'd ruined any chance he'd had for happiness with Laura Pendleton when he drove her away years ago...and into the arms of another man, thousands of miles away. Now she was back, a widow with two small children...and despite himself, he was starting to believe in second chances.*

*Harlequin Special® Edition® presents a new installment in* USA TODAY *bestselling author RaeAnne Thayne's miniseries,* THE COWBOYS OF COLD CREEK.

*Enjoy a sneak peek of* A COLD CREEK REUNION

*Available April 2012 from Harlequin® Special Edition®*

A younger woman stood there, and from this distance he had only a strange impression, as though she was somehow standing on an island of calm amid the chaos of the scene, the flashing lights of the emergency vehicles, shouts between his crew members, the excited buzz of the crowd.

And then the woman turned and he just about tripped over a snaking fire hose somebody shouldn't have left there.

Laura.

He froze, and for the first time in fifteen years as a firefighter, he forgot about the incident, his mission, just what the hell he was doing here.

Laura.

Ten years. He hadn't seen her in all that time, since the week before their wedding when she had given him back his ring and left town. Not just town. She had left the whole damn country, as if she couldn't run far enough to get away from him.

Some part of him desperately wanted to think he had made some kind of mistake. It couldn't be her. That was just some other slender woman with a long sweep of honey-blond hair and big, blue, unforgettable eyes. But no. It was definitely Laura. Sweet and lovely.

Not his.

He was going to have to go over there and talk to her. He didn't want to. He wanted to stand there and pretend he hadn't seen her. But he was the fire chief. He couldn't hide out just because he had a painful history with the daughter of the property owner.

Sometimes he hated his job.

*Will Taft and Laura be able to make the years recede...or is the gulf between them too broad to ever cross?*

*Find out in*
*A COLD CREEK REUNION*
*Available April 2012 from Harlequin® Special Edition®*
*wherever books are sold.*

Celebrate the 30th anniversary
of Harlequin® Special Edition® with a bonus story
included in each Special Edition® book in April!

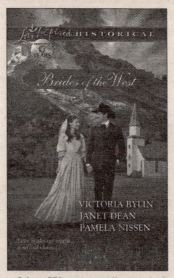

## Harlequin® Blaze™
### red-hot reads

**Sizzling fairy tales
to make every fantasy come true!**

Fan-favorite authors
## Tori Carrington and Kate Hoffmann
**bring readers**

*Blazing Bedtime Stories, Volume VI*

# MAID FOR HIM...

Successful businessman Kieran Morrison doesn't dare hope for
a big catch when he goes fishing. But when he wakes up one
night to find a beautiful woman seemingly unconscious on the
deck of his sailboat, he lands one bigger than he could ever
have imagined by way of mermaid Daphne Moore.
But is she real? Or just a fantasy?

# OFF THE BEATEN PATH

Greta Adler and Alex Hansen have been friends for seven years.
So when Greta agrees to accompany Alex at a mountain retreat
owned by a client, she doesn't realize that Alex has a different
path he wants their relationshiop to take.
But will Greta follow his lead?

**Available April 2012 wherever books are sold.**